SO

DOORS

A murder mystery

set in colonial Africa

by

Eileen Marguerite Henwick

"Death hath so many doors to let out life"

The Customs of the Country

[Francis Beaumont & John Fletcher]

Published by *Marque*

So Many Doors: A murder mystery set in colonial Africa

ISBN : 978-1-912499-04-5

First Published in May 2018 by Marque

Mark Henwick asserts the right to be identified as the author of this work.

Editors' note

So Many Doors is set in Northern Rhodesia, now Zambia. The book was written by our mother, Eileen Henwick, in the early sixties, around the time of Zambian independence. The world of the book has vanished, so it's probably useful to briefly mention some of the terms used.

Northern Rhodesia was often referred to as the Territory. It was administered by the British Colonial Office through a Governor. The Territory was divided into Provinces, each with a Provincial Commissioner (P.C.). Each Province was divided into Districts and each was administered by a District Commissioner (D.C.). The D.C. was based on a station, but these stations tended to be referred to as Bomas. A Boma comprised a cluster of offices and the homes of the officials and staff based there, but the term was also applied to any station of the administration as well as the specific office the D.C. used.

Assisting the D.C. was the District Officer (D.O.), and a troop of uniformed Messengers, recruited from the native inhabitants of the Territory. Messengers had a role which included policemen, mailmen and orderlies.

The word 'bush', used as a term in Northern Rhodesia, generally meant anywhere outside of a town or city.

We have edited the text to replace terms which, while in common use and without implication at the time, are now regarded as unacceptable. We have left in 'Bwana' and 'Donna', terms of respect used by the Bantu.

The names of places and geographic features are largely correct with the exception of the African villages.

Gail & Mark Henwick

Author's original note:

The background of the Colonial administration does, I hope, lend an authentic note to the story. I have drawn heavily from my memories of our time at Feira in the Zambezi valley. Obviously the rest of the story is fiction—the characters and events are imaginary and no similarity to anyone living or dead exists, or is intended.

E. M. Henwick
Broken Hill, Northern Rhodesia.
August, 1964.

DEDICATION

To the memory of
Eileen Marguerite Henwick
née Newman
Born 3rd March 1918
Died 4th February 1975

CHAPTER 1

Ndalisa, sitting in the dust of an African village, mourning the loss of her grandson, set off a chain reaction and Elizabeth Drayton died.

Murder could never have been proved of course, but murder it undoubtedly was.

It's difficult to say what first aroused my suspicions regarding her death, or at what point suspicion became certainty. Looking back on the affair, I think I knew before Father Bravachko came to my office that morning. And yet, how could I have known? Nothing that had happened prior to that could have really justified my assumption that there was something wrong.

I've wondered before whether it was Feira itself which infected my mind. It was a place with an atmosphere peculiarly its own, a reflection of its history. Feira was the eighteenth century name the Portuguese gave the place, and communicated their laconic functionalism. The word *feira* means market, and there was only one market that flourished along the Zambezi then: slaves.

It was mainly a seasonal trade, driven by the monsoon winds. Buyers and sellers needed a place to meet, and this small village, situated on a promontory at the meeting point of the Zambezi and Luangwa, had become that place.

After the slave trade, tribal wars ravaged the district, and this had been a violent place for many years. When Livingstone passed in 1856, he noted that the town had been destroyed and rebuilt many times.

An imaginative mind might suggest that history had bequeathed a dark legacy to Feira—a legacy which would shape the events which took place there. In any event, it was the sort of place to breed strange fancies—and murder.

It was also the most uncomfortable station in the Territory, a punishment station; the place where the Colonial Office sent officials to meditate on the error of their ways.

It lay at 1,500 feet in the Zambezi valley, at the most south-easterly point of the Central Province, staring across the rivers at Moçambique and Southern Rhodesia. There, on the escarpment, the cool season passed unnoticed. Temperatures stood at 115 degrees Fahrenheit in the shade, and they climbed another ten degrees as the dry season came to full term at the end of October.

It was a wicked month, October. A month of stretched nerves and tempers rising with the thermometer and the humidity. A month of dancing heat haze and red dust spiralling in tiny whirlwinds with the faintest whisper of air. A month when the drooping fringe of the river banks sat like a dark green collar against the baked brown redness of the hinterland and a heavy, expectant stillness blanketed the area while everything held its breath and waited for the flooding relief of the first rains.

It was at just such a time I arrived to take over the administration of the District: James Lancaster, District

Commissioner in His Majesty's Colonial Service.

It was 1948, and I was 37.

The swift, tropical dusk chased light from the water as the barge rounded the last concealing bend in the Zambezi River and our destination swung into sight across the prow.

I will always remember Feira as I first saw it that evening. It lay in an impressive setting—a setting of violent beauty, of harsh line and colour. The overall effect was one of unreality, an effect underlined by the darkening sweep of the river and the sullen threat in the still air.

Behind us, as the sun lowered to the west, the river went from the colour of molten copper to something more resembling old blood, with shadows creeping out from the banks.

Faintly across the water came the soft voice of a drum; insistent and repetitive. The staccato beat of the paddles on the side of the barge tapped out a pulsing counter, as we swept into the widening channel of the river.

A gleam of lamps, like distant stars, picked out the station houses, crouched in the rough shape of an inverted 'V' on the slopes of the peninsula which thrust out into the broad confluence of the Zambezi and Luangwa rivers. The peaks of the escarpment loomed over the turbulent wedding of waters, and the paddlers fought to bring the barge around to the landing stage.

In the way of Africa, the jetty, seemingly deserted seconds earlier, became, as the barge drew in, a mass of pushing bodies, each striving for a front seat view. For the remote villagers, anything and everything unusual was a show; that it was the maize shipment of much-needed supplies was a bonus. Hands reached out in the dusk to catch the barge ropes and the ululating cries of the village women split the air in welcome over the throb of the drums. I stepped ashore into the smell of dried fish and hot bodies.

Rush torches jumped into magical flame, as sudden as the growth of the crowd, and in their flickering light, Lameck, my servant, detailed carriers and cleared a path for my kit.

We climbed the steep bank, leaving the barge and the landing stage to the paddlers and the milling mass of their welcoming relatives.

Through the darkness loomed the Boma office; a low, white-washed building squatting on a flattened section of the hill. The flame of the torches we carried outlined the scarlet fez of the duty messenger.

"Bwana D.C.'s house." He pointed to the house on the crest and, in single file, we followed him up the winding dirt road which rose from the Boma.

The noise from the river bank faded away behind us and in the slowly-enveloping quiet—a quiet of shrill cicadas and a million bull frogs—I noticed that the drum had dropped to a sullen murmur. It was an unusual pattern of drumming, but that thought slipped from my mind even as my ear registered the change in the rhythm.

I was tired and lathered in sweat.

Ten days on the barge had been time to grow weary of the heat and cramped quarters; to lend a dream-like quality to six months' leave and blot out the smell of Devon with autumn nipping the air. Even the wedding ceremony seemed impossibly distant. Africa, with her capacity to smother and obliterate, had already erased the fresh memories of my wife, Ann, and the gentleness of the English climate during our brief honeymoon.

Two weeks ago, I had been in the capital, Lusaka, walking the jacaranda-lined streets as the trees shed their soft purple flowers underfoot.

The meeting with the Provincial Commissioner had gone the way I anticipated. I knew the petty, unwritten rule that I needed the P.C.'s consent before I married, and I knew that I could expect some retribution for breeching it.

"You're being assigned to Feira," he had stated flatly. "Drayton is due out in mid-November. You might want to get there early for a hand-over."

"Thank you, sir," was the only possible response, of course.

I got a ten minute briefing on the current and likely situation in the District, most of which I knew already, and then I was dismissed.

Naturally, I was curious about Drayton. Why had he been sent to Feira? Where was he likely to go next? Why was he being moved? The Lusaka Club and the bar at the Ridgeway Hotel were full of chit-chat without significant detail.

Drayton hadn't spent much time in Lusaka and if he had a problem, it wasn't widely known.

Drink? Women? Retirement?

Perhaps.

He'd served fifteen years in the Territory and he had a reputation for being a good administrator. He'd married before he joined the service and still was.

My reasons for asking about him were transparent.

One old-timer fixed me with a pale gaze under beetling eyebrows.

"You're Lancaster, aren't you? Just got Feira." He rocked on his bar stool, and finished his whisky. "My advice, old boy, is to get there and make sure your station reports are as boring as they can be. Nothing to draw anyone's attention and you'll be out in a year or two, eh? Maybe less."

It was the best I was going to get, and there had been nothing more to keep me in Lusaka, so I set about following my orders.

No method of travelling to Feira had been suggested. I decided that ten days down river by barge to Feira was a unique opportunity to familiarise myself with a District new to me. At that time, it was a famine area and a barge ferried maize meal from Chirundu to Feira. I had been fortunate enough to catch the barge on one of its departures.

The rising sandbanks, with the Zambezi at its lowest ebb, made it a slow trip but I had been in no hurry: I had until mid-November. I had made the most of the trip. It had been a time to get into the feel of things again—to acclimatise myself. I even enjoyed the first week—the hot, lazy days on the river and the chill misty mornings in camp: fishing, and the occasional hunt in the evening to bring in meat for the paddlers. It was a world shared with chattering monkeys and game down from the thirsty hills, schools of curious hippo and, it seemed, all the birds in creation. Only the last few days of the trip had been trying. The heat had really started to build up as the barge pushed its nose lower and lower into the valley, and the discomforts of barge touring, normally negligible, had begun to assume a proportion in relation to the rising humidity.

And here I was finally, hot and tired, trying to rein in my grasshopper thoughts.

As we made our way uphill, tracks branching off the main path appeared in the flame of the torches, and then slipped again into darkness. Through the thin screen of bush, will-o'-the-wisp lamps winked and vanished in the houses those tracks led to.

A European mustering of twelve or so, the Provincial Commissioner had said. It was quite sizeable for a remote bush station.

Somewhere out in the impenetrable darkness, the drum stopped, just as we turned onto a path through the terraced garden to the District Commissioner's house.

The heavy perfume of frangipani trees scented the night air. In the light of a solitary pressure lamp on the verandah of the house, their branches were silhouetted like a forest of arms raised in prayer against the mosquito gauze. The lamp shone from one corner. A hush lay around the house like a shroud; the only sounds were the quiet hiss of the lamp and the flight and flop of its attendant barrage of moths.

"Hello there!" My voice sounded loud in the stillness and the door rattled under my hand. "Anyone home?"

"Come in!" The invitation from the shadowed end of the verandah startled me. As I pushed inward, the warped gauze door scraped against the concrete floor.

He was sitting in the shadows with his feet propped on the sill, his head resting lightly on the back of the chair.

"Good evening," I said. "I'm Lancaster. You've probably been expecting me. I've just come in on the maize barge."

For a second he sat unmoving and silent.

"Ah... yes. Lancaster!" he replied at last. "Yes. Expected you sometime. Wasn't sure when you'd turn up." There was a clink of ice and a click as he set the glass down on a table. He lifted himself from the chair and came slowly towards me.

"Drayton." He held out his hand. "Good trip?"

"Pleasant enough. Hot! Reminded me a bit of Barotse." I waved at the front of the house. "My servant's outside with the kit."

"Kit?" He stood there, his face etched in lines drawn by the lamp, eyeing me with the exaggerated and careful concentration of several whiskies. One hand raked his dark, springy hair. He gestured vaguely towards the silent recesses of the house. "Kit?" he repeated. "Tell 'em to park it. Help yourself to a drink."

I watched him weave his way back to fetch his glass. I

7

dismissed the waiting messenger.

Lameck had already disappeared with the carriers to the back of the house. Drayton came back and stood behind me as I splashed soda into the whisky. I could feel his eyes on me, as I fished drowned moths from the melting ice in the bucket. He said something which I thought I must have misheard.

"Sorry, Drayton. You were saying about your wife?" I raised my glass towards him.

"I was saying," he replied slowly, "that my wife died this morning."

His eyes closed as he leaned his head back and tossed the whisky down his throat.

CHAPTER 2

Held against the steaming fecundity of Africa and her own
rituals of death, the European burial service had always
struck me as incongruous. To me, the conventional funeral
with its association of grey skies and slight drizzle, cold
moist earth and banked flowers, fitted uncomfortably into
the tropical background. I felt it particularly that following
morning.

It didn't help that I hadn't known Elizabeth Drayton. I
was an outsider.

Drums had broken the early stillness as dawn streaked
the sky from behind the hills on the far bank of the
Luangwa. The threatened storm of the previous evening had
passed over and, before the sun had climbed far into a sky
already heavy with heat, Elizabeth Drayton was buried with
the unseemly but necessary haste following death in the
tropics.

She was the first woman to be buried in the small
cemetery overlooking the river. Standing sentinel on the few
clustered graves, two giant baobabs raised bare gnarled
branches. Incongruously, as we lowered the coffin from our
shoulders, I found myself thinking of the Bantu explanation
of the baobab's ugliness—that they had been plucked from
the earth by their Maker and thrust back, roots uppermost,

9

for not leafing at the appointed time. They cast no shade, no relief from the heat.

The scent of the freshly dug grave was strong, masking all other smells, and the distant drums stopped as the coffin came to rest.

Relieved of our burden, we pallbearers stood back, merging with the rest of the mourners. The men were in khaki drill, the women in the flimsy cottons of sleeveless dresses. We all looked out of place around the graveside. Surrounding us at a little distance, small groups of villagers merged together to form a growing crowd. They were whispering and pushing. For them, our ritual was another show.

From the bush, the honey bird called insistently, "Follow me. Follow me. Follow me."

Closer, I saw a small marsh warbler on one of the baobabs, and heard him imitate the call with uncanny accuracy.

"Man that is born of woman..." Father Bravachko towered over the grave, an old testament prophet, his calico habit hanging loosely from enormous shoulders, his wiry, salt-and-pepper beard flirting with his paunch. A doctor of medicine as well as of spiritual welfare, it was he who had come in response to Drayton's appeal.

"But there was nothing I could do, my son," he had told me in his deep Polish accent the previous evening, after we'd helped Drayton to bed.

"Receive this daughter of the Church..."

Something plucked at my mind, drawing it away from the soft flow of the priest's voice. I am not an imaginative man—at least, not more so than the next—but something about the ring of people around Mrs. Drayton's grave that morning caught my wandering attention.

By some accident of placing, Father Bravachko and I

stood slightly apart from the rest of those present. As though intruders, we were cut off from them.

It gave me a chance to study their withdrawn faces. There were nine of them, of whom five had joined us at the house to follow the coffin downhill to the cemetery. There seemed a tension binding them, one to the other. It was a disturbing feeling, which I tried to shake off by recalling the brief introductions at the house. David Young, the cadet, ruddy-faced and sweating, stood beside Drayton. He was easily categorised; early twenties, a younger son, minor public school, middling University, Colonial Service. A muscle twitched in his cheek, and was it embarrassment I surprised in his eye as our glances met?

Beside him was Larry Nelson, the game ranger; shoulders braced beneath wilting drill and a secretive, aloof face. He was a more complex quantity than Young. Nelson's wife, Grace, pale beneath her tan, her piquant face framed in a tawny halo of hair, was like a delicate china figurine beside her husband's bulk.

Next to them stood the Prails; Martin and Elsa. He was the biologist from the American Research Institute doing the survey on sleeping sickness. Fortyish I guessed. His had the face of a scholar, but his body was that of a gourmand. On the other hand, Elsa Prail was beautiful; there was no other word to describe her. Her blond hair was drawn severely back from an interesting, angular face which remained expressionless and her fingers performed an unconscious cat's cradle as she stood beside her husband. Early thirties?

The middle-aged couple who had joined us at the graveside had the jaundiced skins of too many African summers and bouts of malaria. There was a likeness about the pair of them I often noted in married couples of many years' standing.

Lastly, the slim, dark girl standing beside them looked

cool despite the heat. Attractive in a pale, thoughtful way. I wondered who she was.

On the surface there was nothing about any one member of that group to account for the impression I had that there was an undercurrent of something unpleasant between them.

"...and to dust thou shalt return..." The calm voice of the priest recalled my mind from its curious analysis as the first handful of red earth dropped loudly on the bare coffin and Mrs. Prail started to cry; a painful catching of breath, sounding harshly against the soft timbre of the priest's voice.

Martin Prail took his wife's arm and drew her away to let the service end. They only got as far as the baobab, before she sank to her knees and covered her face with her hands.

The priest concluded and the swell of noise from the surrounding crowd seemed to act as a release to the ring of people around the grave.

I moved away, alone, leaving Father Bravachko, who had turned aside and was talking in a low voice to Drayton. Mrs. Nelson stood silent, watching her husband and the slim, dark girl as they attempted to raise Mrs. Prail to her feet. Prail stood by, watching his wife, and looking helpless.

The girl knelt and said something I could not hear. Elsa Prail raised a face on which the tears had furrowed the mascara in dirty rivulets down her cheeks; her green eyes were blazing with hatred. The shock of the stinging slap that followed, with her open palm across the girl's face, brought everyone around on their heels.

"You wanted her to die," Elsa Prail said bitterly. "Both you and Barnaby are to blame. You let her die."

We were all frozen in place. I was reminded of that game of statues, played as a child.

Then Nelson pulled Elsa Prail roughly to her feet. "That's quite enough." he said.

She twisted from his grasp. "Don't touch me," she choked. "You know it's true. If Elizabeth had gone away she'd be alive now."

She turned and stumbled away over the scorched grass, still crying. Her words seeming to hang after her in the still, hot air. The slightly unreal quality of the whole morning's proceedings transformed her exit into that of an actress, I thought, leaving the supporting players on stage, awaiting the fall of the curtain.

Nobody spoke for several seconds after Elsa Prail's departure. It was as though her words had tied all tongues. Then, as people do, everybody had started to move and talk at the same time, as if on a given signal. It was the game of statues again, everyone coming back to life suddenly.

Drayton, with a muttered apology, hurried after Prail, who had followed his wife. I crossed over to help the girl to her feet. Violet-flecked eyes looked blankly at me.

For want of anything more sensible to say, I introduced myself. "I'm James Lancaster. I don't think we've met yet. Here, let me help you up."

She made an obvious effort to collect herself and took my hand.

"Janet Frenton. Thank you. Excuse me." Turning, she walked away, followed by the middle-aged couple with whom she had been standing at the graveside. They gave sketchy goodbyes as they left, shock still in their faces.

Like autumn leaves dispersing in a sudden gust of wind, the rest of the mourners had gone and only Father Bravachko remained with me. I walked slowly back toward the house with the priest in the rising heat, the unpleasantness of the scene we had witnessed simmering in my mind.

At the first bend in the path, we stopped and looked back at the labourers shovelling the red earth into the open grave.

"Grief affects people in many ways," Father Bravachko said. "It can distort their outlook for a time. They're not themselves. Thanks be to God it is usually a temporary phase."

"Were they close friends?" I asked. "Mrs. Prail and Mrs. Drayton, I mean."

He hesitated a moment and then said slowly, "They were much together."

He'd evaded the question, but I didn't feel I knew him well enough to call him on it. We walked in silence for a few minutes, before I spoke again.

"Who is Janet Frenton?" I said.

"Miss Frenton's the nursing sister. She's been here since August. She volunteered to take over the African Hospital and Dispensary whilst Spencer was on leave."

Some way ahead of us, the Nelsons and David Young turned off the main path to the right. They were talking animatedly.

"Who were the couple who left with Miss Frenton?" I asked.

"The Jones—they run the trading store here." The priest halted suddenly and took hold of my arm. "Before we reach the house there is something I must say, Mr. Lancaster. I am not a man of idle chatter, neither do I gossip, but this I must say. Feira has not been a happy station for many months now. The atmosphere has been, what is the word I want? Unsettled? I've noticed it, more and more recently."

He hesitated, his eyes searching my face, then added, "It has, I feel, been something more than the little frictions and mutual irritations that arise among a handful of people with nothing in common who have been thrown together on an isolated Boma."

I remembered the odd impression that this handful of people had made on me some fifteen minutes earlier—that there had been a tension between them.

"There is nothing one can lay a finger on," the priest added, "but the outburst we have just witnessed is an example. Of course, Mrs. Prail was hysterical and—"

"Granted she was," I interrupted, "but even so, it was an extraordinary statement to make."

"Extraordinary, I agree, but quite untrue. Miss Frenton is an excellent nurse. Everything possible that could have been done for Mrs. Drayton she had already done before I arrived. There was little more I could do, or any other doctor could have done, for that matter. Mrs. Drayton had been considerably weakened by malaria. She just wasn't strong enough to fight against what was a particularly virulent form of enteritis."

We walked on a little way. There was clearly something more he wanted to say and that he was deliberating how best to put it. He stopped again and turned to me.

"It's not so much that I'm worried about Mrs. Prail's remarks. They were nonsense. Perhaps even dangerous nonsense. It's the outburst itself which worries me. It's symptomatic of whatever is wrong here on the Boma. Whatever it is, it has been growing steadily for months. I can only hope that your arrival here, as a complete stranger in their midst, will bring in a little fresh air."

My hope that I would be able to follow the advice of keeping my station reports 'boring' seemed to be fading.

"It's not uncommon," I began tentatively, "to find that people living on a rural Boma don't quite hit it off—"

He interrupted me as I had him. "I'm certain it's more than that, Mr. Lancaster, and it's because I have been concerned about it that I've tried in the past months to make more frequent visits. Mrs. Drayton was my particular responsibility. She was, of course, of the Roman Catholic Church. I was worried about her."

He was still being vague.

"As a doctor or a priest?" I prompted.

"Perhaps it was a little of both," he said slowly. "As far as I could judge, there was nothing physically wrong with Mrs. Drayton up until this last illness, bar the ongoing effects of malaria." He put his hands behind his back and rocked on his toes. "I know it will sound absurd to you, but my diagnosis on Mrs. Drayton would have been... fear."

He turned away as if embarrassed and we continued up the hill, coming to the path that led through the terraced garden to the house.

"Fear of what?" I asked.

He didn't reply immediately. In fact, we were on the steps leading to the verandah door before he spoke. He stopped and turned, panting slightly from the exertion of the walk uphill. His voice was soft. "I don't know, my son, but let me repeat myself. I only speak of these things to you because I hope your arrival here will put a stop to whatever mischief has been brewing."

Again there was the sense that he was embarrassed when he hurriedly completed his reply. "Two nights ago, Mrs. Drayton, before she lapsed into a coma, spoke to me of being bewitched."

I stood still, startled into silence.

At that moment, Drayton appeared, just as the gong sounded for lunch. He apologised for his absence, and ushered us inside. He made no reference to the incident of the morning nor to his abrupt departure from us.

Lunch was an uncomfortable meal with our host understandably morose and preoccupied.

The priest kept up a desultory conversation with me on his work at Kapoche Mission, some miles to the north of Feira, his visits the local villages and to Zumbo Mission just across the river in Moçambique, but from time to time I saw him eye Drayton speculatively and I felt his thoughts were elsewhere, as were Drayton's. None of us was sorry when the meal came to an end.

Father Bravachko took his leave after lunch and Drayton and I stood watching him on his downhill trudge to the waiting barge which was to take him up the Luangwa river to the Mission. The dry, red dust rose in puffs under his feet as he turned the bend in the path and passed from our view. With his departure, the house and station settled into the afternoon quiet common to this part of Africa.

"Decent enough type" Drayton said. "Thank God he didn't feel I was in need of spiritual comfort."

This remark appeared to call for no comment and in silence we turned back to the house. The coolness of the verandah was inviting after the heat outside.

"When would you like to start the take-over, Lancaster?" Drayton asked abruptly.

"Whenever you feel like getting down to it. I'll leave it entirely to you." As I spoke, I turned to watch idly through the mosquito gauze for the reappearance of the priest on the landing stage, where the barge waited. "In the circumstances I should say the sooner you get away, the better."

"What the bloody hell do you mean by that?"

I turned. He realised his mistake as he saw the surprise in my face and, in the same instant, I understood his interpretation of my remark.

"Exactly what I said." I knocked out my pipe into an ashtray.

He was silent for a moment, the anger slowly dying from his face, leaving it drawn under the sallow tan. He reached for a cigarette.

"I'm sorry, old man. I'm a bit on edge. Let's have a drink".

"Good idea."

It was an excellent brandy and after the events of the morning, very welcome.

"You're right, Lancaster," he said, after we had sipped our drinks for some moments in silence. "It's time I got out of Feira. It's a good district but the last year hasn't been easy."

"Are you referring to the Matafwali affair? I understood from the P.C. that it only started six months ago."

"Matafwali?" Drayton said. "Oh, that. Just part of the day's work; neither here nor there. I wasn't referring particularly to the district, when I spoke of a difficult year."

I didn't pursue the point and Drayton didn't seem disposed to clarify his remarks.

Instead, I went on. "Matafwali was executed in Lusaka the day before I left."

"I know." Drayton said slowly. "Nyrenda, the Head Messenger, told me a week ago. Bush telegraph. It's common knowledge in the Chiabele area." His voice sounded tired.

"The P.C. seems to think that Chief Chiabele, if not a party to the whole business, knew perfectly well what was going on." I said. "He's not at all sure that the chief shouldn't have appeared as an accomplice. He wants a final report from you when you get back to Lusaka, by the way."

Drayton nodded, unsurprised.

"I've brought a copy of the proceedings in the P.C.'s Court along with me," I said. "I'll let you see it this evening, but there's no urgency. In the circumstances, well, we can leave things over for a bit."

"Don't worry about me, Lancaster. I'm not a grief-stricken widower. There'll be no need to 'leave things over', as you put it".

There was an edge again to Drayton's voice, but I reasoned the man needed some leeway.

18

CHAPTER 3

It was past three when I got away to my room, pleading the excuse of unpacking. I was anticipating, with a sense of relief, the prospect of an hour or two alone and it was surprising to find Lameck in my room, folding away my clothes into the drawers.

Mid-afternoon was an unusual time to find him around. From one thirty to four was off-duty for him, as it was for most African domestic servants.

"Still going, Lameck?" I said.

I sat and watched him as he whisked the last batch of shirts from the bed and stacked them into the drawer. His usually cheerful face wore a morose and harassed look.

"What's upsetting you?" I asked.

"Feira not a good place. Too much work, bwana."

Muttering and grumbling to himself, he leaned forward to shut the last open drawer, the flap of his loose shirt revealing his neck and part of his chest. I couldn't help but notice the 'much work' must have taken him the best part of the morning. Where he'd exposed his neck there was an inflamed, raised patch. A thick needle of metal had been pushed under the skin, immediately below the collar bone. I had seen that particular type of 'medicine' before.

19

I made no comment on it and chased him out of the room, speculating on his sudden need for protection; a desire sufficiently urgent to send him haring off to the local witchdoctor within twelve hours of our arrival at Feira.

Witchcraft, despite legislation restricting it, and the slowly growing influence of the missions, still festered like an abscess under the skin of the African continent.

What had convinced Lameck? Stories from other servants? Those drums? There was no disputing they had an eerie and unsettling rhythm.

It was odd that Father Bravachko had mentioned witchcraft. In fact, it had been a peculiar conversation altogether, but there was probably nothing to it. A handful of people isolated in the bush, living cheek by jowl with little or no outside interest, getting on each other's nerves—things could get a little out of proportion; I had seen it happen before.

I settled on the bed with my brief case, but there was no escape from the topic. Witchcraft was the basis of the Matafwali incident. I pulled out the report and flicked through it; Drayton might choose to discuss it that evening and I needed to be completely in the picture.

The affair had started a year earlier. I read that Drayton had become suspicious about the disappearance of five people in a short space of time and within a radius of fifteen miles in the Chiabele area. There had been a whisper from the bush of 'banyama', a practice of human sacrifice, which entailed the eating of certain parts of the victim in order to acquire magical powers. Drayton had set out with a mustering of District messengers to investigate, ordering Chief Chiabele to accompany him.

The general suggestion was that lions were responsible for the disappearances. Certainly, the Chiabele area had the reputation of being good lion country. On the other hand, a

lion kill leaves evidence. What's more, a lion turned man-
eater does not revert to a game diet, and there had been no
further reports of missing people, either in the Chiabele or
the adjacent areas.

These considerations, added to the obvious fear in the
villages, and a history of similar disappearances five years
earlier, had left Drayton disbelieving the theory about lions.
But he discovered nothing. The villagers were evasive and
sullen. At the end of the week, leaving three messengers to
organise search parties in the thick bush surrounding the
villages, he had returned to Feira. There he found, waiting
for him in the shape of Ndalisa, the first link in the chain
which eventually led to Matafwali.

"They have taken the son of my son," the old woman
told Drayton, "and I will speak. Let them work their spells.
Let them do what they want to me. It does not matter. I am
old. My death comes soon."

That had been the beginning. Ndalisa's evidence had
implicated the headman of her village, who in turn had
accused the headman of a neighbouring village. Despite the
lies and prevarications, quickly and surely, the net had
tightened. Finally, Drayton, in a swoop on the village of
Tanga, had found the appalling evidence buried beneath the
hut of Matafwali, the witchdoctor.

The discovery of the deformed foot of Ndalisa's
grandson was what had hanged Matafwali; this he had
preserved, attributing magical properties to the deformity.
Had it not been for that foot, his explanation of corpse-
stealing, a common enough practice for witchdoctors, to
account for the presence of human bones might have carried
the day.

The Provincial Commissioner's Court had found
Matafwali guilty of murder and after review of the evidence,
the High Court had authorised his execution. Three

headmen of the Chiabele area had been hanged with him and seven gaoled as accessories.

The report did not make pleasant reading. I turned back to the Provincial Commissioner's covering minute.

"Before he died, Matafwali made a curious statement (I attach a copy) and this statement, reviewed in the light of previous suspicions of Chief Chiabele, and supported by the trend of evidence, would indicate that the chief himself was aware of what was going on; in fact, it would appear exceedingly likely that he was a party to these rites, for whatever reason.

"A strict watch is to be kept on him and, if further investigations turn up proof of complicity, you will advise me immediately and take no action until I arrive. In any event, I propose to visit you in late January, failing previous advice from you."

I pushed the papers aside. Obtaining proof of Chiabele's guilt would certainly be no easy matter. I wondered what ideas Drayton would have on the subject.

In the soporific heat, I let my mind wander.

Drayton was a strange fellow. Did his reference to a difficult year have anything to do with the unpleasant scene at his wife's graveside? Wife trouble? Woman trouble generally? 'I'm not a grief-stricken widower', he'd said. Drink? He could certainly put it away, as he had proved on the previous evening.

And Bravachko; he had left so much unsaid, he'd been positively evasive. He was at least reluctant to talk about this 'bewitched' nonsense, but why had he brought it up at all? Why pass on the delirium of a dying woman?

My thoughts turned lazily around; picking and pecking in ever-widening circles: Drayton, his wife dying, witchcraft, his comment about not being a grief-stricken widower. How to make my district reports unexceptional and boring with all that going on.

It was a hot, sticky afternoon.

I stretched in that state between sleep and consciousness. I was back on the river, on the barge, feeling the pull of the paddles, hearing the smooth slap, slap of the water.

Then a sudden change in the beat of the paddles wakened me with a start.

But I was here, in the District Commissioner's house at Feira, not on the barge.

I'd slept much longer than I'd intended. Dusk had turned the room into an unknown place of deep shadows and vague outlines; the beat of the paddles that I'd dreamt of was a clenched fist thumping on a table somewhere in the front of the house.

"You mind your own bloody business, Young. Keep out of it." Drayton's voice carried clearly through the still house.

He was alone when I joined him later.

CHAPTER 4

In the following days, the task of taking over the station from Drayton fully occupied my waking hours and I pushed the events surrounding my arrival to the back of my mind, albeit with an uneasy feeling of unpleasantness temporarily shelved.

The hours of duty at the Boma were arranged to suit the climate. Work started at seven in the morning, broke off for the afternoon heat and continued for an hour or so in the evenings, before the light failed.

Each morning, in the grass-thatched office, I paged through the files, estimates and tax registers and discussed with Drayton the general policy on district administration, the chiefs and their areas.

The District, covering roughly twenty thousand square miles of the Lusaka Province, comprised of five areas, each area under the control of its own Chief. Of these areas the largest was Chiabele.

Feira was the seat of district administration under the Colonial Government and was sited within the Chiabele area.

It was a moderately important station, being strategically placed to control the movement of cattle into, and from, Portuguese territory. A veterinary depot at Baluti, eight miles from Feira and under the control of a Livestock Officer, enforced a strict quarantine to prevent the introduction into healthy areas of cattle sleeping sickness, still prevalent in some parts of the District.

Feira was also the focal point of investigations into the habits of the tsetse fly, the carrier of the deadly germ of sleeping sickness, fatal to both man and beast. This explained the presence of Martin Prail, the biologist on loan from the Delaware Institute and whose research operations were financed by the World Health Organisation.

Various methods were, at that time, being tried to combat the spread of the tsetse fly, and with some success: to prevent the movement of game which carried the fly to uncontaminated areas was one; the shooting out of game in a series of cordon sanitaire around healthy, fly-free areas was another; and a third was the destruction of mopani trees, a natural breeding ground of the tsetse. All of these operations were directed from Feira.

All in all, it was an interesting district.

If I'd thought it was hot when I arrived, Feira soon showed me how wrong I was. As we progressed from October to November, the thermometer topped the 120 degrees Fahrenheit mark, with no sign of rain.

In the evenings, whilst Drayton packed, I browsed through the District Notebook, that fount of accrued knowledge of the District, written up gradually over the years by every District Commissioner who had held the office. The Notebook had been started in 1906 and made fascinating reading: blurred photographs, faded inks and a variety of handwriting styles. The journal covered all subjects, it was an anthropology by authors, some long since dead or retired, some legendary figures in the history of the Territory, some safely seated in the golden secretarial chairs of many years' service—and others still breaking backs and hearts on the greasy pole of promotion.

Feira might be a punishment posting, but it was not necessarily a dead end. I wondered how many of those authors had been required to make their district reports boring so they could get back into the main stream.

As the days passed, I realised Barnaby Drayton was an able officer. I came to appreciate his grasp of relevant detail on situations was sure and adroit. His knowledge of the District, culled over the previous two years, was extensive. He had an astute mind and I found him quite likeable once we got past the initial embarrassment of our first days together. There was a certain charm about the man which leavened the general acidity of his remarks and his brusque manner.

On the subject of Chief Chiabele, I learned that Drayton's mind had followed much the same line of reasoning as the Provincial Commissioner's. He had already posted messengers throughout the area, ostensibly on tax and labour returns, to listen and report. However, he expected little, if anything, to arise from this, and confessed as much to me.

The general atmosphere of unrest in the surrounding area he laid at the door of Matafwali's execution. "But give them time. They'll settle down." he said, "Though for my money, if we could get rid of Chiabele, I think the process would be a helluva lot quicker."

And that something was bubbling in the background was obvious. The smell of trouble seemed to hang over the place: labourers were deserting; the tax office was idle a greater part of the morning; and the African staff on the Boma were jumpy. Nelson, the Game Ranger, reported difficulty in recruiting carriers in the Chiabele district and he had had one of his touring camps gutted by fire.

The drums stayed silent now, except at night. In

sweating, restless sleep I sometimes dreamed that I heard a single beat of a drum, like the toll of a muffled bell.

David Young's manner to Drayton, when work brought them into contact in the office, was impeccably polite... and arctic.

"Yes sir, no sir, bloody young fool." Drayton muttered under his breath on one occasion when Young had left.

"What ails him?" I asked.

"A little green monster sitting under his topee." Drayton shrugged and glared at me, as though daring me to press the question further.

I declined, continuing with my work, conscious of a rising sense of irritation at the intrusion of discords I barely understood.

A few minutes later, Drayton spoke again.

"It's time you were officially introduced to the Boma." He cleared his throat. "It'll be too difficult at my house with all the packing going on, so I've told Young to arrange something in his house, at my expense. A short, informal drinks thing. Sundowners. I've invited everyone."

He kept his face turned away from me.

"That's kind of you, Drayton, but under the circumstances, don't you think—"

"No, I don't. It's all arranged."

I wanted to get to the bottom of what was happening with the station staff, but I didn't believe that was best handled by crowding them into a room for a couple of hours and giving them drinks.

I tried to appreciate Drayton's effort on my behalf, and hoped that the singular lack of enthusiasm I felt for the whole idea was not apparent.

CHAPTER 5

Whatever my misgivings, that evening, as the sun set, we strolled over to Young's house—a matter of five minutes' walk.

May a good time be had by all, I thought, as we walked through Young's garden. Who will end up slapping whom? But it was Drayton's idea, so it would be on his head.

Martin Prail's voice with its strong, nasal twang floated down from the verandah as we reached the bottom of the steps. He was apologising to Young for his wife's absence.

"And for these small mercies..." Drayton muttered.

Maybe no one would be slapped, was my answering thought.

Prail's obese body overlapped the sides of the verandah chair, which creaked beneath his weight. Heaving himself up, he came towards us.

"Ah, there, good evening, gentlemen. I was just explaining to David here how upset Elsa is not to be here this evening, but this heat has got her beat. Yes sir, taken it all out of her."

"I can imagine it would," Drayton said shortly, "but what a whipping boy we tend to make of the heat."

Prail's eyes flickered but he did not pursue it. He turned to me.

"And you, Mr. Lancaster," he asked, "How are you settling down in our little place?"

I made a vaguely worded response and looked around.

Most of the people present I had seen or met at Elizabeth Drayton's funeral but, as though by common consent, that occasion was ignored and re-introductions were made as though I had just arrived at Feira.

It was the sort of thing you might see in an outstation; slaps and hysterics one day and a jolly evening a few days later, when the prime concern of everyone present was to ignore what had happened before to the point where it faded out of existence.

On most stations, it usually worked out well: these 'little unpleasantnesses' had to be overcome, and they were, no matter how detailed and endless the individual discussions were over the tea cups or glasses of beer. Perhaps it was that a small number of people on an outstation needed to keep that communal contact unbroken, to preserve the comfort of their day to day living; one breach of that communal front and the whole fabric of social life dissolved in feuds and cliques.

Hence Prail, presenting his wife's apologies, and not one eyebrow raised.

Tolerance? Good manners? Hypocrisy? Whatever it was, I found myself thinking that it was a step ahead of my time at my last station, Mendizi, where two of my fellow officers had lived a stone's throw apart without communicating, except through intermediaries, for a solid eighteen months.

From the long, low verandah, people had trickled into the sitting room, where the tobacco fog was already thick. The wreaths of smoke drifted almost imperceptibly upwards, undisturbed by any current of air. In the background, a slightly scratched record of "Begin the Beguine" ground to a halt. The room was really too small for the number of people.

Young appeared at my elbow with a whisky and soda. Behind him loomed a new face; that of John Drobinall. It was not prepossessing. He was the Livestock Officer who lived out at Baluti, the quarantine station. Looking him over as Young introduced him, I wondered whether the theory that owners grow to look like their dogs, could be applied to Livestock Officers and cattle. There was something peculiarly bovine in the long soft face and spiked lashes fringing the large, slightly protuberant eyes.

"What sort of accommodation have you there in Baluti? Bush or permanent quarters?" I asked him.

"Brick-built by Mr. Drayton's predecessor. 'Chez Baluti' we call it."

"We? Are you married?"

"Oh, goodness me no!" he laughed immoderately. "I say 'we' meaning the Boma there."

He was thirty-three or so, I judged; an unusual type of Livestock Officer; fussy but loud.

I found myself cutting his description of 'Chez Baluti' short.

"I will be out with Mr. Drayton to have a look around, once things sort themselves out at the Boma. I'll give you due warning."

His smile stuck slightly. "Warning? That sounds frightfully ominous, Mr. Lancaster."

"Advice then, if you prefer. I mean I'd like you to be there to show me around."

"Oh, I see." His smile loosened.

"Are you kept pretty busy out there?"

"Busy enough; but not too busy to prevent my popping over here for the odd weekend to see what's going on." He hesitated. There was a speculative look in the protuberant eyes. "I should, of course, have come in for Mrs. Drayton's funeral, had I known about it," he said slowly, "but it was all rather sudden, wasn't it? Is it true—"

"I wouldn't know," I cut him off. "I've just arrived."

I didn't like him, however unfair that might have been after only a minute's talk, so I left him and went over to talk to a couple who also hadn't been at the funeral. Seeing it, Drayton joined us to make the introductions.

"Grobler here's the road foreman," he said, "he's working on the new road to connect up with the Great East Road. The present effort tends to wash out in the rains and it's our only efficient route to Lusaka."

Grobler was a big, grizzled man with hands, rough and pitted with labour, sticking out from his arms like bunches of bananas.

"Honest, forthright and a bit of a rogue—but a good one." Drayton grinned at Grobler. "And talkative," he added.

Grobler returned the grin and silently shook my hand.

His wife was a small dumpling of a woman with smooth, greying hair and eyes framed in laughter lines.

"My wife does enough talking for the two of us." Grobler patted her arm affectionately.

"And if I didn't exercise my tongue, I'd lose the use of it," she retorted, "Sitting out there in the bush. You know we live under canvas, Mr. Lancaster? We don't see many people, unfortunately, and we don't get into Feira often."

"Well, you're coming in once the rains set in. Can't be much longer," Drayton said and moved away to the door as Janet Frenton arrived.

The renewed buzz of conversation underlined the momentary lull which had greeted her appearance. The slim delicacy of the white throat rising from the scooped neckline of the blue linen dress was accentuated by the severity of the hairstyle; drawn straight back from the pale face, the dark hair was twisted into a vertical knot behind her head. Her

31

eyes, enormous above the finely moulded cheekbones, looked unsmilingly up at Drayton. She shook her head in reply to his question and moved away.

"I actually prefer being out in the bush," Mrs. Grobler was saying, her back to the door, "where you don't get all these..." she paused as Janet Frenton moved across her line of vision. "Well, you know what I mean, Mr. Lancaster. Life's simpler."

"Now, there you have something, Mrs. Grobler," I said.

Mrs. Nelson joined us.

"How about you?" I asked her. "How do you like bush life?"

She looked very different from the woman I'd seen at the funeral. The black dress clung to her diminutive figure and her earrings seemed too large. The lamplight caught and gleamed in folds of her burnished hair which was piled luxuriantly above her face. Her blue eyes were veiled and she regarded me coolly.

"I hate it," she said and smiled.

"An extravagant word, if I may say so, Grace." Drayton's voice broke in over my shoulder. "Bush life has its points— its advantages. Material and otherwise."

"Tell me some," she said.

"Now why should I do that when there are others present, better qualified to speak on the subject?" Drayton's voice was silky. He turned away to speak to Mrs. Grobler.

The flash of hostility in Grace Nelson's eyes before the shutters came down was unmistakable.

"Would you get me some ice, please, Mr. Lancaster?"

We moved away together and had to edge around Drobinall, who was looking across at Drayton over his drink, open enmity in his expression.

"What is it you don't like about bush life?" I asked Mrs. Nelson. I used the tongs to fish in the ice bucket for the last pieces of unmelted ice.

"The people I have to live with." Her voice was angry. She turned her back on the corner of the room where Drayton was standing and eyed me warily. I think she had immediately regretted her remark and changed the subject. "When is your wife joining you?" she said with an effort.

"Not sure." I realised such a brief answer would only beg more questions I didn't want to answer. "Perhaps after the Christmas holidays. Hopefully it will be cooler then."

I could feel that she was still angry and, when Drobinall came in fruitless search of ice, I took the opportunity to move away towards Young, who was busy with the drinks.

"It's good of you, Young, to go to all this trouble," I said.

"Pleasure, sir. I'm sorry, it's a bit awkward. I mean, so soon after..." he stopped.

"A masterpiece of understatement." I topped up my drink and went over to Janet Frenton, who was sitting on the arm of a chair. Nelson stood beside her.

I could feel Young's eyes following me.

It wasn't a good move and I regretted it the moment I had made it. The nursing sister was listening to Nelson, but without giving the appearance of really hearing him. A pulse throbbed visibly at the side of her neck.

Nelson's face was even more secretive than I remembered from the funeral.

"Bad time of year to arrive at Feira," he said to me.

We chatted. The expected rains, my wife, my last station, the good game country in this corner of the Territory, the looming threat of tsetse fly, even what shows I'd managed to catch in London.

All the time, I wondered how much longer the stem of Janet Frenton's glass could take the pressure of those rigid fingers.

Young joined us and his arrival seemed to act on Janet

Frenton like a call.

She stood. "I must speak to you, Mr. Lancaster. Now. Alone, please." She thrust the sherry glass towards the table. Her hand was shaking.

"Janet!" Young laid a protesting hand on her arm. She shook it off and Young turned on his heel and left us. Nelson, with a muttered 'excuse me', moved off to the drinks table.

"If you feel this is a suitable time and place, Miss Frenton."

"I've got to get away from here," she said.

"The house or the station?"

"Feira. I must get away!" The intensity in her voice was disquieting.

I took out my cigarette case and held it towards her, my eyes on the tightly interlaced fingers.

She shook her head.

"Go on. Take one," I said.

She did and I held a light towards her.

"Pull yourself together." I said it softly.

"Sorry," she murmured and drew hard on the cigarette.

"Up and out?" I said. "Just like that? You're a Government servant, Miss Frenton. I don't know the background, but—"

"I put in my transfer application weeks ago."

"Then I presume Mr. Drayton forwarded it. I haven't yet taken over the station. But, in any event, you know it isn't up to the District Commissioner. The powers-that-be take weeks over these things. It's a wearisome business."

"You must do something, please. I've got to get away!"

She looked very young and at bay somehow. Twenty-five or six? Difficult to judge with some women.

"At the risk of rushing in where angels fear to tread, Miss Frenton, let me say this: I know it sounds trite and pompous, but nothing is ever solved by running away."

"You don't understand." There was a hint of tears in her voice.

"Obviously. How could I? But I'd like to. Come and see me at the office."

I took a deep breath. This whole welcoming party was even more of a disaster than I had anticipated.

I tried smiling at her. "Despite the studied lack of interest in our conversation, the whole room is waiting for you to throw a fit of hysterics. Disappoint them."

There was an answering flicker of a smile, so brief it was gone in a blink.

"Let me get you another sherry," I said.

"No. I..." she stopped and swallowed. "I shouldn't have come, but I felt I had to."

"Quite right; but having made the effort—don't spoil it." It sounded cruel, even to me, but the tinge of colour which crept into her face seemed to justify the brusqueness of my voice.

From the corner of my eye I could see Drayton making his way towards us.

I could also see Grace Nelson, staring coldly at my companion, with a grimace pulling her mouth.

"How's your drink, Lancaster?" Drayton asked as he arrived, but his attention was on Janet Frenton's face. "You don't look well, Janet," he said. "Would you like someone to take you home?"

"No. I'm staying. I've changed my mind about that sherry. It's all right, I'll get it from David."

"Hmm," Drayton said to her retreating back. Then he turned to me, all business again. "There are only two people not here tonight: the Brackenhursts. They farm about fifty miles north. They're the biggest farmers in the District. They come in only very occasionally. Brackenhurst runs a couple of lorries to Lusaka every month. We sometimes get supplies through him."

He was speaking idly, his thoughts were obviously elsewhere.

I was rescued by the Jones. They were the middle-aged couple I had noticed at the funeral; the ones the priest had mentioned ran the store. Drayton made introductions and moved away.

They were pleasant and amiable, a blessed relief after the conversation so far. We talked about the stations I had worked on and I dodged the inevitable questions about when Ann would be joining me here.

"We've made this our home," Jones said. "We've no ties now to the UK. We'll leave our bones here."

He broke off suddenly; hesitating, perhaps feeling he was sounding disloyal or unpatriotic. His wife came to his rescue.

"We've settled here for good, Mr. Lancaster. We've got our roots down here now. Our son farms in the Northern Province. He's doing very well, too."

There was a placid, solid quality about Mrs. Jones. She looked the type that would work cheerfully in the store all day, cook well in the evening and then sew until bedtime.

Jones was a sound enough type, but with that over-freeness of manner and slight aggressiveness of speech which some self-made men appear to acquire as a corollary of their years of individual effort.

"I took up the option and never looked back," he said of how he'd started.

"Good for you, Mr. Jones," I said. "Must have been a lot of hard work."

While we spoke, I watched Drobinall talking to the Nelsons. Was it my imagination, or was there an air of conspiracy about the three of them?

Nelson inclined his head towards Drobinall's face, listening; but his gaze, hostile and watchful, was fixed on Drayton who was leaning against the verandah door, talking to the Groblers.

I heard Drayton promise Grobler that we should make an early trip out to inspect the finished strip of the new road, but it was clear his attention was focused on the other side of the room, where David Young appeared to be reasoning with the nursing sister, with no obvious success.

"...for twenty-five years." Jones was still talking.

"...twenty-four years." Mrs. Jones corrected her husband absently. I realised that she too, was watching Janet Frenton, a worried frown between her eyes. Suddenly, with a muttered apology over her shoulder, she left us to join David Young and the girl.

I continued to talk to Jones with half my mind on it, but I was more interested in the by-play in the room. Despite the studied nonchalance of turned backs and averted eyes, the girl and Drayton were the focal points of interest.

I sensed sympathy for the nursing sister. Quite the opposite for Drayton.

I decided, looking around me, that the usual division of interests, common to these sundowners, would have been pleasanter with the men clustered near the drinks, talking shop, and the women discussing the delays in the mail, the latest reports on children at far-away schools and the most recent gossip from wherever it came.

Prail came in from the verandah door at the far end of the room.

"Just been getting a breath of air. It's mighty hot in here. When are you likely to be over to see our little set-up, sir?" he asked me. There was the slightest slur to his speech.

"Hope to get over one day next week. There are quite a few bits and pieces to tie up when a station is being handed over. First things first. Have I got it right, that you're hoping to complete your survey within three months or so?"

"That is so."

"Does the Foundation feel that the survey has served a useful purpose?"

"Well, I guess so. There've been four teams in Central Africa and collated field reports seem to be getting them that much ahead."

"What are your plans when you leave here?" I asked.

"The Institute is talking of a possibility of a similar survey in South America on mosquitoes. In the Lower Andes. But as you say, sir, first things first. So back to the States for a spell when we finish up here. Mighty fine butterfly country, South America though. Shouldn't mind at all getting down there for a bit."

A thin trickle of sweat slipped down from the sparse hairline and dripped unnoticed on to his collar.

"You're interested in butterflies, then?"

"And how!" With the enthusiasm of the collector he described his latest specimens.

I had to stem the flood of Leptomyrina lara and Danaus chrysippus, and asked: "How has your wife settled down here?"

"Oh, Elsa's an adaptable woman. She makes out wherever we happen to land up." Over the rim of his glass, a gleam of something flickered and died in the pale eyes. "But I don't think she'll be all that sorry to get back to the States." he added slowly. "As I told Mr. Drayton, she's been finding the heat trying just lately. I want to get her away to Lusaka for a break. We had the notion of skipping off there a week or two back but circumstances decided otherwise. But we'll try to make it now. Elsa is bound to feel a bit of a gap with Elizabeth... I mean with Mrs. Drayton gone."

The introduction of the name seemed to act as a brake on

his tongue. He gazed down at his glass, swirling the last dregs round and round.

"Pity" he said at last. "So sudden. A great pity."

"It was the suddenness of it all, wasn't it?" said Jones.

Before Prail could respond, Drayton returned and interrupted.

"I'm off," he said to me. He sounded angry. "Would you like to stay on?"

"No, I'm ready." I tossed back my drink.

It had seemed a long hour.

I waited for him at the top of the verandah steps whilst he hunted around for his torch. David Young hovered. From the room behind, voices seemed to die suddenly. I heard Grace Nelson laugh.

Drayton was silent as we walked back to the house for dinner.

A hippo snorted from the river, a trumpeting bass in the orchestra of cicadas and bull-frogs.

I did not think it quite the right moment to broach the subject of Janet Frenton's transfer, even had I felt inclined to. I would no doubt hear more about it.

There was also something else on my mind.

It was not unknown for a District Commissioner to be disliked by members of his staff, or their wives, on an outstation. The man in authority could be quite unpopular.

But at Feira that evening I realised that it was a little more than that; at least as far as the Nelsons and Drobinall were concerned. As Prail might have expressively put it: they hated Drayton's guts.

CHAPTER 6

The following day, Drayton elected to pack during the afternoon. I left him to it and went down to the Boma office, looking to use the quiet time to get ahead on my reading of the station files. Afternoons were usually a good opportunity to work without interruption.

It was not to be.

I'd made a reasonable start when Mrs. Jones poked her head round the open door of the office. I had an idea what it would be about, and making myself available would be part of my duty when I formally took over, so I pushed aside the files and smiled in welcome, while I sighed inwardly.

"Come in and sit down, Mrs. Jones. Hot afternoon to be abroad. What can I do for you?"

At the party, I'd pigeonholed her as the placid type, but like many such, they have an alternative side. She had barely seated herself before the words tumbled from her mouth with a rush born of nervousness and banked excitement.

"Elsa Prail mustn't get away with this. You must put a stop to it, Mr. Lancaster, or Mr. Drayton must. She's letting her tongue run away with her. You can't let Janet go off like this; she's packing this very minute." She paused for breath. "You don't know where this sort of thing will end. It could ruin the girl's life."

"I presume you're referring to Mrs. Prail's remarks at the funeral?"

"That, and the rest." Righteous anger succeeded the nervousness in her voice. "Don't you think that Elsa Prail has stopped at that. If it had been only that, well, we all know she was upset and everything, and we all say things we are sorry for, but..."

"Has she said anything more?"

"She must have. Mr. Drobinall was in the store this morning, hinting and smirking. Where would he have got it from if not from her? He and the Prails are as thick as thieves and I wouldn't put it past them—"

"Perhaps you'd better tell me exactly what he did say." Sweat stuck my back to the chair and I felt thirsty; thirsty and irritated. I needed to deal with the problem, but this felt as if it was the wrong way.

"Well." She composed herself. "He was saying something about his having missed all the excitement and the 'goings-on'. He said it just like that, 'goings-on'. You know the way he talks. I pretended I didn't know what he meant. But that wasn't the worst. Two minutes later I heard him asking her when the post-mortem was going to be held. Of course he was joking but—"

God!

"Hang on a moment," I interrupted her again. "Do you mean to say you overheard him asking Mrs. Prail about a post-mortem?"

"No. No. He was talking to Grace Nelson. She came into the shop whilst I was in the back getting a case of soap brought in for Mr. Drobinall. He buys stores in bulk, you see, when he comes in from Baluti."

"Hold on, Mrs. Jones. Why assume he was referring to Mrs. Drayton's death? She died from enteritis and she's buried. There wasn't and won't be a medical post-mortem.

41

Perhaps he was talking about something unrelated—a post-mortem could be about anything. Perhaps about the government's decision to nationalise the gas industry."

Heaven knows it had been on everyone's lips in England, though I had to admit it was a weak example for a discussion in the middle of the African bush.

"Not him," Mrs. Jones said. "I heard him mention Mrs. Drayton. And if it was all innocent, why should Grace Nelson hush him up when she saw me coming? Oh, no."

"Suppose you tell me, if you can remember, exactly what he said to Mrs. Nelson."

Mrs. Jones pushed back a strand of greying hair from her damp, flushed face and frowned in concentration.

"I think... no, wait a minute, this is how he put it: 'spot of excitement at Mrs. Drayton's funeral'. Then 'our Elsa's the girl! I'm sorry I missed that' and 'I mustn't miss the post-mortem. When's that going to be?'" She leant back. "It was then that Grace Nelson saw me coming back and shushed him."

Mrs. Jones had aped Drobinall's manner of speech in repeating his words and I could almost hear him saying them. I hadn't liked him at the sundowner, and I liked him less now.

"All right, Mrs. Jones. It does sound as though Drobinall was, in fact, referring to the incident at the funeral and some conversation that followed it. But why do you assume Mrs. Prail is responsible for spreading gossip?"

"Of course she is. She, and nobody else, started it. And Drobinall went back to the Prail's house last night. I saw his car turn into their drive as we passed on our way home. That poor girl, Janet. If she were my daughter..." She looked away, caught between being angry about it all and pleading the case to me.

"Did Miss Frenton ask you to come and see me?" I said.

"No. I haven't seen her since last night. But I know she's packing; she sent down her servant to see if I'd got any old tea chests. I wouldn't repeat to her what I've just told you. It would only upset her more." One hand was floating up to push her hair back again. She stopped it and folded her hands in her lap. "And, please don't let on to my husband that I've been here. He'd chide me for interfering. It can be bad for business getting mixed up in this sort of thing. But I like the girl. I'm old enough to be her mother."

I found myself wondering whether a genuine concern for the nursing sister's reputation was her only motive in coming to see me with such a story. Not that it mattered; I thought she was telling the truth.

"What on earth did Elsa Prail tell him," she was saying, "that would make him joke about a thing like a post-mortem? It must have been libellous, whatever it was."

"Slanderous," I corrected mechanically, under my breath. But I appreciated her point. Had something more been said by Elsa Prail, or by anybody on the Boma? Or had the original incident been embroidered and the words twisted to a degree sufficient to evoke such a facetious comment from Drobinall?

It didn't sound healthy, whatever it was.

"Yes. Quite. I agree." I stood up and gently urged her toward the door. "Of course you were right to come and see me about it. Leave it with me."

I watched her go, conscious of a rising tide of frustration with the station and with the people living on it. This wasn't a good omen, certainly not this early in a tour. I needed to put this gossip and slander to one side; concentrate on getting a grip of the important detail of the administration of the district.

So I sent the messenger up to the house in search of iced water and turned back into the office. The smell of pencils, dust and old paper settled afresh in the returning quiet.

Reading through files was a necessary but dull occupation, essential on taking over a new station. I knew that. Within another fifteen minutes I found out it was a waste of time to attempt it at the moment.

Eventually, I gave up. I shuffled Political, Awards, Instructions, Codes and Security back into the steel safe set in the concrete wall and pulled out the file on Staff.

The only paper in the file relating to Janet Frenton was a memorandum from Health, dated July, announcing that she would take over Spencer's duties whilst he was on leave. There was no note of an application for a transfer having gone forward which an administrator like Drayton would normally have filed.

Deliberate omission? If so, why?

Or just an understandable slip? A busy man making an uncharacteristic error?

I paged through the rest of the file.

I noticed that Drobinall was a comparatively new arrival to the Territory and had been at Baluti for two years and Nelson appeared to be the longest serving European in Feira. This was his second tour of duty there.

It was mainly unexceptional, but of David Young, Drayton had written: 'Reliable, conscientious, though I feel he lives up to his name on occasions; a failing which time and experience will undoubtedly eradicate.'

Apart from that comment, the file was as bland as could possibly be. Certainly no hint of a source for the problems that seemed to afflict the people here so badly.

Frustrated, I pushed the Staff file back into the safe. As I did, a slim file marked 'Unofficial' caught my eye and I pulled it out.

It contained a miscellany of notes in Drayton's hand. It was an odd collection, more in the nature of an aide memoire, I judged. There were brief notes of conversations and the dates on which they took place; notes on the movement of elephant and buffalo herds; the distilling of the kachasu alcoholic drink from maso berries; the native custom of hanging the bodies of dead lepers in trees; treatment of snake bite with the 'snake-stone' and barks of certain trees; poisonous plants; notes on a discussion with Brackenhurst regarding the cross-breeding of African cattle with Zebu bulls from North Africa.

Some of the notes I recalled having seen written out at report length in their relevant files and the District Notebook. Nelson's name appeared frequently and the dissension between him and Drayton was obvious from the content. I wondered what the significance was of a large question mark which Drayton had scrawled under a list of dates and numbers and headed 'Nelson'.

Then I came to the last sheet in the file. It was dated August and below Drayton had written:

'Warned Drobinall that further complaints from the Baluti headman regarding the local girls will necessitate his transfer—with explanations in his file.'

God!

Drayton had made a remark at the sundowner the previous evening about the advantages of bush life; Drobinall hadn't liked it. He'd also reacted oddly when I spoke about a visit to Baluti. Clearly, with that warning, the man would be on edge, and I'd no doubt Drayton's handling of him could be at least part of the reason Drobinall hated Drayton.

But thinking carefully through my recollection of the reactions to the comment, Grace Nelson hadn't liked it either, and I had the feeling that Drayton's remark had been directed at her. Drobinall had been a bystander. Had his guilt made him feel the comment was directed at him?

With a sigh, I slipped the file back on the shelf and locked the door of the safe.

I lost all pretence of trying to update myself on the administration of the station and simply sat, thinking through everything I'd heard and seen of the staff in light of what I had learnt that afternoon.

What exactly had Elsa Prail said at Elizabeth Drayton's graveside?

'You let her die…' No, that wasn't quite it. 'You wanted her to die. Both you and Barnaby are to blame. You let her die.'

Yes. That was it. And then: 'if Elizabeth had gone away she'd be alive now.'

I poured a second glass of water from the thermos and drank it while I watched the lazy progress of a stink beetle across the floor between the door and the desk. From time to time the insect paused and rested as though, it too, felt drained in the afternoon heat.

When I learnt that Janet Frenton was our nurse, I'd taken Elsa Prail's words to be an accusation of medical incompetence, perhaps with Drayton somehow contributing by not being helpful enough.

However to link Drayton and Frenton together like that, with all the further gossip and poisonous rumours…

Was she accusing them of an affair? Suggesting Elizabeth Drayton killed herself because of it?

Or was it something much more sinister?

I couldn't just leave it and I certainly couldn't assume the situation would resolve itself when Drayton left.

An allegation had been made, and at least one of the people who'd had it made against them might suffer ramifications if this wasn't cleared up now.

More selfishly, I had to admit to myself, I had my marriage to think of. Ann wasn't fully recovered. It was going to be difficult enough to persuade her to come back out to Africa, especially to Feira, without it also being to a station riven by this sort of venomous undercurrent.

Of course, her parents weren't helping. They'd insisted on a full marriage ceremony while Ann was still pale as a ghost. Their unceasing hints that I should transfer to a different branch of the service while I was in England had no doubt changed to comments about my shirking my responsibilities. I wouldn't put it past Ann's father to find out some rumour of what had happened in Feira and paint it all in the worst possible light.

Well, I could wallow in self-pity, or I could solve this puzzle and ensure my district report was as bland and boring a recitation of the solution as was possible.

I had an idea where to start. On a shelf fixed to the wall above the safe was a collection of books to be found in every Boma Office: Colonial Regulations, bound copies of the Government Gazette and General Orders. I found the book I was looking for, wedged between Stone's Justice's Manual and Robson's Local Government; I slapped it free from dust and thumbed through it:

> 'Defamatory statement', 'slander if spoken or conveyed in some form which is not lasting', 'Special Damage', 'slander is not actionable without proof of actual damage'.

I paged through the exhaustive legal definitions until I came to the terms I wanted.

> 'Words spoken of the plaintiff in relation to his profession, trade or office, which impute to him

47

unfitness for, or misconduct, in that calling.'

I read it through until I was sure I had the wording right. That certainly covered it. Of course, it was all contingent on whether the allegation was true or not.

I replaced the book on the shelf.

'You don't know where this sort of thing will end,' Mrs. Jones had said. How right she was.

I sat and thought about that while the harsh sunlight that slanted through the open door reached slowly across the floor.

CHAPTER 7

My private sundial had almost reached its limit when the Head Messenger turned up, accompanied by his second-in-command.

There was an embarrassed, foot-shuffling air about them; a hint of deputation in their general demeanour.

"Well, Nyrenda? What is it?" Given how the afternoon had gone, I was more abrupt than I intended.

"Bwana, we cannot find the one who beats the drum in the night." He cleared his throat. "The people are very afraid."

"What drum?" I shuffled my notes together and checked the safe door was locked, but then I gave them my full attention. The issue itself might or might not be important, but the messengers were essential for the smooth running of the station.

Of course, I had a fair idea of what drum they meant, and that Drayton would have sent them to investigate, but I wanted to hear their approach to it.

It was a strange story they told.

The heart of it, when finally extracted from a certain amount of verbal camouflage, was that the sleeping inhabitants of the compounds were being disturbed during the night by the beating of a drum; an invisible drum, beaten by an invisible drummer. In the gradually increasing terror evoked by this ghost drum, the main body of the compound inhabitants had stayed indoors, but the messengers had formed a night watch to try and locate the drum. They had been unsuccessful; tracking the will-o'-the-wisp drumming in one direction, when it would fade and die as they seemed to approach. Then it would start up again behind them. Sometimes, it would grow louder and louder and seem to pass over them.

"Outside my hut I hear it, just there," said the second messenger pointing at the ground in front of him, "but there is nobody."

"A drum harms nobody; why are the people afraid?" I asked.

"The people fear Matafwali, bwana." Nyrenda's voice lowered and the name seemed to echo in the still airlessness of the room.

"Matafwali is dead. Why fear him now?" I said, frowning. "And anyway, what's Matafwali got to do with the drumming?"

"The drumming, it starts and it finishes at the place where the Donna D.C. lies," Nyrenda said.

Elizabeth Drayton's grave.

"The people say it is Matafwali," his colleague pitched in. "They remember his words before he was taken from Feira."

"What words were those?"

I stacked the general files into the out basket and swept the odd bits of paper rubbish into the waste bin, signalling that the new Bwana D.C. didn't want a long-winded explanation.

Nyrenda stayed silent, and it was the second messenger who eventually answered. "Matafwali said death come to the house of the Bwana D.C., sure as it come to him at Lusaka."

"And it is as he said," Nyrenda added. "The Donna D.C. is dead. The people say it is Matafwali who is beating the drum, so people remember his power is great and—"

"Rubbish!" I broke in before they got completely carried away. "If that is what people are saying, they're speaking nonsense. Matafwali is dead. He can beat no drum. The Donna D.C. died of the sickness carried by the little bugs that you cannot see. It is they who are powerful, not Matafwali."

"The people say it is Matafwali who brings death to the Donna," Nyrenda said softly. "They are afraid."

"Well, go tell the people what I say, Nyrenda," I answered sharply. "Matafwali is dead. If he had power, it was only a power given to him by the villagers' belief. Any power he had was broken as surely as the rope broke his neck. As for the drumming, it sounds as though someone is making fools of all of you."

I stopped myself and went on in a different tone. "Leave these fears and fancies to the women and children. You are messengers. You wear the uniform. You are proud and strong, so Matafwali can never have power over you."

I dismissed them, and through the open door, I watched them give an account of the discussion to the duty messenger squatting beneath the fig tree.

Even if they had gone out with their heads higher, I hadn't completely convinced them.

It would do no good to pay more obvious attention to their mysterious drummer, I thought, but I could well gauge the effect on the minds of the local population of the coincidence of Elizabeth Drayton's death occurring within days of Matafwali's execution. The apparent fulfilment of his prophecy would be more than enough to account for the unease on the Boma.

I wondered whether Drayton had heard about it.

And the drumming itself? I toyed with the idea of a lone drummer on the other side of the river. Some effect of echoes? A mirage of sound rather than vision, caused by the geographical formation of the escarpment? It certainly sounded more plausible to me than the drumming of a phantom witchdoctor, dancing through the village.

I looked down at the files on my desk. Among them was the Court file which I had already read through, finishing earlier that afternoon. It had contained little of great moment: assault, theft, even witchcraft; but nothing outside the usual run of Court cases in the bush. I drew it towards me. Drayton's Preliminary Enquiry on Matafwali was in there. Having read the account of the proceedings in the Provincial Commissioner's Court, I had skipped the enquiry report that afternoon. I paged through it. There was little new, but I thought what odd reading the list of exhibits made:-

3 military buttons
several strips of animal skin
two dried claws of an eagle
one stuffed owl
one kalilosi gun
one calabash rattle
one wooden mask with fabric ornamentation
bundles of herbs, barks, leaves
roots [unidentified]

And on and on.

I read it to the end. Most of it was the usual paraphernalia of the witchdoctor.

Some of the stuff, I'd noticed, still lay, coated in dust, on the trestle table which ran the length of one wall of the office. There were beads, animal bones and unusual shells;

perhaps one or two items of possible interest to a collector.

Attached to the end of the report were notes on additional investigations being made in the Chiabele area. I slipped the file back into the basket and went over to the trestle table. I picked up a few pieces to inspect them; the mask, the rattle, the hollowed rhino horn.

It was while I was looking down idly at that collection, speculating on the fear it could engender, that the ancient telephone, set on the wall, gave a rusty tinkle.

The telephone system at Feira was a Heath Robinson affair; a party line, connecting some of the houses on the station with the office. It was seldom used. Its reliability, like its age, was an uncertain quantity.

It tinkled again and, dropping the horn which I had picked up, I went over and unhooked the ear piece. "Lancaster here."

In my ears came a surging roar like floodwaters, a crackling, and a faint voice.

"Lancaster here," I repeated. "Speak up! I can't hear you."

The voice seemed barely a whisper, but for a few brief moments, it hissed above through the background noise. "Find out how she died," it said.

"What the hell? Who's there?" I shouted into the mouthpiece.

There came a sigh and a click, then only a booming surge, as of distant seas.

Outside, the shadows had lengthened over the Boma lawn.

CHAPTER 8

The house and garden was as still as an old photograph.

Drayton was nowhere to be seen, and I decided to take a bath before he returned.

From my bedroom window I scanned the sky. Surely there was a storm in the offing. With a drop in the temperature tongues and tempers might settle down. There would be less of this nonsense all around, drummers and anonymous phone calls included.

But damn it, I then thought as I climbed in the bath, Mrs. Jones was right: the gossip had to be stopped. It was no good counting on a change in the weather. I'd have to discuss it with Drayton. I swore softly under my breath. Why had he taken no action? Was it what I'd come to suspect—he'd actually been having an affair with the girl?

'You and Barnaby,' Else Prail had said, coupling them together.

If it was a false allegation, an apology to Drayton and the girl should cover it: a written retraction posted at the Boma should quieten tongues. Faced with a suit for slander, it shouldn't be difficult to persuade Mrs. Prail to fall in line; and perhaps a few words with Drobinall wouldn't come amiss either.

My mind turned it over as I lay in the tepid bath.

I dressed slowly afterward, but by the time I joined Drayton on the verandah my clothes were again stuck to my body with fresh rivulets of sweat. The air itself felt hot, like the exhaust from a truck.

"Help yourself, Lancaster," he motioned towards the drinks tray. "God, this heat! Where are the bloody rains?"

"Feels like there's a storm brewing now. The rain can't be far off." I poured whisky over some vanishing ice cubes. "How's the packing going?"

"Slowly."

In the gathering shadows of the verandah, Drayton looked pale and tired. Of course, he would be packing his dead wife's effects as well. Whatever he said, that had to take some toll.

"Where's Kalinga with those confounded lamps?" He hoisted himself abruptly from his chair and went off to the back of the house, alternately muttering under his breath and shouting for Kalinga.

He seemed calmer when he returned, as though the yelling had eased some inward tension. I decided to postpone the discussion of the rising station gossip until later in the evening, and started talking idly.

"I've been looking through the safe this afternoon," I said over my shoulder as he diverted to the drinks tray. "I found your 'Unofficial' file. Interesting bits and bobs."

"Much of it's duplication." He splashed soda on his whisky. "Most of the items you'll find written up in the appropriate files. Some of it I've written up in the District Notebook. For the rest, well, I'll take the file. Might write it up privately, make a book of reminiscences, if I ever get down to it." He snorted. "I'll be in the company of host of other retired District Officers of H.M. Colonial Service, I'm sure."

I didn't comment on the thought of another colonial

memoire, but there was some information in the file that needed to be kept on-station.

"I gather that Drobinall has an unhealthy interest in Africana," I said to prompt him on that.

"I think his interest has waned considerably," Drayton replied drily, "since I made him copy out the law regarding defilement of girls before they reach the age of puberty." He raised a hand to stop me interrupting. "Not that it amounted to that. It was bottom pinching and lewd suggestions, but that's beside the point. It could lead to something damned unpleasant. I shouldn't hesitate to report it and get him out if you hear any more of it."

I relaxed. For a moment there I had thought Drayton had allowed Drobinall to get away with rape.

"No, I think I've frightened him off. The headman at Baluti will tell you soon enough if it starts again. I'll leave those sort of notes with you."

"Fair enough. What's his work like? Drobinall?"

Drayton shrugged. "Adequate, when he keeps his mind on it. Not so good that I would risk trouble at Baluti to keep him there." He glanced at his watch. "I suggest we eat out here. The dining room feels like a Turkish bath."

"That's a good idea."

We drank in companionable silence for a few minutes, but I had a list to get through with Drayton, and this was as opportune a time as any to talk of staff issues.

"What's your opinion of Nelson's work?" I asked, starting from the neutral end of the issues. "It's quite obvious from the files that you and he don't often see eye to eye."

"I think he's fiddling Government trophies," Drayton said. "Ivory. You must have seen the list in my file, of dates and numbers?"

"Yes, I saw it, but it didn't mean anything to me."

But now his comment to Grace Nelson at the sundowner made sense to me; that life out here had material advantages.

"No, I suppose not. Well, I've noticed discrepancies in the weights register. The numbers of tusks have shrunk during the journey to the Boma. Now, it could be clerical errors, but I don't think so. Not that many." He took a long drink and sighed. "He's unpopular with the Africans... has trouble with his carriers. Always a bad sign. And they talk. I'll go through the register with you tomorrow. I think he's getting the stuff shipped out of Dar es Salaam but don't ask me how he's getting it there."

That had been the first thing that occurred to me.

"I'll make a report to the P.C. on the way out; can't do any more this end," Drayton said. "You'll have to watch it in the meantime."

"You've not discussed it with Nelson then?" I asked.

"No. He doesn't realise I'm on to it, I'm sure."

I had a suspicion that Drayton was wrong there, but I said nothing. Certainly if he was making comments like that to the man's wife, one or both would suspect.

"He's a good enough game ranger," Drayton went on, "the main trouble is that he's been in Feira too long to take kindly to authority in the shape of the new boy." He gave a bark of laughter, pointing to himself. "Me? I've been in Feira for only two years. Nelson wants to be a law unto himself. I don't have to tell you, you know the type, Lancaster, a few years in the Territory and they know all the answers. They resent the authority of the Provincial Administration and what they term 'unknowledgeable interference' with their own little corner."

"I've met the type." I admitted.

Kalinga interrupted us with dinner and conversation became general during the meal; fishing, game, the Staff List, the last promotion list, the new salary review.

From a discussion over coffee on the tsetse fly problem and the value of the research work done over the past year, talk naturally turned to Prail.

"He's a good biologist," Drayton said, "but a soak."

He smiled faintly and looked at the glass on the table beside him. He had just refilled it. "I know," he went on, "glasshouses and throwing stones. I admit I'm drinking too much, but I don't stupefy myself with the stuff. Prail blots it up until he's out for the count. Goes on a bender every weekend. Still... I might do the same if I had the bitch of a wife that he's got."

From the hills came the first blessed rolls of thunder. It was a good opening and I took it.

"Well, as we seem to have got round to Mrs. Prail, I must tell you I've had a session with Mrs. Jones this afternoon. There's some unhealthy gossip going the rounds, I think possibly triggered by Mrs. Prail's remarks at your wife's funeral." I related briefly to Drayton what Mrs. Jones had said.

Drayton swore fluently for a few seconds.

"There's no proof," I finished, "that Mrs. Prail has added anything to what she said at the funeral. No proof that anybody else has, either. But if her original remarks are giving rise to this sort of comment, I think some action should be taken before Miss Frenton leaves. According to Mrs. Jones, Miss Frenton is packing now to leave—posting or not."

Drayton raised his eyebrows but said nothing.

"What happened about her application for a posting, by the way?" I said. "I didn't see any note of it in the Staff file."

"I sent it off three weeks or so ago. I've heard nothing." Drayton's answer was abrupt.

I realised suddenly, as I looked more closely at him, that

he hadn't known about Janet Frenton's impending departure until I'd mentioned it.

I had to follow this questioning through. The necessity to do that with Drayton, within days of his wife's death was painful. But he appeared to have chosen not to pursue it, and so I had to.

I took a turn or two about the verandah.

"You know the Prail woman better than I do." I said. "She was clearly overwrought, but it was a stupid, dangerous remark to make. One guaranteed to set tongues wagging. It's not that gossip on an outstation would be anything new, but this is damaging."

Drayton didn't respond.

"Even if you're inclined to ignore it as far as it concerns yourself," I said, "have you thought of the possible harm to Miss Frenton's career, in that an unfortunate interpretation could be put on Mrs. Prail's words?"

"I have," Drayton said tersely. "I told Prail the other day, the day it happened, that I'd slap a slander suit on his wife if she didn't watch her tongue and apologise. For my own part, I couldn't care less what she says, but Janet's a different matter."

He spoke as though I knew the whole background to the story and, in the prickle of embarrassment at the necessity to pry further, I felt my temper rise.

"Look here, Drayton," I said as mildly as I could, "little as I feel inclined to hear more of this wretched business, I can't help but think it reasonable to put me in the picture. You'll soon be off and I shall probably end up with the backwash of it. What led up to this outburst of Mrs. Prail's?"

"Jealousy. Jealousy and superstitious nonsense," he said. "She's jealous of Janet Frenton. She, in common with the rest of the Boma, thinks I'm having an affair with the girl. My wife certainly thought so." He put his glass down with a thump. "They're all completely wrong."

From the faint, cynical smile that twisted his mouth, I knew he realised that I'd suspected it too.

He got up and pumped the spluttering lamp. Attracted by the revived light, the flying ants beat desperate wings against the mosquito gauze.

He lit a cigarette and leant against the back of his chair, looking out sombrely into the darkness. I felt that more was coming, so I sat quietly and waited.

"No. It wasn't Janet," he said. "It was Elsa Prail I had the affair with."

That I really hadn't anticipated.

Drayton pulled on his cigarette and flicked ash into the ashtray.

"You know how it goes, Lancaster—or perhaps you don't." He sighed and ran a hand through his hair. "You know, looking back on it, I'm not sure that I do myself. You wake up one morning and wonder how and why the bloody hell it started."

The chair creaked as he shifted position.

"It was a brief episode and it finished weeks before Janet Frenton came to Feira, but Elsa wouldn't accept that it had. I don't think she ever doubted that I'd go back to her, right up until Janet arrived. She was jealous of Janet from the moment they met. She got it into her head that Janet and I were having an affair, and there was hell to pay."

Drayton grimaced and slapped at the flying ants which had found their way under the door.

"Well, thank you," I said. "That, I guess, is the first part of the picture. What about the superstitious nonsense you mentioned?"

Drayton snorted.

"I suppose you've heard that on the last day of the Preliminary Enquiry in Court here, Matafwali made some stupid threat about this house?"

"Yes, I heard something about it at the Boma this afternoon."

"Well, I don't know how it got back to my wife, but it did. Her monkey died within a day or so of Matafwali being sent off to Lusaka. That started it. All absolute nonsense of course. The animal was probably poisoned by one of the servants. They hated the bloody thing."

He ground out his cigarette and refilled his drink.

"Elizabeth and Elsa both got the idea that it was this damn fool curse. Then once Elizabeth was sick, there it was: proof. You know what Elsa said to me the night before my wife died? 'I told you so'. She told me it was all my fault and that I should have sent her to England, or anywhere, so long as it was out of this house."

He looked suddenly weary of the subject.

"Perhaps I should have," he said. "Perhaps it would have been wiser in more ways than one."

"The Africans on the Boma share the nonsense," I said, and told him of Nyrenda's report of the afternoon.

Drayton looked at me over the rim of his glass. There was a curious, guarded expression in his eyes.

"Well, there's at least some excuse for them to think that way," he said. "They suck in a fear of witchcraft with their mother's milk, but that educated women should..."

The thunder rolled again, threatening, nearer. The first jagged streaks of lightning lit the far ridges of the hills and there was the slightest change in the air.

"Of course, when you're ill," Drayton muttered, half to himself, "these things can prey on your mind. Maybe more than I realised."

He got up restlessly, brought the drinks tray to the table between us and moved the lamp away. When he sat again, his face was in shadow.

"For a long time now," he said softly, "I've been rated a prize bastard for my treatment of Elizabeth. She played up to that. She lived on the sympathy of the world. But the truth is, Lancaster, that Elizabeth hadn't been my wife—in the accepted sense of the word—for years. She was my housekeeper. She stayed with me as a matter of face and social standing and she positively enjoyed the role of the neglected, little woman at home. In a way, I think she was glad of my extramarital activities because they eased her conscience."

I wondered if he was trying to convince me, or himself.

"She was a bitter, neurotic woman without the slightest interest in me as a man. As her husband, I was a badge of respectability. If she had any affection for anything at all, it was for her monkey. Divorce?" He snorted. "She was a Catholic. God knows I gave her enough grounds. Elsa Prail wasn't an isolated instance by any means, though strangely, it was the one she didn't know about. In fact nobody knew. I didn't broadcast it. I wasn't proud of it. The others I've made no secret of, but they were outside our own circle."

I had no doubt that Drayton was telling me the truth as he saw it, but in my experience, someone always knows. Always.

"We had no children," Drayton said. "Perhaps that had some bearing on it. We found we'd grown so far apart after the war, but perhaps we'd never been really close. I don't know, but the sum total of everything is that I can't pretend that I'm a heartbroken widower."

We weren't drunk, Drayton and I. I'm not trying to extol the virtues of whisky or claim in vino veritas, but he told me many things that night. He told them in an extremely matter-of-fact way, without emotion and without inhibition. It was a compelling statement of account which he compiled in the manner of an independent observer. He drew no lessons or conclusion from his recounting and I didn't get the impression that he spoke in extenuation of his own conduct. It was just that he had to tell someone.

Despite what he said about his wife, there was an unacknowledged grief there, and this was a sort of ritual he needed to exorcise it. As he talked, he visibly relaxed. That core of tension I had seen since I arrived started to loosen.

I felt instinctively that it helped that I was a comparative stranger, that it was too dark, with the lamp behind us, to make out each other's faces, and that I said almost nothing in response. I was taking over his position here in Feira. Perhaps that made him see something of himself in me, or feel that he was speaking to a shadowy mirror of himself.

"That's how it was," he finished, "so you see, a little more unpleasantness such as this wasn't unexpected after the past months." He poured himself another drink.

I made no comment on what he had told me. Any comment, I felt, would have been inadequate; neither did he expect one.

We sat for some time in silence, watching the slow, teasing progress of the storm. Lightning lit up the grounds in ghostly, momentary splendour. The scent of rain came wafting in on a fresh breeze. For the first time since I'd arrived, I wasn't hot.

"Well," I said eventually, rising to go to bed, "a written retraction by Mrs. Prail, circulated to the Boma should quieten tongues and act as a deterrent to further talk."

We discussed briefly which of us should take the task. I reluctantly agreed that my voice, as an outsider's, would be carry more weight with Mrs. Prail. I looked forward with no degree of pleasure to tomorrow's interview.

I decided on the spur of the moment that there was no point in telling Drayton about the telephone call.

The first savage onslaught of rain against the corrugated iron roof woke me from a deep sleep. It was long after midnight. Cool currents of moist air carried the smell of freshly flooded earth into the room and set the mosquito net swaying. The windows blazed as lightning struck.

I pulled up the sheet and shivered, listening to the storm for a while, savouring the blessed relief of the dropping temperature.

I soon realised any prospect of sleep had gone. I moved a couple of chairs up to the window and I sat there with my feet up, watching the immense flashes of lightning around the ridges of the escarpment, listening to the drumming of rain on the roof, the suck and gurgle of water draining down to the greedy earth.

My mind back-pedalled idly over my conversation with Drayton. That a man of his calibre could have got bogged down in the marital mess he had described so dispassionately, surprised me. It seemed alien to his character as I read it, but I had no feeling that he'd lied.

A simple written retraction about that specific allegation, that Drayton and Frenton had had an affair, would protect Janet Frenton's reputation. Drayton declared himself utterly unconcerned about any other gossip directed at him. Finally, any implication that Janet Frenton had fallen short in her care of Elizabeth Drayton, I could counter with Father Bravachko's professional evaluation that Frenton was an excellent nurse, and that everything possible that could have been done for Mrs. Drayton, had been done before he arrived.

Neatly tied up?

As a child, I had been given a present by an uncle one Christmas. It was a set of oddly shaped bricks. It was a puzzle, the objective of which was to find the one way in which a stable tower could be built using all the bricks. There had been, of course, many ways unstable towers could be built.

Why did that old memory surface and nag at me?

My thoughts turned to the general unease of the African population on the Boma and the unfortunate coincidence of Elizabeth Drayton's death having followed the execution of Matafwali. It was not surprising that the superstitious mind should accept her death as a fulfilment of the witchdoctor's prophecy; nor that they should hear in the itinerant drumming, the boasting of a triumphant, avenged Matafwali. No logical explanation of the drumming, no reasoned medical opinion as to the cause of her death, would alter it. Down the years, the children would listen to the story at their mother's knees of the white woman killed by the magic of the witchdoctor, and of how he had returned to crow over her grave in the guise of the invisible drummer.

But as Drayton had said, 'that educated women should...'

I stretched in the chair, enjoying the cool dampness of the night air, my head nodding as the eye of the storm passed overhead and the ferocity of its attack lessened.

The sound of rain was replaced by the roar of waters from the rivers below. They were in flood, and the unimaginable weight of their meeting and churning below the promontory made a constant, oddly soothing roar.

It was at that point, as I was about to return to my bed, that I heard the drum.

Its throb echoed across the Boma—an eerie, regular beat, a lonely call. Then it was swallowed up in the reverberating roll of the thunder crashing from the hills and I heard it no more.

The early hours of the morning are perhaps the wrong

time for thinking reasonably. That time is better suited to the strange, intuitive fantasies born of the darkness.

I lay back down. As I slipped towards sleep, sounds and images of my recent thoughts churned together like the waters below. They rose in flood, demolishing little brick towers, and roared down the wide Zambezi toward the distant, waiting sea.

And above their roar, I heard again that whispering voice on the telephone. 'Find out how she died'.

CHAPTER 9

I breakfasted early and left the house without seeing Drayton.

The wet earth steamed in the sun, its fresh, damp smell invigorating after the dust and heat. Along the river banks, a mantle of grey scum frothed over floating rafts of dead wood blocking the inlets. Young trees wrenched from the banks upriver, tumbled and twisted like green islands rising and submerging in the brown water. The smaller sandbanks had disappeared overnight and, with them, much of my dark mood of the early hours.

A working party of prisoners was busy clearing the accumulated debris of the storm from the rain drains around the Boma office. On the path leading to the flag pole, the district messengers were parading for inspection.

The title of messenger was, I always felt, a completely misleading one. I once heard a Chief describe a messenger as the eyes, ears, hands and mouth of the District Commissioner. It was a good description. The messenger force was a distinctive feature of the Territory and over the years had built up a reputation for integrity, courage and loyalty. Being regarded as agents of the District Commissioner, messengers were held in high regard by the villagers.

The complement of a station ranged from fourteen to twenty-four messengers and their duties were as varied as those of the D.C., whose orders they were there to enforce. With his district messengers, the Administrative Officer maintained law and order throughout his District. The blue and red uniform, the leather belt and red fez, came to be recognised as a symbol of that law and order—an integral part of the Administration. Guard, mail carrier, messenger, orderly, labour supervisor, prison warder, policeman and general factotum; the district messenger was a man of many parts, and utterly essential to a well-run station.

If I had them onside, I had a good chance of getting everything else running smoothly.

In the office, an orderly mopped the pools of water which had dripped from the leaking thatch while I wrote a note to Mrs. Prail, asking her to call at the office later that morning.

I sent for Nyrenda.

"Have this letter sent over to Donna Prail. Ask the D.O. to come to my office when he arrives, and detail a messenger to make a bonfire of the storm debris at the back of the office."

I walked over to the trestle table and stood looking down at the collection taken from the late Matafwali. It looked such an insignificant jumble of rubbish, it was difficult to appreciate the terror it could arouse in the mind of the villagers. Dirty pieces of knotted string and bandage, military buttons, tortoise shells, bundles of dried herbs, leaves and barks, beads and shells such as a child would play with. The stuffed owl was entirely covered in beads of varying colours and swivelled on a rough pedestal. I set it rotating and wondered how many poor wretches had watched the swivelling bird, with the fear of death in his heart that the hooked, yellow nose would come to rest, pointing at him—smelling him out.

The kalilosi gun too, was a sinister-looking thing. It was made of human shin bone, fashioned in the shape of a gun. Everyone in Africa had heard the tales of paralysis and death of people from having the gun pointed at them.

The horn was the shorter, rear horn of the rhino; about twenty-one inches long, and the lip of the horn was decorated with ivory chips. At the base of the hollow, a few grains of white, crystalline powder clung. I grimaced with distaste and wiped my fingers. Goodness knows what that might be.

I had the strange feeling there was something out of place about the collection, but I couldn't pin it down. I was swivelling the owl and puzzling over the elusive thought that teased my mind when Young arrived. His red, scrubbed face shone and an unruly twist of hair, standing up from the crown of his head, made him look absurdly like a schoolboy.

"Good morning, sir." He eyed the owl. "Going into the witchdoctoring business?"

"I might do that, if I thought I could find out who's scaring the pants off the Bantu with this drumming at night."

"Oh, yes. I heard something about that from my cook. He says it's Matafwali."

"That's what they all think."

I told Young what the messengers had reported the previous day.

"It's not surprising," I finished, "that there's this general feeling of unrest on the Boma."

"But it was Mr. Drayton who was threatened by

69

Matafwali, not his wife," Young said.

"No," I replied. "According to the messengers, it was his 'house'. Not that it matters, you can bet your last penny that any mishap that comes Mr. Drayton's way from now on, will be laid at Matafwali's door by the locals."

"What's to be done, sir?"

"I'm considering what to do. That isn't what I wanted to see you about." I pulled the labour file towards me. "The messengers up at Tilala seem to be having some difficulty in recruiting labour. Go up as far as Grobler's current position." I pointed it out on the wall map. "That's just short of Tilala. See how the new road strip's coming along. Pay the labour gangs. Whilst you're there, practice a little witchcraft yourself and see if you can smell out what the problem is with the recruiting. We're getting a bit short. You can be there today, spend tomorrow and return the following day. I understand the Land Rover's still out of commission, so you'll have to cycle. Take a couple of messengers with you."

"I'll get off right away, sir."

"Have a good trip."

After he had gone, I went back to look at the witchdoctor's collection.

What had I been thinking earlier? Nothing relevant, considering what I had planned.

I swept the oddly assorted effects of Matafwali into waste paper baskets; everything except the horn, the owl, the kalilosi gun and the interesting looking rattle. Those might have some interest to collectors, and their exclusion wouldn't detract from what I intended.

Taking the baskets outside, I called over the remaining messengers and made sure they watched as I emptied the contents into the flames of the bonfire they'd made of storm debris. I didn't know how I was going to persuade the rest of the Boma, but I knew I had to start with the messengers.

Elsa Prail was undoubtedly a beautiful woman; the mature beauty of the early thirties; the cold beauty of the northern fjords.

She sat opposite me, looking cool and assured in a green linen dress which accentuated the neat lines of her figure and matched her eyes. Her smooth, blonde hair was drawn severely back from the triangular face, and twisted in soft, gleaming coils into a coronet around her head.

"You do realise," I repeated, "that failure to do as I suggest will lead to your being sued for slander? Mr. Drayton is quite prepared to bring a case against you, quite regardless of any action Miss Frenton might contemplate."

She listened to me in silence, those green eyes watching me steadily. Only in the faint tremor of the hand that held her cigarette, could I detect any hint of nervousness.

"I realise it, but..." she stopped and seemed to become fascinated by the way the smoke from the cigarette swayed like a misty snake before disappearing.

"Well then, Mrs. Prail?" I waited.

She got up, with a grace few women can command when rising from a chair, and walked over to the window. The long, slim legs showed to advantage as she moved. Watching her, I could better understand how Drayton had got himself involved. There was something about her that hadn't been apparent at the funeral, something sensual and seductive.

She spoke at last, without turning.

"When I spoke at Elizabeth's funeral, even making allowances for the fact that I was upset," her voice mocked my own words earlier in the discussion, "I only meant that, if Barnaby hadn't had his mind on other matters, he would have realised that Elizabeth should have been sent away.

71

And as far as Janet Frenton was concerned, she saw to it that his mind stayed on other matters." She turned towards me. "But now, I'm not sure. Perhaps I did mean more than that, without realising it at the time."

"What do you mean, Mrs. Prail? I must advise you to think very carefully before you say any more."

She leaned against the window.

"I've thought of nothing else since Elizabeth died," she said slowly. "I saw her the day before she died. She was sick, yes, but not that sick. Then the very next day, she was in a coma and dying. It was all so quick, and very convenient. Barnaby—"

I cut across her angrily. "Do you seriously propose to make allegations based on nothing more than your opinion that Mrs. Drayton's death was 'quick' and 'convenient'? The certificate of death was signed by a competent medical man. What gives you the right—"

"I don't believe it," she said, turning back and interrupting me with surprising forcefulness.

"What, exactly, don't you believe?"

"That Elizabeth died of viral gastroenteritis following malaria." The words rolled smoothly from her lips. "I know that's what the certificate says, but I don't believe it."

I don't know exactly what answer I had expected, but I felt a sense of unreasonable relief at the negative quality of the accusation.

"Are you medically qualified? Or do you have other grounds for questioning the opinion of Father Bravachko?" I asked. "As well as questioning the competence of Miss Frenton?"

"None," she admitted, faltering. "Well, none that you would accept."

"Then let me warn you, Mrs. Prail, to say no more about it. Not here, in this office, or elsewhere. Take my advice and let me have the retraction I outlined to you. I'll send you a draft of what is required. If not..." I shrugged.

She came back to the desk and stood looking down at me, her eyes expressionless beneath the finely arched brows. A faint flush had crept into her face, beneath the warm tan of the skin.

"I'll think about that, but, in the meantime, let me give *you* a warning, Mr. Lancaster. Before you dismiss what I've said as unsupported allegation, find out exactly how and why Elizabeth's monkey died."

A trace of her perfume hung in the still air long after she had left my office; as insidious as the uneasiness which her last words had aroused in my mind.

CHAPTER 10

By mid-day, it was as though the rains of the night had never been. The cool promise of the early morning had vanished and I walked slowly uphill in the steadily rising heat.

I was relieved to find a note from Drayton saying he would not be in for lunch. I wondered whether he had gone to see Janet Frenton. If he had, it was hardly a wise visit in the circumstances, but it was a welcome respite for me. I needed time to think before reporting on the interview with Mrs. Prail.

What was I going to tell Drayton?

Should I merely tell him that she was thinking about it, and leave it at that? Or should I warn him? Warn him of what? That she was still harping on some supernatural influence of Matafwali, as Drayton had suggested? But was she? That even though she might produce the written retraction I'd asked for to avoid any action by Drayton, that she didn't intend matters to rest there?

The questions chased through my head as I sat at a solitary lunch.

Was it Mrs. Prail who had telephoned me the previous evening? What had she meant today, about the monkey? And what would be her next move? That there would be a next move, I was certain; she was out for blood.

I stretched my legs on the cane chair. From where I sat on the verandah, I could look straight down the river to the deserted landing stage. The early morning spate that had followed the storm had died down and the barge swung gently in the oily flow of the water.

The file of Annual Reports stayed unopened on the table beside me as I went over the events of the days since my arrival at Feira again.

The hot, still afternoon passed slowly. The sun beat down on the deserted station. Summed up, there seemed little enough in all conscience, to justify my unease.

After all, what was it?

An unhappy marriage. An affair between the D.C. and the wife of a drunk scientific officer. An ending of the affair. A new woman on the station. Gossip giving rise to vague accusations. A jealous woman intent on revenge.

Why did it not seem to me to fit together as a

whole?

Why was she so adamant on that final point? 'Find out how and why the monkey died'.

I tried to recall exactly what Drayton had said about the monkey.

'The monkey died within a day or two of Matafwali being sent off to Lusaka. Probably poisoned by one of the servants... they hated the bloody animal.'

Had Elizabeth Drayton, a cultured, educated woman really been connecting the death of the monkey and her own illness with the mumbled nonsense of an old witchdoctor when she spoke to Father Bravachko of being bewitched? It sounded incredible.

I was still sitting there when Lameck padded in with the tea tray.

There was an unfamiliar quiet about Lameck, I thought, as I watched him emptying ashtrays and tidying up the verandah. Not even at the back of the house had I heard his customary, cheerful patter.

I tried some questions and his replies were uncharacteristically brief.

Yes, his house was rainproof and he was comfortably settled in.

No, he was not missing his wife, who had been left behind to follow with the rest of my kit. He was happy at Feira.

I was sure that last was an outright lie and he was telling me what I wanted to hear.

"Have you heard any talk of what happened to Donna Drayton's monkey?" I put in casually as he turned to go.

"The monkey die, bwana." He moved off.

"No, don't go Lameck. Wait. I know the monkey died. How did it die?"

Had I not guessed what his answer would be, it would have been unintelligible.

"Matafwali," he said simply.

"Nonsense, Lameck. Matafwali went to Lusaka before the monkey was sick."

"Matafwali, bwana." he repeated obstinately.

"Find out how the monkey became sick, Lameck. How many days was he sick? Did food return after it had eaten? Did it sleep a lot? These are the things I want to know."

"Ndi, bwana."

"And it is Lameck who wants to know about the monkey. Not the new Bwana D.C."

He nodded glumly.

It had been the impulse of the moment to ask Lameck about the monkey and after he had gone I regretted it. Why had I asked him?

Then again, perhaps it would be useful to find out something about the monkey's death. Anything which might explain Elsa Prail's present attitude.

I turned back to the Annual Reports without having decided what I should tell Drayton, but when he returned later that evening, I had already gone to bed.

It was three in the morning when I left the silent house. The note of the drum which had woken me carried softly on the still air. Its echo bounced back from the hills of the escarpment.

A brilliant moon flooded the Boma in cold, pale light and silvered the river. I hugged the shadows of the trees as I made my way downhill to the cemetery. I felt a little foolish; I wanted to see rather than be seen. Not that I really expected to find anything; but it was once again too hot to sleep and I was curious.

The throaty chorus of the bullfrogs drowned all sounds except the drum beat. I reached the narrow path leading to the cemetery and it was here that something caught against my leg as I turned off the main path. I flicked the torch switch. Across the path, a bark rope had been stretched a foot above the ground, the ends disappearing into the undergrowth. By the light of the torch I found the ends of the rope. Each was firmly tied to a forked stick in the ground. One stick was draped with tufts of hair and threaded shells and, at the side of the other, leaned a broken pot, filled to the edge of the break with a dark, sticky fluid. It was a common enough 'medicine'. In theory, the rope barrier prevented the passage of whatever sickness or evil it had been raised against.

It seemed that the villagers had tried to combat Matafwali in their own way.

Further on, inside the cemetery, the baobabs shone in grey brilliance, like trees in an enchanted forest. The curtain of surrounding shrubs enclosed the place in its own pocket of silence and a warm, rank smell hung in the air.

Elizabeth Drayton's grave presented an odd juxtaposition of European and African customs.

At its head were spread a confusion of faded flowers; at the foot of the grave lay a bundle of blood-soaked feathers. It was a chicken. Its head had been chopped off and it had been disembowelled. The freshness of the blood meant it had happened shortly before I arrived. The entrails of the sacrifice, except for that part of them filling the broken pot left at the entrance to the cemetery, had been scattered over the grave. It was obvious that one or two of the villagers were brave enough to visit the cemetery after dark for a ceremony of appeasement.

I walked around the place but found no other sign of recent activity. Faintly on the night air came the sound of the drum with its single, tolling beat. Neither approaching nor receding as far as I could tell.

I walked past the other graves, my torch searching out the brief stories on the sunken headstones. Africa marked them all: elephant, lion, leopard, malaria, dysentery. The dead reached back through the years and to far-away places: Australia, New Zealand, Canada, Holland, and now, with Elizabeth Drayton, England.

The bleached skull of an elephant straddled one of the graves. According to the headstone, it was the same elephant whose dying frenzy had torn life from the man whose bones lay below. In the shadowed effect of the moonlight, the skull seemed to grin grotesquely.

I sat in the shadow of the shrubs with the torch switched off and waited.

It must have been an hour later when I realised that the sound of the drumming had started to draw nearer.

Louder and louder, the note swelled in volume. I stood, gripping the torch and, despite myself, my heart started to pound.

The drummer was on the main path.

Then the cemetery path.

Closer. The next second would bring him into view. The echoing note of the drum seemed to fill the cemetery and swirl around the graves.

Now!

I stepped out.

But I saw nobody, and abruptly, on that very instant, the drumming stopped.

Hairs stood up on my arms as silence flooded back to smother the last echo.

CHAPTER 11

Phantom drummers, Elsa Prail and dead monkeys were successfully relegated to the background by the events of the following morning.

"Something's up." Drayton poked his head around the bedroom door before I was up. "The Head Messenger's outside; He says that Kimya, the Paramount Chief, has turned up with fifty of his able-bodied and he's asked to see me this morning. I don't understand it. Kimya's a stickler for due ceremony; this sounds off."

"Weren't we due out at his court this weekend?" I said. "At least, that's what was in the calendar."

"As you say. That's why I think this is something more than a courtesy call. Added to that, he doesn't as a rule travel so well escorted. I've got a twitching in my thumbs."

"Let's hope you're wrong." I drained the last of my tea

and threw back the sheet.

"I've told Nyrenda to tell Kimya that we'll be down straight away."

"I'll be with you in five minutes," I said.

Drayton left and immediately returned.

"Sorry, Lancaster. It hasn't sunk in yet that I'm no longer the D.C. This is, of course, your call."

"Forget it. I'm the new boy as far as Kimya's concerned. He's come to see you. I'll just sit in on this. Anyway, I'm only acting D.C. until you leave."

Drayton insisted on a cup of coffee while he briefed me about the Paramount Chief.

"He succeeded to the Paramountcy two years ago on the death of his great uncle. Matrilineal succession, of course. Kimya's a good type; clever, reasonable, moderately progressive and reliable. He and his Court Assessors and Elders make a good team He might need jogging a bit from time to time, but less than most. He's popular with the Chiefs. That is, with the exception of Chiabele and perhaps Shuwima."

I ransacked my brain for something on the Paramountcy.

"Hold on, wasn't it Chiabele who laid claim to the Paramountcy? I seem to remember something in the files about a dispute."

"Yes." Drayton topped up my cup. "It's always been a sore point with him. He thought he had a prior claim through his great aunt. There was something to be said for the claim. The wrangling went on for a year or so before the Elders eventually decided against him and named Kimya instead. Good move, I thought at the time, but even more so since the trouble in the Chiabele area."

"The Matafwali incident?" I said.

"Yes. I'm damned sure Chiabele knew more about the killings than ever came out but I couldn't prove a thing, and

I don't think we ever shall. It's not that Chiabele's all that popular with his own people, though he has a strong following among the younger men. But he's still the Chief and the Chief can do no wrong."

"So, there wouldn't be any love lost between the Paramount and Chiabele."

"No, there isn't," Drayton said, "but on the surface, things go reasonably smoothly at the Councils of the Chiefs. I had heard that there were one or two little bust-ups shortly after Kimya became Paramount, but Chiabele came off second best and drew in his horns." Drayton shrugged. "He now pays lip service and falls in line, though Kimya would be a fool to accept that at any more than its face value, and I don't think Kimya's a fool."

As we walked down, Drayton enlarged on the hierarchy of the Chiefs in the District—their characters, their areas and the tribal set-up generally. I was struck anew by his detailed knowledge of the District and its people.

At the Boma, in the shade of the giant fig tree, the Lion men of the Paramount stood, the handles of their spears turned towards us. They were tall and straight-bodied with paint gleaming on their oiled, black skins. Around each neck hung a twist of elephant hair from which hung a single lion's tooth. Flaps of lion skin, back and front, covered abbreviated loin cloths. They formed a crescent behind the Paramount Chief and his court.

Kimya, squatting on the ceremonial lion skin, carried the fly-switch of the Paramountcy. It was made of long sable antelope hair attached to a carved, ivory handle. Around his neck hung a double necklace of lion's teeth and on his head sat a hat made from a lion's mane.

Around the ceremonial skin, the Paramount was flanked by elders. As Drayton and I approached, he raised his switch and the soft, rhythmic clap of hand on thigh from the assembled escort welcomed us.

The initial courtesies exchanged, Drayton invited Kimya to join us in the office with one of his elders.

Kimya was a solidly built man possessing a natural dignity. He had shrewd, bright eyes and he greeted Drayton warmly. The elder, a man with a grizzled white wool cap of hair took over the interpreting for a round of welcomes and good wishes.

"Well," Drayton finally brought the lengthy civilities to a close, "suppose you tell me what brings the Paramount Chief to see me so unexpectedly."

"Great trouble," he answered through the interpreter. Kimya's face, turned towards Drayton suddenly looked old and tired. "We hear Bwana D.C. is going. This is bad time."

"The new Bwana D.C. will look after you well," Drayton said.

"Yes," replied Kimya, which was more along the lines of 'I hear you', than agreement. I hoped I could be in the same position at the end of my time here, but right now, Kimya wanted someone he knew.

"Does the Paramount Chief think that his people would agree on any time as being a good time to change D.C.?" Drayton asked. "There are always reasons: famine, small pox, drought. Anyway, what's this great trouble?"

The Paramount Chief smiled faintly as the interpreter translated and replied in a soft, swift undertone.

The elder turned back to Drayton.

"This is not as other time," he said. "The Babenye have been stolen."

Drayton swore under his breath. This about equivalent to saying that thieves had made off with the British crown jewels. There was a mystical and religious significance, difficult to convey in words, attached to the Babenye. They were regarded as the repository for the spirits of the tribal ancestors.

"When?" he asked.

"Seven nights," the elder said. "It was marriage party for Paramount Chief daughter. All village watch Lion Dance. The one who keeps the Babenye, she watch too. When she go back to hut, the floor dug up." He made a shovelling motion with hands, then spread them, empty. "The Babenye gone."

"What does the Babenye consist of?" I asked.

It turned out they comprised an ivory axe handle, a lion-shaped stone, a ceremonial spear and a bead crown.

At present only the Paramount Chief, two of the elders and the Mukabenye, the woman who guarded them, knew of the loss, but such a secret could not be kept long.

"The theft should have been investigated at once." Drayton said. "Why this delay of seven days?"

The Paramount's soft sibilant voice contrasted with the harder notes of the elder's English.

"Chief Kimya says Babenye not like stealing chicken. Not come for help to find person. Chief has ways to find. Babenye are in Chiabele. Chief Chiabele make men to steal Babenye."

"Why does the Paramount Chief think Chiabele is behind this?" Drayton asked, raising his brow.

"He knows. We look. We find."

There was a finality in the voice of the elder that I recognised. No more would be said on the method used and Drayton did not pursue the point.

I was sure what they'd done, and that they would never admit to having called in a witchdoctor. Drayton seemed to be in agreement about that.

"Tell us what is known," he said after a short silence.

"Two men come to hut of Mukabenye. They dig under wall, take Babenye. After, they go Ziapunde forest. All the way, come out at Mvuu swamp. Next night they reach

Ifwefwe. After, we do not know."

Drayton went over to the wall map and traced the route given. The Ifwefwe Hills marked a rough border between the Chiabele area and that of the Paramount Chief.

"The first village over the hills there is Kacinda," he said. "That's ten miles south of Chiabele's own village."

Kimya spoke quietly to the elder who turned back to us.

"Chief Kimya can go to Chiabele," the elder said. "He can say give back."

"You will not take the law into your own hands." Drayton interposed.

The elder waited politely. "Or Chief Kimya can wait for Chief's meeting. Both bad. He comes to Bwana D.C. first."

"But without evidence to produce in my Court of Chiabele's guilt..." Drayton said slowly, almost to himself.

Both Drayton and I knew Kimya would also have to produce evidence at the meeting of Chiefs. Evidence that was based on witchcraft. This would be accepted by the other chiefs, but it definitely wasn't the direction we wanted them to take.

Worse, the other chiefs were likely to respond violently to Chiabele's theft of the Babenye. Things could get out of hand.

We were going to have to do something.

I could tell Drayton was convinced of that, but exactly how we should go about it was another matter. He started digging more.

"What is in Chief Chiabele's mind? What good can the possession of the Babenye do him? Has he taken them for the trouble their loss will cause the Paramount Chief? He knows that only the Paramount can produce them as his seals of office and, even if their loss has to be made public, the authority of Chief Kimya cannot be questioned."

Kimya's voice quickened in his replies, but the

interpreter kept to the same unhurried, toneless translation.

"Loss of Babenye cannot keep secret. Then people say tribal ancestors not happy with Paramount Chief. Bad omen: disease come; famine come. He is not true Paramount."

"But even so, Chief Kimya could still not be deposed." Drayton said.

Kimya shook his head and the elder replied. "Must go. Spirit of chief is in Babenye. Then Chiabele find Babenye. Chiabele claim Babenye choose him."

"It's a little tortuous." Drayton said gruffly.

The elder lowered his voice and leant forward.

"The Paramount Chief ask: What Bwana D.C. think of banyama in Chiabele area? Only say missions not good? Only say old way better?"

Drayton swung around and studied the face of the Paramount Chief, his own expressionless.

"I wouldn't say," he replied at last," that I believed that that was the only thing behind the ritual killings... but it had never crossed my mind that they were connected with Chiabele's wish to be Paramount. Is Chief Kimya now saying that they were?"

"The Chief say Lion Skin of the Paramount lie behind all trouble in Chiabele. Matafwali vow Skin come to Chiabele. All killing for this. Chief Chiabele know."

"Do you mean that the Paramount Chief knew what was going on in the Chiabele area? That he knew of the ritual murders? That he knew of this motive behind them?" An ominous rumble had crept into Drayton's voice.

Kimya interrupted the elder, shaking his head in agitation. "The Paramount Chief say not know then. Know now."

"We'd certainly need more evidence than that. If the Paramount Chief has—"

CHAPTER 12

A rising hum of voices in the distance had slowly been gathering volume and, from outside the office, shouts drowned Drayton's last words.

He pushed the window wide and leaned out.

"What's all that noise about out there, Nyrenda? What's going on?"

I couldn't quite hear as Nyrenda's reply was lost in the confusion of raised voices.

"The hell you say," Drayton said and leaped towards the door. "It's Young!" He threw the words over his shoulder at me. "He's been in some trouble."

A knot of curious sightseers milled around a central point and we had to push a way through. Four district messengers carried the improvised machila—a rough stretcher of bark string between bamboo poles. On it was Young. The messengers had spread his camp bedding beneath him to cushion his journey. The pillow was stained an ugly red. He was unconscious.

"Bring him inside!" Drayton called out. "Messengers, clear this crowd away. Come on, break it up! Nyrenda, send a messenger to the Donna Nursing Sister."

In the office we bent over Young. The drained edges of the ugly gash at the side of his head gleamed like the mouth of a clown against the congealed blood matting the hair; his pulse was slow and faint.

Drayton turned to the four messengers who'd carried him.

"All right! What happened?" They all started to answer and he had to stop them. "No. One at a time! You, Chipupu." He pointed at one of the messengers.

"We find him behind the camp at the village, bwana."

"Which village?"

"Kacinda, bwana."

A faint sigh came from the Paramount Chief.

"I sent Young to Tilala yesterday," I said to Drayton. I crossed to the wall map. "Here it is—about fifteen miles east of Kacinda. I told him to pay the labour gangs and see if he could find out what the trouble was with labour recruiting up there. What was he doing in Kacinda?"

"Bwana D.O., he camp Tilala," Chipupu answered. "I hear he come. I go Tilala. Say trouble Kacinda. Bwana D.O. say he go there. We move camp—"

"What trouble was this?"

It took a little time to get a clear story out of the messengers.

Trouble had arisen at Kacinda over labour recruiting. The men of the village had refused to supply any labour on the grounds that they had duties to carry out for Chief Chiabele. They had made vague threats that mischance would befall

Chipupu and his fellow messenger should they return to Kacinda on such an errand. After Chipupu's report, Young had broken camp and set off for Kacinda, arriving at dusk. The headman's story was that he had not been at the village when the messengers came but they had obviously misunderstood what had been said; he claimed that they had not been threatened or chased out of the village.

Young had arranged a village inspection for the following morning and stipulated ten volunteers from the village for road labour; failing volunteers he had said that he would recruit ten men from the tax register—the first on the list being the headman.

Chipupu had seen Young at the stream early the next morning, talking to one of the villagers. A little later he had gone off towards the hill behind the camp, telling Chipupu to wait at camp and supervise the packing up.

The same villager who had been talking to Young at the stream had later come to Chipupu and said that the bwana had fallen. They had found him in a gully behind the camp.

"Who is this man, the one who found the Bwana D.O.?" Drayton asked.

"He is son of headman, bwana. He is man, but head like child. He say only he find the bwana in the ditch. He not see him fall."

"The village idiot," Drayton muttered, "a lot of help."

We were interrupted by the arrival of Janet Frenton.

"Take a look at Young, please, Janet, and see what you think."

Drayton turned back to the messengers. "Was there any indication, any sign, that the Bwana D.O. had fallen into the gully? Tree roots? An earth slide?"

They shook their heads.

"Was the ditch where you found him far from the camp?"

"No, bwana, not far. Bwana D.O. come back from the hill, but I not see him."

"The camping equipment was left out there? All right! Go and get food and then report back. We're going to Kacinda. Hurry it up!"

The messengers trooped out.

"I'm no doctor," Janet Frenton said, squatted back on her heels beside the machila, "but I'd say he's concussed. We must get him to bed."

"He'd better be taken to our place." I suggested. "Miss Frenton can stay with him there until we can get Bravachko here from the mission, or until we get back from Kacinda."

"How long will he be out?" Drayton asked.

"It's a little difficult to say. The sooner we get him settled, the better."

I detailed two messengers to carry Young to the house. Janet Frenton left with them, shading Young's flushed face from the sun with an empty file she had whisked from a shelf.

I turned back into the office.

"This is a bad thing, bwana," the elder was saying.

"Bwana Young could have missed his footing." Drayton banged out his pipe.

"Is it not strange, this trouble at Kacinda?" the Elder asked softly.

But Drayton refused to be drawn.

"The new Bwana D.C. and I leave for Kacinda this morning. We will find out what happened. We will think on what the Paramount Chief has told us this morning. If anything more is heard concerning the Babenye, let us know, but he should take no action himself. Is this well understood?" Drayton turned and spoke directly to Kimya. "Something will be done. Go well."

"Something must be done," I echoed as the door closed

on the Paramount Chief. "But what?"

Drayton grunted. "If Chiabele's got the Babenye and I can't frighten them out of him, I'll eat my pith helmet," he said.

"Do you really think he has got them?"

Drayton puffed his pipe and considered the question behind a wreath of smoke.

"Yes," he said finally. "If the Paramount Chief says he's got them, I think he has. Anyway we'd better get out there and see what the bloody hell is going on. Nyrenda!"

The Head Messenger was detailed to rustle up carriers and two extra messengers. "Six should be ample," Drayton said, then looked at his watch. "Radio transmission scheduled to the P.C. in ten minutes. Would you like to report? I'll get a message off to the mission. Perhaps Prail will go, he's got a working car."

I went off to the wireless room. It was a large hut at the side of the Boma office. Reports were made to the Provincial Commissioner twice weekly as and when reception allowed. The transmitter hadn't been functioning for the past few weeks, awaiting a spare part, which had finally turned up in the last mail bag.

I connected it and snorted at the advice I'd been given in Lusaka. Submit boring reports? Feira did not seem to be that kind of station.

Contact was difficult that morning and reception poor.

"Feira calling Lusaka, come in. Feira calling Lusaka, come in Lusaka."

I got them eventually and faintly over the spitting ether came the voice of the District Assistant. The Provincial Commissioner was on tour.

I reported briefly on what had happened to Young and our proposed action.

"It may be a complete mare's nest but we'll call within a

couple of days, same time. Over," I finished.

There was a hiss and crackle, a long wait and then, faintly: "Lusaka calling Feira. Lusaka calling Feira. I am not receiving you. I am not receiving you."

CHAPTER 13

The theft of the Babenye, with its underlying threat to the peace of the District, distracted me from thinking too much about the death of Elizabeth Drayton and all that surrounded it. I was distracted but my unease was not entirely dispelled.

I met Drayton back at the house where we found Young cleaned up and in the guest bedroom. Janet Frenton was shaving the side of his head to allow treatment of the wound.

"How is he?" Drayton asked.

"His pulse has pulled up a bit, and that's encouraging, but it's a nasty gash," she said. "It's bled a lot. It looks fairly clean but I'll get some penicillin over from the dispensary, just in case there's any infection."

"Has he shown any sign of coming around yet?" I asked.

"He's been mumbling a bit. Nothing coherent."

"Could you make sense of anything?" Drayton was at the door ready to leave.

"No. It sounded like nonsense," she replied. "Something about guards and monkeys in a cage."

Drayton grunted. He was actually outside the bedroom door when he swung on his heel and turned back into the room again.

"Cave! Not cage, cave. Could it have been cave?"

The girl slipped the razor into the bowl and turned. "It could have been."

Drayton motioned to me and I followed him from the room to the verandah. He had a copy of the map from the office which he laid out on the table.

"The Cave of the Monkey," he said softly and pointed with his pipe.

"Here, just above Kacinda, in the Ifwefwe Hills. I surveyed that area thoroughly last year when there was talk of moving the village to get away from the tsetse fly. The Cave of the Monkey is the burial cave of the Chiabele chiefs. The body of a chief is left in his hut for a few months and, when practically only the skeleton remains, it's taken to the Cave. Chiabele himself visits it once a year to make offerings to the tribal spirits. It's usually quite a session they have there."

It rang a bell. "I've read about it in the Journal," I said.

Drayton turned away from the map. "Let's see. The Babenye disappear over the Ifwefwe Hills. We have trouble recruiting labour at Kacinda because the villagers there have a duty to perform for the Chief, and Young is found with a broken head talking of guards and monkeys in a cave."

He banged out his pipe. "I wouldn't mind taking a look inside that cave," he said and grinned. "What about you?"

I did and I didn't. Drayton's gut instincts seemed correct.

On the other hand, the colonial administration was under the strictest instructions to respect the culture where it was not actually breaking the law. The possibility existed we could blunder into something and be shown to be completely wrong. Wouldn't that make an interesting report to write? But either I trusted Drayton or the whole mess landed in my in-basket.

"Why not?" I said.

The carriers, already waiting at the back of the house were briefed quickly and sent ahead with Lameck and four of the messengers.

We sat down to discuss details over a hurried meal and Janet Frenton joined us.

This was a different Janet Frenton, quite unlike the nervous and distraught girl who had spoken to me at the sundowner. Dressed in her white, drill uniform, there was a cool, professional calm about her, completely at variance with her behaviour at the party.

There was something else too: she and Drayton had obviously reached an understanding. It was obvious in her manner. Her violet-flecked eyes no longer avoided his glance, though something she read there brought a faint flush to the smooth pallor of her skin.

Drayton too, was more relaxed and less abrupt.

It made for a less tense meal, but, reluctantly returning to Elsa Prail's words, I realised the overall situation wasn't improved. Whatever trouble was brewing from that quarter, it would, I felt, involve Janet Frenton. Studying the girl, I was sorry about it. There was a freshness, an innocence about her, which persuaded me that she was no willing contributor to any circumstance that would provide ammunition for Mrs. Prail.

It was I who unwittingly re-introduced the feelings of tension as we finished the meal.

Oddly, it was the mention of Father Bravachko that did it. I remarked that Prail had gone to fetch him from the mission and, that unless he happened to be out touring the villages, he would arrive that evening.

A silence descended.

Was it that they both remembered the last occasion on which Drayton had sent for the priest? The time he had arrived too late?

A few minutes later, Drayton and I set off by cycle in the noon heat accompanied by the two remaining messengers.

If it hadn't been so serious, I might have laughed at it: the might and majesty of the British Empire, called out by a man with a fly whisk, and represented here by four men on bicycles, winding our way through narrow, bush paths, cross country towards Kacinda.

But my mind instead went back to Feira and to what Lameck had reported to me before he left with the carriers.

'Find out how the monkey died,' Elsa Prail had said. And Lameck had found out.

But what was his information worth? For him, it was enough that Matafwali had threatened; Matafwali had carried out his threat; death had indeed come to the house of the Bwana D.C., and like monkey, like mistress. Superstitious fear would naturally tend to find points of similarity between the monkey's death and that of its mistress.

That didn't work for me.

My eyes were drawn to Drayton's broad back as he cycled ahead and I found myself wondering what sort of man he really was.

I found him, in his professional capacity, admirable. Would I be able to maintain complete detachment as I investigated his wife's death?

It was a pointless train of thought at this point, but so

much for posting boring reports back to the P.C.'s office in Lusaka. One way or another that wasn't going to happen.

I put it to one side.

Our route that afternoon roughly followed the northward sweep of the Luangwa and, on winding, snake-like paths through thick bush, we pushed or rode our cycles, as terrain allowed, towards Kacinda.

CHAPTER 14

We arrived at camp towards evening. The tent had been erected under trees shading a clearing and the welcome fragrance of coffee mingled with the tangy smell of wood fires. Lameck was already busy over a pit of hot embers, with pots and pans and the evening meal.

In the swiftly settling dusk, coming up the path from the stream, swayed a line of village women. The water pots balanced on their heads looked like a strange new fashion in millinery.

"The carriers must have put a spurt on and the village seems to be co-operating." I remarked to Drayton. The piles of logs for the camp fires were swiftly mounting and a grass-walled enclosure already screened a steaming bath.

Drayton grunted. "They'd better. I'll toss you for first bath."

I lost.

I drank while he went off, the beer slipping easily down my throat. It was warm but refreshing—it had been a dusty, sweaty trip here from Feira. Apart from the one massive storm, there had been little or no rain in the area.

Brushing the tree tops, the moon bobbed into the sky—a giant, carnival face. From the bush came the distant howl of hyena. It was the hour of the day in bush touring which I had always enjoyed; back at the camp; feet up, the first beer; the fatigues and challenges of the day slipping away with the fading light; the sounds of water splashing in the tin bath and the crackle and spit of the fires; the smells of the evening meal and the burning mopani branches.

Drayton and I swopped over, and I had just rejoined him when Nyrenda brought the village headman and his elders to see us.

"He's not a bad headman really, just a bit weak." Drayton murmured as they squatted in half circle and began the soft, slow greeting—a rhythmic clapping of hands together and on thigh. Nyrenda loomed over them like a sergeant major, suspiciously inspecting a company of raw recruits. They were nervous.

Drayton made a short speech in passable Bemba. He had brought the new District Commissioner to meet the people, he said. There would be an investigation of the messengers' charges of trouble during labour recruiting, and also an enquiry into the 'unhappy accident' which had befallen the District Officer. This enquiry would start the following morning; this evening he wished only to speak to the villagers when they arrived.

The villagers had already started to congregate; they filtered through the trees in little groups, moving slowly into the clearing and massing together at one side. In ten minutes they presented a sea of shining faces, glowing with the flickering blaze of the fires.

I sensed a strange discomfort in the unnatural orderliness of the crowd; there was none of the usual laughing, no joking, no pushing—and the children were too quiet.

Despite that, proceedings began normally. We listened to the perennial complaints of elephant and warthog depredations of early gardens and requests for extra game guards.

It wasn't my imagination, there was an unusual listlessness in the complaints; their hearts weren't in it.

Drayton brought that part to a close abruptly. "I will talk of these matters with the Game Ranger but I want to hear no more of them now. This is not my usual visit—I have not come to see who has not planted his garden or who has not paid his tax. I have come to find out what happened to the Bwana District Officer this morning. Why my messengers tell me there is trouble with the people of Kacinda. These things we will speak about tomorrow. Tonight, you are here to greet your new District Commissioner. You will give him the same loyalty and obedience as you have given to me."

Drayton might have been a retiring professor, introducing his successor to a class of students.

"This is the man who will now be your father and mother and who will help you in all things. In times when your gardens fail, he will see that you are fed; when sickness strikes the village, he will bring you medicine and help such as I have done, and others before me have also done. Seek his advice in all matters and listen to his voice... his voice." There was a bare shade of emphasis on the penultimate word.

Against the crackle of the mopani wood shooting cascades of sparks into the air and the whisper of breeze in the branches, there came the faintest sound of released breath from the silent squatters.

"Sometimes the voice of another is also heard," the headman said, breaking the long silence which had followed Drayton's words.

"No voice is louder that the Bwana D.C.'s—and no arm is longer than his. Remember this!" Drayton spoke slowly, throwing the words like pebbles into a stream. There was no threat in his voice. He made it a statement of fact, and it would be up to me to live up to it. There was no alternative.

It was the compact which formed the bulwark of colonial administration. It was this acceptance which enabled one man—a man such as Drayton or I—to keep law and order throughout a District like Feira, covering 20,000 square miles of bush, without military or police support.

In the gradual surge of volume in the chorus of hand clapping which followed, I felt a lightening of the atmosphere.

"First score to you." I said to Drayton as they started to break up.

He grunted. "It's a double-edged knife. What I can do, others can do as easily. With a trouble-maker it would work in reverse. We need to close this down quickly. Still... I don't have to tell you that."

He produced a flask. "Lameck," he called out, "time for dinner. Bring a couple of glasses first."

CHAPTER 15

During the meal, we went over the plan, with Drayton's map unfolded next to us.

"Here we are... here's Kacinda... the hills." His finger traced the line. "If we go up here and around, we can approach the Cave from behind. From memory, there's one small ridge of rock here which might be tricky, but once over that, I don't see why we shouldn't reach the Cave without detection. I'll bet my pension there'll be nobody in or near the Cave—they'd be too frightened to get too close, especially at night. They'll be guarding the approaches uphill only."

We were going to depend on his memory of a survey he had done a year ago in broad daylight to guide us around an unfamiliar hill in the darkness.

I knew I was being swept along.

"Let's make it midnight," he said. "Everyone should be asleep by then."

"There'll be hell to pay with the P.C. if we don't find what we're looking for—and it gets back to him that we've been in there," I said. "You know the line he'd take... desecration, etc."

He nodded.

"But I think it's worth the risk," he replied. "The Cave is

the ideal place—the most logical place for Chiabele to choose as a hiding place for the Babenye; fear would keep his people out and we're forbidden to enter the Cave. The Babenye could lie there for a year undisturbed—receiving the blessing of his own tribal ancestors! And, after all, where better for Chiabele to 'rediscover' them—the Babenye having returned to the Paramount of its choice. I think someone on the hill this morning must have lost his head when he saw Young and clouted him before he thought it through. All he really had to do was tell Young that he was approaching forbidden territory."

"I'm guessing Chiabele only posted the guards to cope with the possibility of Kimya's men coming this way," I said. "I wonder if they actually know what they're guarding?"

If they did, they'd be more alert.

I was only raising the points. I'd made my decision back at Feira, so we continued to sit there, chatting and sipping our whisky and warm water.

"I don't think so. Chiabele's nothing if not cunning. He'd want the fewest people possible in on his secret. But you're right about it being a problem if we're caught. We'll need to get in and out of there, unseen and unsuspected."

Out here, on a 'mission', there was an enthusiasm in Drayton—a 'cops and robbers' air about him which was infectious.

I had to keep reminding myself; he might be both an admirable colonial officer and a murderer.

Despite everything, as midnight approached, I felt a rising surge of excitement.

The camp slowly settled into a relative quiet, swamped by the million voices of cicadas and punctuated by the squeals and grunts of unseen animals.

We fed the fires and a quick check seemed to show everyone else asleep.

"All set?" Drayton whispered, and we were off.

But we had reckoned without Nyrenda. He appeared silently beside us as we slipped into the shadows at the back of the camp.

"Go back to sleep, Nyrenda," Dayton whispered.

"No, bwana. You sleep, I sleep. You go, I go."

"Nyrenda," I struggled with what to say. "Go back. This isn't part of your duty."

Even in the darkness we could see enough of his face to know there was no persuading him.

Drayton eventually shrugged and we resumed.

Nyrenda followed us silently through the thicket skirting the camp, a thicket bathed in cold moonlight filtering in weird patterns through the tree tops.

Perhaps it was the whisky, or the rush of excitement at our midnight escapade, or Nyrenda's stubborn insistence on coming with us, but for the first time I had a feeling for the station at Feira. This wasn't just a job, or something to be endured.

Twenty minutes walking silently through the moonlit night brought us to the foot of the rising ridge of rock which Drayton had described.

"Now, Nyrenda! No bloody nonsense. Wait here," Drayton whispered.

He seemed to obey, and I followed Drayton on the uphill climb. It took us a further hour; an hour of slipping and sliding, stopping and stumbling, pushing and panting, but eventually Drayton proved to have been quite right. Once around the last ridge of rock, nothing could have been simpler than our downhill progress to the Cave. We hugged the shadows.

"There it is," Drayton breathed, catching my arm and pointing. Moonlight showed up the cliff-face in stark detail: under an overhanging shelf of rock, the mouth of the Cave was narrow, dark and uninviting.

"Bad luck about the moon," Drayton said, squinting upwards to see if there were any friendly clouds gathering. There were none. "We'll have to chance it. Here goes."

We flitted silently across the brilliant strip of moonlight and dived for the shadows of the Cave mouth. We waited— waited to hear outraged cries announcing our presence—but only the sound of our breathing broke the quiet around us.

"All the guards snoring their heads off," he said softly with a quiet snort. "I'll go first."

I followed him, feeling my way through a rock passage, turning sharply to the right. The sudden chill of the air enveloped me like a cold shower. My feet sank into what felt like damp marsh, and the rank smell pricked my throat.

Ahead of me I heard Drayton grunt and something whisked past my face. "Bloody bat. Must have overslept," he whispered. Then: "Can't see a thing now. Going to have to use the torch."

The beam pierced the blackness ahead.

"Well, there's a pleasant-looking reception committee," he said over his shoulder. A faint echo of his words bounced eerily back from the walls.

Bones. The dark emptiness of the eye sockets sprang into sudden macabre life in the bleached whiteness of the skulls as the light hit them. Skeletons had been arranged in sitting postures, at intervals around the rocky walls, each one supported by two elephant tusks. Earthly possessions lay beside them; cooking pots, beads, spears and axes.

"Meet the tribal ancestors!" Drayton said softly.

"Somebody's been here quite recently," I said, peering at the floor.

He shone his torch down and followed tracks in the thick carpet of guano. They ended abruptly at a rough, stone table in the centre of the cave. It reminded me of part of

Stonehenge in miniature—two upright slabs being connected by an horizontal lintel stone.

"Well... it hasn't been a wasted journey." His torch picked out the gourds on the stone platform: cobs of maize, grains of millet, cassava roots and strips of dried elephant meat, all powdering to dust. But it was the arrangement of objects in the middle of the slab to which Drayton referred: a large stone, a short ceremonial spear, the ivory axe handle and the bead crown.

We stepped up and he reached out to pick up the stone.

"Unpolished malachite" he turned it in his hand, "a fair likeness to a lion couchant".

"Thank God the Babenye didn't include any of those." I indicated the tusks supporting Chiabele's ancestors. "I shouldn't have fancied making the return journey with anything of that size strapped to my back."

To keep my hands free, I pushed the axe handle down my sock and thrust the bead crown into my pocket. Drayton took the stone and the spear.

"Let's go," he said. "No! Don't make fresh tracks—go backwards in the ones you've already made. That's it."

Moving slowly backwards towards me, he carefully smeared the imprint of our feet in the guano, leaving as much as possible of the tracks we had found leading to and from the table.

"Let's see if the tribal ancestors can tell Chiabele who's taken the Babenye."

Once we were clear of the guano, Drayton lead the way again, switching off the torch half way along the passage. We crept cautiously back in the blanketing darkness of the cave towards the waves of the fresh, warm air of the outer world.

We stopped at the barrier of bright moonlight—waiting–listening.

"On the home stretch now," he said, his voice barely a whisper.

"Thank God. I'm stiff with cold. That place is like a mortuary."

We laughed quietly and crossed the moonlit area as quickly as we could without making a noise.

Again, we stopped, crouched in the shadow of rocks, and listened.

Silence.

Relief as welcome as breathing the fresh night air fell on me, and we started the climb back up. We were skirting the tail end of the rock ridge when the shadows ahead of us moved, nearly giving me a heart attack.

It was Nyrenda.

"I told you to wait down below." Drayton hissed angrily.

"There are many men in the bush behind the camp now, bwana. They watch. This way, I lead."

"Well, they're a little late," Drayton said to me with bravado.

Nevertheless, we had to put our trust in Nyrenda. Twice he halted us and crept ahead—returning only to make us double back on our tracks.

It made for a long return journey to camp and I was very pleased to see, at last, the light of the fires through the trees. We had come in almost a complete circle and even here, we approached cautiously.

Finally, we stood in the shadows behind the tent.

Drayton brought bottles of beer out.

"Good show, Nyrenda." He handed him one. "Now go and get some sleep."

"Bwana." He smiled and left us.

I let my welcome beer slide down my throat and heard Drayton begin to laugh quietly; it was an infectious laugh; despite the scares on the way back, the whole thing had been simple.

We hid the Babenye in bed rolls and lay down on the camp beds at what must have been nearly five in the morning.

"We've earned our keep tonight" Drayton's voice came softly in the warm darkness.

"You mean you have," I answered. "Thank God Kimya turned up before you left. I wouldn't have had a clue as to where to begin."

He snorted. "All in a night's work... goodnight."

But sleep wouldn't come and I sensed Drayton's wakefulness too. The exhilaration of the night's activities faded slowly.

I had wondered what sort of man Drayton was; now I knew... a little more. He was a gambler; he played his hunches; nerveless, tough; the sort of man to have along in a spot of bother; a sound type.

Was he also the sort to murder his wife?

I didn't think so, but I had to keep my thinking clear.

Eventually I slept to the muted orchestra of dawn in the bush and I dreamt of a monkey dancing on the grave of Elizabeth Drayton.

Her husband stood to the side, dressed in a highland kilt and with a lion's mane on his head.

CHAPTER 16

Breakfast came at seven; eggs and bacon, lots of coffee and a incongruous glass of bubbly health salts for Drayton. "Take 'em every morning, even on tour," he said. "Keeps the body in balance, settles the stomach. Take my advice..."

I smiled, not taking much notice of his advice. I was enjoying the fresh coolness, watching fingers of mist rise over the stream and vaporise in aerial whirlpools in the early sun.

We found little to complain of during the actual village inspection; the place was reasonably clean and the bins and huts were in good repair. Gardens had been stumped and burnt for the first rains planting; sanitary structures were adequate and far enough removed from living quarters and the nearby river.

At an identification parade, after the inspection, three men were picked out as the ringleaders of the trouble with the messengers. I held a Court at camp and gave them three months apiece for threatening violence. They would be taken back with us to Feira, acting as carriers en route.

Drayton returned from his inspection ofthe site of Young's camp as I finished writing the case records. He was grinning.

"Lameck! Bring coffee, please. Well..." he threw himself

down into a chair. "The old man of Baker Street would have been proud of me. I crawled around the ditch, examining the ground inch by inch—watched by a very anxious audience of the headman and senior men. I marched them up and down the hill on the track that Chipupu saw Young take—examining every broken leaf en route and every scuffle mark in the sand. I sat and deliberated ponderously within sight of the Cave."

He laughed. "They were wetting themselves. I had the devil's own job to keep a straight face. And then, my dear Watson, I gave them the results of my logical deductions. Their faces were a sight to see. I've told them they have got until this evening, when we return from Chiabele's village, to produce the man who knocked Young over the head and the men who helped carry him downhill and dump him in the gully; I don't want them to have time to contact the Chief. Failing this, I've said the whole village will be moved to Feira for questioning and possible identification by Young. I've pointed out that such an enquiry might take a very long time—that they'd all have to stay at Feira until it was finished—which would be very inconvenient for them to say the least, what with the early gardens and planting and suchlike on their plates. I think they'll co-operate."

There was no doubt but that Drayton was a gambler. If his guess was wrong, if his bluff failed, and he was forced to implement his threat to evacuate the whole village to Feira, I could see the fur flying. I could almost hear questions in the House.

"...is the Secretary of State aware... forced march of a whole village... resultant hardship... no gardens... famine... Colonial Administrators becoming dictators... "

The shower of irate minutes descending from Lusaka would need another in-basket.

Drayton looked at his watch. "Nearly eleven," he said.

"We can be at Chiabele's village in two hours."

Skirting the lower reaches of the Ifwefwe Hills to strike north across country we had to leave the river, which I regretted. The green, fresh vegetation fringing the banks was kind and cool to the eye. Inland, rain had not yet fallen and the summer sun had bleached the coloured brilliance of the spring leaves to a faded tapestry of yellow, orange, brown and red shades.

From time to time, we lost the thread of the brown path and had to push our cycles over dry, stunted bush. The dead leaves of the previous seasons fall crackled underfoot, waiting for the rains to start the rot which would, in time, return them as natural compost to nourish the trees which had borne them.

It was good game country through which we made our way. I could have wished our trip had taken a more leisurely course. Game was down from the hills in search of water and signs of their passage were plentiful.

It was near mid-day, with the back of the journey broken, when we sighted buffalo; buffalo in strength of hundreds. The herd moved as a dark, compact mass over the narrow plain lying between the escarpment and the first fringe of bush—they were heading for the Luangwa. We called a brief halt and the messengers dismounted and flung themselves flat in the shade. Drayton and I sat and smoked, watching the slow progress of the herd.

"Pity we're a bit pressed for time." Drayton echoed my own thoughts. "Could do with some buffalo steak."

It was afternoon when we reached the surrounds of the Chief's village; the bush was stumped and burnt, ready for seasonal planting, stretched in humped, dry mounds towards the Luwima Stream which, rising in the hills, joined the Luangwa farther east.

The village clustered on the side of a hill which, on its far side, dipped and then climbed towards the Ifwefwe plateau. A trickle of brackish water sludged over the rocky bed of the stream, skirting the eastern approaches to the village.

The afternoon drowsiness common to villages lay over the outer compound, resting below the crescent of huts which formed the kraal of Chief Chiabele.

Or was it only that, I wondered: no children played in the dust; no women sat in communal hairdressing sessions; no smoke rose from the dead ash of fires in front of the huts.

The high yelp of dogs as they hurtled from the shade and then retreated again, cracked into the silence with the force of an explosion and through the village could be felt a rustle of movement as of an animal disturbed in sleep.

Flies rose in swarms from the excreta of those dogs as our passing disturbed them—and settled again.

"They all sleep, bwana." Nyrenda returned from a cursory inspection of several huts.

"Well, wake them up! Find the headman; throw some water over him. Get him here. Get the people on their feet. Hurry it up!"

The messengers went off at a trot. Their shouts, rebounding from the hills, echoed in a receding and diminishing wave to the river bed below.

"Too much beer?" I suggested.

"Could be." Drayton stopped and pointed to a flourishing patch of green at the side of a hut. "Or that. Most likely both."

The plant looked much like a wild growth of marigold.

Drayton broke off a leaf and, bruising it between his fingers, sniffed it and passed it to me.

"Dagga," I said. "We've timed our arrival very nicely if

that's what they're sleeping off. They'll be dead on their feet."

"Yes. Let's take a look at the inner kraal."

The Court ground was a litter of gourds and empty food bowls; stools, upended and overturned, covered the dais flanking one end—the seat of the Chief. Scrawny chickens scratched in dried patches of vomit.

"They must have had quite a party!" Drayton surveyed the mess with a frigid eye.

Behind the Court House stood the Chief's house, barred and shuttered.

"When we get hold of the headman, he can go and wake the Chief. We'll wait here."

We squatted in the sparse shade of a baobab.

"Look here, Lancaster," he said, "would you like to handle this?"

"No. Handle it your own way. I'll back whatever line you take." I spoke without hesitation. I was quite happy to play second fiddle to Drayton. It wasn't just his better knowledge of the situation. There was a shrewdness and strength which I sensed in the man out here, oddly at variance with the domestic mess into which he appeared to have got himself bogged down in at Feira.

Presently, the messengers brought the headman: a slob of a man who stumbled along between them, bewildered alarm on a faced creased with sleep. His hands trembled as though with fever as he clapped out his greeting. Drayton sent him off to rouse the Chief, signalling a messenger to accompany him.

"I wonder how much of the stuff they're growing?" Drayton rolled the dagga leaf between his fingers. "Leonotis leonura - Cap.127. - Section [k] Dangerous Drugs." he quoted.

"Every hut," I answered. "That's quite a crop."

A thin trickle of men had started to move towards the court ground—eyeing us warily as they passed – sleep bemused and holding their heads in their hands. From the outer compound, the raised voices of the messengers and curses of disturbed sleepers grew in increasing volume.

"Do you notice what I do, Drayton?" I indicated the assembling villagers.

He nodded. "Only men and boys. Yes. There are, of course, one or two of the initiation ceremonies which are never held with the women and children around. I wonder..."

We watched the growing crowd on the court ground, sipping the scalding coffee which Lameck had produced from the thermos. Roughly an hundred, I estimated, and still coming. This was an excessive gathering for a village of this size and they were a sorry sight in the aftermath of beer and dagga.

"Here's Chiabele now." Drayton's voice brought my head around to see the group issuing from the door of the Chief's house. "Well, I'll be damned! That's Chief Shuwima on the right—well, at least, we now know where he stands. I've often had the idea there was something between these two."

The two Chiefs in black robes and carrying their staffs of office walked slowly towards us. The councillors fanned out behind them.

"Shuwima's got his men with him. He's here in force. That's why there are so many." Drayton indicated the still swelling crowd on the court ground. "I wonder what they're up to, eh?"

"Perhaps Chiabele thinks he may need a little support, if Kimya's right and a claim on the Paramountcy is behind all this."

"Could well be." Drayton grunted and we had no time to

say more before they reached the court ground.

My preconceived ideas of Chiabele turned out to be so ludicrously inaccurate as to be almost disconcerting. The sleek, gross picture I had built up in my mind certainly fitted Shuwima; he was a barrel of a man, his small eyes embedded in rings of fat; but Chiabele was an emaciated creature, the cadaverous face and angle of the skinny neck giving him a vulturine look.

As we exchanged greetings, an echo of the schoolroom came to mind: 'Let me have men about me that are fat; Yon Cassius hath a lean and hungry look. He thinks too much.'

Though the prospect of having Shuwima constantly around would hold no appeal either, I thought.

A dazed air hung over the whole party and there were obvious signs of their rude awakening from sleep. The tails of Chiabele's headdress hung at a tipsy angle but the general effect was more macabre than amusing, framing as it did, the pitted face, twisted in an obsequious smile which did not reach the glazed eyes.

The formal greetings over, Chiabele motioned us towards the raised dais.

"No," Drayton turned down the suggestion. "We will sit out here away from that mess. Have your people bring seats for us." Drayton spoke in the vernacular and, although the word he used could be translated as mess, it had a more subtle meaning in the native tongue. It referred to a mess as from people as against a natural litter of vegetable or mineral origin.

If Chiabele resented the choice of word, he hid it.

The silent crowd on the court ground must have numbered around two hundred and, at a signal from the Chiefs, they broke into the long, slow clap of greeting. Drayton began to speak as it finished and had Chiabele on the run within a minute.

"What have you heard of the trouble at Kacinda?"

"I hear there was some small trouble there. I have no details."

"Do you call an assault on one of my staff a small trouble?"

"Your District Officer—"

"Then you did hear details," Drayton cut in. "What have you done in the matter?"

Chiabele hesitated, his gaze fixed. One could feel the effort he made to collect his dulled wits.

"I sent a Councillor at once to bring me the full story," he said at last.

"Which Councillor?" Drayton cast a sardonic, appraising eye over the full council flanking the seat of Chiabele.

Chiabele had an answer to that one.

"My nephew. He enters the council next planting time."

"When did he leave for Kacinda?"

"Yesterday."

"It is strange we did not meet. The new Bwana D.C. and I came from Kacinda this morning."

Chiabele made no reply.

"Listen well to me, Chiabele—and your people, if they are wise, will also listen well. Trouble started at Kacinda with labour recruiting; my district messengers were threatened. It has been suggested that special duties which you have given to the village interfered with the normal quota of labour from Kacinda for the new road strip. The young men of the village think that in acting as they did, they were following the wishes of their Chief. What is your answer to this?"

"They are mad." Chiabele's thin fingers plucked at the dusty robe.

"Mad or not, three Kacinda men will be gaoled at Feira for three months for threatening violence. What were these special duties of which they speak?"

Chiabele hesitated. He couldn't decide how much Drayton already knew.

"I ordered them to clear the path to the hill," he ventured at last, his eyes fixed on Drayton.

"Why?"

"The path is overgrown; the time comes near for our ceremonies at the Cave of the Monkey." He paused. The lack-lustre eyes watched to see whether the name had any special significance for Drayton.

"Oh, yes." Drayton's voice was casual. "But why choose this time for path clearing? With the early planting to be done, and the road strip to be finished before the rains set in. It was unwise."

"Unwise, I agree, bwana." He spoke more easily. He could accept being unwise. "But I did not order that no labour should be given for the road. The young men have misunderstood my—"

"Obviously, and the misunderstanding will cost the people of Kacinda a fine of one shilling a head through the Native Authority Court. You will be responsible for the collection. The money and the tax register will be brought to me at Feira four days from now. Instead of ten men, the village will now produce fifteen for labour on the road."

"My Councillor will come to Feira with the money—"

"No, not a Councillor," Drayton interrupted. "You, Chief Chiabele, will report to Feira in four days. The people of Kacinda have disturbed the peace; they have broken the law; they have flouted the Rules of the Native Authority; what trouble will they be causing next do you think? These are things of which we must talk."

Jerked out of his momentary sense of security by Drayton's words, Chiabele stayed silent and, except for those plucking fingers, motionless; a vein throbbed on the bony temple.

"It shall be done as you say," he muttered eventually.

"Now," Drayton continued, "let us go on to the matter of the Bwana D.O.. What did you hear of this?"

"I heard that the Bwana D.O. had fallen into a gully. His head was hurt. I sent my nephew."

"The one that has not yet returned. When he does return it will be with a different story. He will tell you that the Bwana D.O. did not fall, as was suggested; that he was hit over the head; he was later placed in the gully so that I would believe that he had fallen. This I have told the people of Kacinda. I have also told them that if the men responsible for this have not been discovered by the time I return this evening, the entire population of the village will go to Feira for the enquiry."

Chiabele was looking at Drayton as he finished speaking as though he saw in him the devil incarnate. Fear and fury battled for top place; fear at the accuracy of Drayton's reading of the incident and the consequences to himself were he to be involved; and fury at the fool who had lost his head and gone too far.

Somebody coughed and spat in the silence.

Shuwima sat silent, his loose mouth drooping; a ventriloquist's dummy awaiting a master's voice.

"If the men of Kacinda have done this thing," Chiabele muttered at last, "they must, of course, be punished. But how could you know?"

"I do know; and punished they will be. Of this we will speak further when you come to Feira." Drayton got up. "Now to other matters! Why is this plant growing in your village?" He tossed the dagga leaf in front of the Chief.

Chiabele looked at it vacantly, his thoughts elsewhere. "It is a weed."

"A weed certainly, Drayton agreed, "but one which the

119

Government forbids you to grow."

"Can I see everything my people grow? Do I look behind every hut?" A little of the fight was coming back into Chiabele. His voice was waspish.

"You have a deputy headman; he should see that such things are not grown. If he fails in this duty, he must be changed. It seems that Kacinda is not the only village in your area where the law is broken—here in your own village, authority is flouted. I shall report on these matters to the Provincial Commissioner."

Chiabele's momentary flicker of spirit lapsed into sullen bewilderment as the talk went on.

"And where are all the women and children?" Drayton suddenly shot off at a tangent.

"They have gone for two days. We hold initiation ceremonies for the young men." "And Shuwima's young men too? Since when have the men of Chiabele and Shuwima joined hands for these ceremonies?"

Shuwima's mouth opened.

"Chief Shuwima came on a hunting trip." Chiabele interposed quickly.

"Shuwima travels with a strong hunting party, does he not? Can it be that he appreciates the possible dangers of hunting in the Chiabele area?" Drayton's voice was silky.

And so it went on; Drayton inexorable; Chiabele floundering; Shuwima silent. The crowd on the court ground sat listless and uncaring. I'd had been quite right; we could not have timed our arrival better. The stimulation of beer and dagga had burnt itself out, its enervating reaction reducing most of them to a state of dulled apathy.

"And now," Drayton said, "dismiss your people. We will inspect the village."

In the tour of the village and its surrounds, accompanied by the Chiefs and the Councillors, we found several thriving patches of dagga which were uprooted and burned whilst we stood watching.

It was nearly three in the afternoon when the inspection finished; an oppressive afternoon. The sun had vanished behind a warning sky and the first stiff breeze of a threatening storm swept through the village.

"Listen well, Chief Chiabele." We stood before the Chief's house and momentarily Drayton's voice echoed the dark threat in the air. "Your people are restless; everything is not well in this area; think well and walk carefully. Remember, if trouble comes, it is you and your people who will suffer. And you," he turned to Shuwima, "before your homeward journey you will come to Feira. I have things to say to you and your hunting party."

And on such a note we left Chiabele's village that afternoon to return to Kacinda. Back at camp, we found that Drayton's bluff had worked; three men were turned over to the messengers. We did not bother to enquire closely into their story.

"Let them stew until we get back." Drayton said. "They probably aren't the real culprits; but they've been chosen because they'll say what they've been told to say. Whatever their story, it'll be a pack of lies. They won't give Chiabele away."

It was farcical in a way; incidents which could have undermined the peace of the whole district exploded with no more force than damp squibs.

I slept soundly that night.

My sleep would not have been so untroubled had I known what awaited our return to Feira. It was no damp squib.

CHAPTER 17

The wailing of women could be heard a mile from the Boma.

"Go ahead, Nyrenda," Drayton said. "Find out what that's all about and report to the house. That's a keen if I ever heard one."

Back at the Boma, I paid off the carriers and signed the orders for the detention of the Kacinda men. We questioned the duty messenger but he knew very little.

There had been a death. Maoma, nephew of Chiabele, had been brought in that morning from the village of Jatwa Nkwanga by Sikanga, one of the senior messengers.

"Maoma!" Drayton said, on our way up the hill. "I wonder what happened to him?"

Janet Frenton met us at the door to the verandah. She looked ill. The flecked eyes were too large in the pale face.

Drayton's hand rested lightly and briefly on her shoulder. "Hello there! How's Young?"

"Father Bravachko seems quite happy about him. He's there with him now. Tea's just coming if you want."

"I'm for a cold beer. What about you, Lancaster?"

"Sounds just the job. I'll rustle some up." I left them alone for a moment.

"You really look as if you've been overdoing things." Drayton was saying as I came back. His eyes searched the girl's face, questioning and curious.

"It's the heat." She turned sharply away. There was something in her voice which belied her. I didn't believe it was the heat at all.

A frown appeared between Drayton's brows.

"Has anything happened whilst we've been away?" There was puzzled speculation in the sidelong glance he gave the girl.

"Nothing."

She was lying. Suddenly it was as though Drayton and I had never left the Boma. The situation as it had rested after my conversation with Elsa Prail flooded back, ugly, unchanged and imminent.

Although, it wasn't unchanged. Something had happened during our absence. I wondered whether Elsa Prail had made any further move.

"How did your trip go?" she said.

"Satisfactory trip," Drayton replied, "but are you sure you're feeling all right?"

"Quite sure," she said.

She leaned back against the mosquito gauze, her face shadowed. "What's all the noise from the compound? It seems to have been going on all day."

"And will likely go on all night. Maoma, one of Chiabele's nephews was brought in this morning; dead. He was next-in-line for the chieftainship." Drayton's eyes still searched her face, as though he would find there the answer to the question which was puzzling him.

"Oh, that must be why they sent up for me from the dispensary this morning. Father Bravachko went down as he happened to be here. But he said the man had been dead for some hours."

She pushed back the damp tendrils of hair clinging for her forehead.

"What did Bravachko say about it? What was the matter with Maoma?"

"Maoma?" Father Bravachko repeated the name as he joined us on the verandah. "The man whose body I saw this morning? I could not say how he died."

There was an odd note in the priest's voice which caught my ear. I saw Drayton, too, glance curiously at him.

He took the tea which Janet Frenton poured for him and stirred it slowly. Twice he stopped and raised his head as though on the point of saying something further. Twice he changed his mind.

I broke the sudden silence which had fallen. "It was good of you to come so quickly to see Young. How is he?"

"Young... oh, yes. Young," he said absently.

He made an effort to collect his thoughts and turned to me. "I think he's going to be fine. There are one or two indications of a slight fracture at the base of the skull but it's impossible to be sure without an X-ray. There was probably some cerebral bruising which is now righting itself. I've stitched his head and he must have rest and quiet for a week or so. I shall be here to keep an eye on him. I have a camp down by the river. I've quite a few villages I want to get round to whilst I'm here. But tell me, what happened to him?"

"Hasn't he told you?"

"The last thing he remembers is walking up the hill behind Kacinda." Janet Frenton interposed.

"We'd better go and see him." Drayton finished his beer.

As we walked towards the room where Young lay, he said softly. "I don't think we'll mention the Babenye. The fewer people who know about this business the better."

But Young was asleep and we returned to the verandah without disturbing him.

We were all still there shortly afterwards when Sikanga

came up to make his report about bringing Maoma to the Boma.

Sikanga had been one of the senior messengers posted out in the Chiabele area on the 'laze, listen and report' exercise which had been mounted after Matafwali had been committed for trial.

Two days earlier, he said, on his way back to the Boma to report, he had been contacted by Maoma's son who said that his father, having heard that Sikanga was in the area, wished to see him. Sikanga had returned with the son to Maoma's village. There, Maoma fed him and suggested that as he intended to go to Feira to complain about a mistake in his tax, he should travel with Sikanga the following day. Sikanga had agreed.

But later that same evening, Maoma had come secretly to the hut where the messenger was preparing to sleep. He had told Sikanga that the visit to Feira was not for the purpose of complaining about his tax; he wanted to speak to the Bwana D.C. but he wanted to travel with the messenger because he was afraid. He refused to tell Sikanga why he wished to see the D.C. but said when pressed: 'If the Chief finds out that I go to see the Bwana, he will kill me. Do you think he would let me live to unseat him?'

Then Moama had proceeded to convince himself not to go.

Sikanga had tried to reassure him that he would be safe travelling with him but Maoma had left the hut saying that he would not go to Feira. By the next morning, however, he had changed his mind again, and he and his family left the village with the messenger.

That evening they stopped at Jatwa Nkwanga. During the night, one of the wives had come to Sikanga and told him that Maoma was sick and wanted to speak to him. He found Maoma vomiting; he complained of pain in his head and stomach.

Here the messenger hesitated.

"Well, go on, Sikanga! What did he say?" Drayton prompted.

"Maoma said, 'Chiabele has sent the jilombo of Matafwali to creep into my body and destroy me. I must die.' Then Maoma slept."

A jilombo was a witchdoctor's familiar.

"Is that all he said?" Drayton asked.

"Later," Sikanga said, "He said he could not move his head, and he whispered to me 'This is what Chiabele threatened if I betrayed him, but how can he know? I have told no one of the promise of Matafwali, nor of the Babenye.' Then he slept again. When the first light came we made a machila and came to Feira. He was sleeping deeply. His body shook and twitched and froth came from his mouth. We were still far from here when I saw that life had gone from him."

It was at this point that a slight sound behind me made me to turn towards Father Bravachko. His hand was shaking as he put down the teacup. His face was pale and there was a look of shock in the eyes he fixed on the messenger.

Janet Frenton also watched the priest—her face a pinched mask.

Drayton appeared to notice nothing.

"Did anybody else hear what Maoma said to you?" he was asking the messenger.

"Maoma's wives were there in the hut, bwana, and the wife of Jatwa Nkwanga."

"All right, Sikanga. Report to the Boma tomorrow morning. We shall need to go through your story again." Drayton had dismissed the messengers.

When they had left, Drayton turned to Father Bravachko.

"Tell me," he said, "Could you venture any opinion on

what caused this man's death when you saw his body this morning?"

I watched the colour seep slowly back beneath the white sweep of the priest's hair line. At last he said, "I did not, of course, know this story when I saw Maoma this morning. On a superficial examination I could only confirm that he was dead. I could not tell how and why he died."

"And now?" I asked, curious as to why he was being reticent.

"No." The priest sounded angry. "I still could not give an opinion."

"Well, in that case, perhaps you'll be kind enough to do a post mortem tomorrow morning. What do you think, Drayton?"

Drayton agreed.

"Very well," Father Bravachko muttered. "And now, if you'll excuse me."

He left.

"I'm going to check on David," Janet Frenton said and went back inside.

"A quick and convenient death as far as Chiabele's concerned." Drayton had broken the ensuing silence.

"Certainly sounds a bit fishy." But my mind was still centred on the strange behaviour of the priest. What had the messenger said to produce that reaction?

The nursing sister returned at that moment with her medicine bag. "I've settled David," she said. "If you can manage now, I think I'll get home."

"I'll walk back with you." Drayton got up.

"No!" The vehemence of her refusal had brought a flush into the pale face. "I prefer to go alone."

She left, avoiding Drayton's eyes, and before he could protest any further. If she'd delayed any longer, I thought, she would have been in tears.

Drayton's eyes followed the neat figure in the white, starched drill until she was out of sight.

"Women are bloody odd creatures," he said.

He made no further comment on what must have been uppermost in his mind and, after some desultory conversation on the implications of Sikanga's story, he swallowed the rest of his beer and left with the Babenye for Kimya's camp, which was not far from the Boma.

I sat on, feeling a sudden chill in the sweat that beaded my face, at the idea that had presented itself to account for the look of shock and bewilderment which I had seen in the priest's eyes.

I worked through the crushing heat of the remainder of the afternoon at the Boma office.

Evening brought no relief to the oppressive heat, nor to the questions in my mind.

The sun, sinking behind the hills, clutched the sky with greedy fingers of fire which dyed the waters of the confluence to tangerine red. The dim shapes of fruit bats swooped from the mango trees over the darkening lawn.

Drayton had not returned. I sat alone again on the silent verandah, my mind given over to speculation on the events of the afternoon.

Lameck slipped in with the lamps.

"Turn on the bath, Lameck—the cold tap."

It was Father Bravachko's reaction to Sikanga's report that had really set me thinking; had I not noticed that strange reaction, I would perhaps have overlooked the coincidence.

Could it be? Impossible! And yet. I went over it again, trying to recall Sikanga's exact words. I saw again the look of blank despair in Janet Frenton's eyes. The pallor of the priest's face.

Both suspected something. Neither had voiced it.

Around and around I worked it. Was it pure coincidence that Sikanga's description of Maoma's death had a familiar ring to it? Elizabeth Drayton had died in such a fashion. As had her monkey.

Neither the priest not the nursing sister would attribute the deaths to witchcraft. That would not have caused their reaction.

Long after the slow trickle of water from pipes choked with algae had ceased in the back of the house, and the silence had surged back, I still sat—my beer had grown warm.

'Quick and convenient death' Drayton had said, referring to Maoma. Exactly the same words as Elsa Prail had used to refer to the death of Elizabeth Drayton.

CHAPTER 18

The following morning, the hand-over papers were signed and I officially took over the station. My first signature as District Commissioner, Feira, appeared under the order for a post mortem on Maoma.

The men of Kacinda, I remanded in custody, until such time as Young would be fit enough to give evidence at their trial. I had seen Young that morning before leaving the house. He still remembered nothing of what had happened on the hill behind Kacinda and I had not pressed the point. It could wait.

Further questioning of Sikanga and the wives of Maoma added little to what we already knew. The two wives denied knowledge of any reason, apart from tax, behind Maoma's intended visit to Feira. They obviously knew more than they admitted but fright had taken over. I suspected that one or both had been instrumental in persuading Maoma to inform against the Chief—hence Maoma's change of mind on two occasions within twelve hours whilst still in his own village. However, it was impossible to get them to talk.

During the morning Grobler came in to report that the bridge—a bush poles and ballast affair crossing a culvert over the Upupulu River on the road sixty miles north—had collapsed in a sudden storm spate.

"It'll take a week or more, Mr. D.C. man, to fix it—and then only if the rains hold off."

"You'd better get up there right away—take labour and materials from the new road strip."

"And hurry it up," Drayton broke in, "I don't fancy battling up river by barge to Chirundu."

"Perhaps your wife would like to come into the Boma whilst you're away." I suggested to Grobler. "It could be easily arranged."

"I'll see what Sarah wants to do." There was an hint of embarrassment in his manner as he turned away. "She'll probably prefer to come to the bridge with me."

"Is there no way round to Lusaka, avoiding the bridge?" I asked Drayton when Grobler had left.

"No." He traced the line of the old road on the wall map. "Ten miles this side of the Upupulu River, the road forks— just here. This little link road which joins up with the main road on the other side of the river is only useful in the dry weather—it cuts off fifteen miles. But once the Luangwa and its tributaries rise at the beginning of the rains, it's completely washed out—the wet-weather link has to be used. If the bridge is down on that strip, you've had it. We were cut off for two months last rains—hence the new road strip."

The Head Messenger knocked.

Drayton turned. "Well, Nyrenda, what is it?" He stopped. "Sorry, Lancaster. Habit."

I waved it off.

"The Paramount Chief wishes to see the Bwana D.C. before he leaves," Nyrenda said to me.

"Come in, Kimya, come in."

As the door closed behind Nyrenda, Kimya prostrated himself, slapped the ground with his hands again and again, incidentally raising a cloud of dust in the process from the

131

old coir matting.

"Look after them well, Kimya. Next time Bwana Lancaster and I mightn't be so lucky." Drayton said softly. "And this matter must not be spoken of—do you understand?"

Kimya raised himself and shook the dust from his robe.

"It will be as you say, bwana." He opened the door and beckoned and the white-haired elder, who had accompanied him on his previous visit, carried in two magnificent leopard skins. One for me, one for Drayton.

No further mention was made of the Babenye, which I suspected were safely held in the thonged bundle strapped to the elder's back.

Kimya spoke rapidly and the elder turned to Drayton.

"The Paramount Chief has heard of the death of Maoma, Chiabele's nephew. Many tales go from mouth to mouth of the manner of his death. What will happen?"

"That," said Drayton, and his lips thinned in a sort of smile, "only time and your new Bwana D.C. can decide. In the meantime, should the Paramount Chief hear any useful gossip regarding anything—he should let Bwana Lancaster know of it."

"So it will be," Kimya agreed. "Tsalani bwino!"

"Pitani bwino." Drayton raised his hand in farewell.

We watched them move off with the Lion Men and, long after they had gone, snatches of their song came back in distant echoes from the rivers and hills.

It was a gruelling morning and I was in a poor frame of mind after a disturbed night. I attacked the accumulation of routine work without enthusiasm and little concentration.

"I'll do the radio transmission to the P.C. if you like." Drayton looked at his watch and pushed back the last of the journals he had been looking through. "Then I'll get back to the house and my packing. I'll ask him to make a response tomorrow. He'll need that time at least to consider what action he wants taken on Chiabele."

"If you would," I said. "Mind you, I couldn't get through last time."

Drayton nodded as he stood and glanced through the window towards the Court House where Bravachko was doing the post mortem. "The old boy's taking his time. I'll tell the P.C. about the bridge washout but, even apart from that, I think he'll be agreeable to my hanging on a while here, until we see a little light on Chiabele."

"Fair enough," I said.

He went out, and as the door shut behind him, I found myself wondering whether Chiabele would provide the only factor which would require Drayton to postpone his departure.

I looked over to the small Court House.

How much longer would it take?

It must be a damned unpleasant job for Bravachko in the heat. Hats off that he was being so thorough.

A half hour later, I saw Drayton leave the wireless room and walk uphill toward the house.

Almost as if he'd been waiting for Drayton to leave, Bravachko emerged from the Court House and strode across.

The Boma drum thumped out the hour of noon as the priest sank into the chair which I pulled forward.

"Well? What's the verdict?" I said.

"I have found nothing, my son."

"Maoma died a natural death?"

"I can find no indication of the cause of death—natural or otherwise. I cannot say why the man died."

I was puzzled. The sudden death of a healthy man, foaming at the mouth and there was nothing?

"Is there anything suspicious?"

"Suspicious? Perhaps. But that is a different matter. The liver and kidneys show a gross degeneration. The heart muscles are flabby. There is slight discolouration of the stomach lining and a reddening of the gut."

Behind the wreathing smoke from his pipe, the seamed face looked old and tired and wary.

"Could these things present a clinical picture of death from natural causes?"

"They could, but I would not be prepared to give a death certificate." The grey eyes regarded me steadily over the bowl of the pipe. "I have removed the vital organs and sealed them in formaldehyde with which Mr. Prail kindly supplied me. The jars must be sent to Lusaka for investigation by a pathologist with the necessary facilities."

I grimaced. "They'll have to be sent by barge up to Chirundu, then by rail. The bridge is washed out over the Upupulu River."

Bravachko got up and went to the window, looking out across the Boma. "That will take time." He seemed to be speaking to himself. "But there is nothing more I can do. We must await the report of the laboratory investigation."

"Which will probably leave us right where we are now," I said, "if one of the African vegetable poisons is involved. I've had this sort of thing before. In any event, I'll have to get out to Jatwa Nkwanga and ferret about a bit. Even if you can't be sure about the clinical evidence, the circumstances of the man's death are certainly suspicious."

"Yes, but one cannot be sure. Suspicion can be a terrible canker in the mind. If I could..." he stopped and seemed to withdraw behind a veil of his own thoughts.

I waited.

He turned at last from the window. "I cannot decide. I must think more about it." He went towards the door.

"Is there something worrying you, Father Bravachko?"

He stopped, facing the door and replied without turning. "Yes, my son, there is. I have been trying to decide whether the devil is prompting my tongue to mischief or whether my mind is sick from too much standing in the sun. I must pray and consider more." He opened the door.

"One moment more, before you go." I crossed over and closed the door. "I've got a worry of my own, which I think you might help me with. Please come back and sit down."

I ushered him back to the chair, but found it difficult to start speaking.

His pipe was dead and I gave him a cigarette and lit it. That occupied us for a minute or two.

He waited.

"There's a spot of bother brewing here on the Boma," I said. "I felt that a talk with you might help to forestall it."

He was sitting with his head bent down and appeared not to be listening to me.

"Tell me," I went on, picking my words carefully, "did any doubt ever cross your mind, that your diagnosis on Mrs. Drayton was incorrect?"

The face he raised to me was grey. "If you, as a layman can ask me that, then it's not my mind which is sick." His voice was a whisper.

It was not a pleasant moment. In his face and his words I read the death of any hope that my uneasiness was born of nothing more than an over-fertile imagination and unhappy coincidence.

"So, whatever is worrying you is connected with the death of Mrs. Drayton?" I asked at last.

"Yes. But how did you know?"

"I didn't know. I was guessing, and eager to be proved

135

wrong."

I told him briefly of the reasons which had led me to pose such a question to him.

"I had hoped that a talk with you would clear the air. Mrs. Prail may be out to make trouble, and this seems fertile ground."

"I know nothing of these matters of which you speak, Mr. Lancaster. I can only tell you what has been worrying me since I saw the body of Maoma yesterday." He crushed out the cigarette and relit his pipe. "This again is something which may mean nothing, but I heard the story of the man's illness much as you heard it from the messenger, in less detail, and without the significant background of the reason for his journey to Feira. Now, you know as well as I do, that the African people are not always reliable in describing an illness; a man might faint and be described as dead, killed by the spirits. I have always found it difficult to give a firm opinion based on their observations. In a case like this, with no obvious signs in the body itself, it was impossible. However, I can say that there are few sicknesses which can kill so quickly. Cerebral malaria could. On a snap judgement yesterday, I might easily have picked on that. It was during my examination that I noticed oddities. Maoma had a peculiar furring of the tongue a white furring with a slight ulceration at the edges of the tongue. The skin of his hands and feet had become friable."

He paused, looking into space as if seeing his work again. He rubbed his fingers against his thumb. "The skin had become almost crumbly, you might say. Now, neither of these things is of sinister significance in itself. A man suffering from a bilious attack would have a furred, yellow tongue, which could very easily appear white—temporarily that is—after drinking a glass of milk. The ulceration of the tongue, like cracked, sore lips could be caused by high fever—as could the peeling of the skin from the hands and feet." He waved his pipe and continued as if addressing students. "Though in the latter case, a sustained high temperature over some time would more likely cause it, not a twenty-four hour illness."

After another pause, he shifted on his seat and his eyes came back down to meet mine. "But there was a third thing. The pupils of the eyes were contracted as though the man had taken some narcotic."

He stopped and drew deeply on his pipe.

"Bearing in mind the circumstances of the man's death," I asked cautiously, "do you suspect that Maoma was poisoned?"

"Well, as you say, on a snap judgement: yes."

He was silent for a long time and I waited rather than prompting him.

"This was the second body in which I have found these unusual signs, and that in the last two weeks." He shrunk a little in the chair and spoke very quietly. "Mrs. Drayton was the first."

The damp stickiness of the air seemed suddenly oppressive. I went over and pushed the window wider. The cicadas were in full chorus and, in the shade of the fig tree outside, the messengers squatted, sleepy in the grip of the noon heat.

"The clinical picture of Maoma's death could well be that of Mrs. Drayton." His voice was a whisper behind me. "And may I be forgiven if I have allowed a devil of suspicion to work evil in my mind."

"This has by no means confirmed anything." I turned back, but he was not listening; as though, once having started, it was a relief to get it off his chest. In his agitation, the accent of his native Poland became more noticeable.

"I ask myself why Maoma bears the same signs in his

137

body as Mrs. Drayton—Mrs. Drayton who died of gastroenteritis? Is it only a coincidence that a post mortem on a person dying of that disease would present exactly the same picture as that on Maoma? What caused Maoma's death?"

"We can't be—" I said, but he took no notice.

"The night I arrived in Feira to see Mrs. Drayton she was a very sick woman. The nursing sister reported that she had vomited a great deal and had attacks of severe abdominal pain. She was complaining of a bad headache and her pulse, which had been fast, had become weaker. She appeared to be slightly delirious though her temperature was not high. I was certain, sure, that she was suffering from a viral enteritis." He stopped and seemed to be going over the recital in his own mind—remembering—trying to reassure himself that even now, he could not have been wrong. He shook his head and went on. "There is little one can do for this condition, except to try to combat the dehydration. I did try streptomycin but she did not respond. She relapsed into a coma that night. This was quite typical, as were the symptoms which followed: twitching muscles and convulsions. But I don't have to tell you—you heard it all yesterday."

"Isn't it a little unusual for an adult to die from a viral enteritis?"

"Yes, but Mrs. Drayton had been considerably weakened by the malaria in the previous week. She was in a poor physical condition."

"Did you make any comment at the time on these symptoms? The ones you say were similar to those you saw in Maoma?"

"The white furring of the tongue, I attributed to the milk she had been drinking. There was still some of it in the glass beside her bed. The ulceration of the edges and under side of her tongue, could well have been due, as I said, to the high temperature of malaria. That applies equally well to the sloughing of the skin of the hands and feet. I attached little importance to these things. When I noted the slight contraction of the pupils, I asked whether she had been taking sleeping tablets; this was the most likely source of a narcotic. Her husband told me that she had been taking them regularly; she had been sleeping badly. I thought she might have been overdoing it a little and I removed the pills. But there was no significant contraction, you understand. It was barely noticeable."

"You had no hesitation in giving the cause of death as a viral gastroenteritis following malaria?"

"None whatsoever."

"And no doubts would have arisen in your mind, had it not been for Maoma's death?"

He shook his head.

I sighed. "It's extremely disturbing, but there is nothing conclusive here, Father Bravachko."

"Conclusive? No. But, disturbing."

"Do you recall what Maoma said, as quoted by Sikanga? 'Chiabele has sent the jilombo of Matafwali to creep into my body and destroy me. This is what he threatened if I betrayed him'."

"You are suggesting that Maoma thought he was bewitched, Mr. Lancaster; but men who believe themselves bewitched do not die in this fashion. I have seen such cases; they waste away without any physical sign of illness in their bodies. Tell me, what does the death of Maoma suggest to you?"

I hesitated. "I would say the odds are that the man died from poisoning; one of the African vegetable poisons."

"Just as you say," the priest said. "So, I ask myself why does his illness and death follow the same pattern as Mrs.

Drayton's? Why do I find these unrelated signs in his body, which I first saw in her?"

"Do you rule out completely, the possibility that Maoma also died of a viral enteritis?"

"Most unlikely, Mr. Lancaster. He was a strong, healthy man in the prime of his life. Even had he done so—stretching the arm of coincidence rather far—it still would not explain these disassociated symptoms which only assume an importance, insofar as they are peculiar of both of them. Do you realise where this leads?"

"Into a mess, obviously." I scowled. "Let me get this straight. Am I right in saying that had you performed a post mortem on Mrs. Drayton, the report would have been identical to that on Maoma?"

"Yes. Death from a viral gastroenteritis would present the same picture in a post mortem examination."

I sat back. In some ways it was the worst of situations. Suspicions and no proof.

"Then none of this is conclusive," I said. "But I shall have to tell Mr. Drayton that you are now questioning the accuracy of the death certificate on his wife. Is this how you see it?"

"Yes. I regret but that is so." He shrugged his great shoulders and arose. "This is a very unpleasant business," he said slowly.

I watched him walk back to the Court House. And if that's all it turned out to be—just 'an unpleasant business'—we would all be very lucky, I thought.

Many distasteful duties fall to the lot of a District Commissioner, but I cannot remember any which I approached with more reluctance than the one which then confronted me.

As it turned out, Drayton already knew something of it.

CHAPTER 19

"Good God! Did you think I'd murdered Elizabeth?" Drayton's voice, raised in anger, carried clearly from the verandah as I reached the steps and, as I opened the gauze door, he was shaking Janet Frenton as he might have shaken a disobedient child.

At the sound of the door opening, Drayton's hands dropped from her shoulders. The girl's shadowed eyes gazed blankly at me from her white face.

Drayton was the first to recover. He pushed the girl into a chair.

"Nicely timed, Lancaster," he said brusquely. "There's something you have to hear."

"Barnaby! Please!"

"My dear girl, I've had more than enough time to think about this. I'm sorry that it has to come out like this, in that it might involve you, but if things have got this far. If I'm suspected—"

"I didn't say that!" Emotion put a raw edge on Janet Frenton's voice.

"Perhaps you didn't. I'm sorry I lost my temper." He bent and picked up a sheet of notepaper lying on the floor between us. "It seems, Lancaster, that station gossip is holding an unofficial inquest on my wife. I suspect, Elsa

Prail is acting as coroner."

"Well, Drayton," I took a breath. "I very much regret to tell you this, but as of this morning, it has become a little more than station gossip."

"Oh?" he said sharply. "What's happened this morning?"

"Perhaps you'll bring me up to date from your side, before I go into that. The word 'murder' has an ugly sound. Has it got as far as that on the Boma?"

"No, perhaps not. I lost my temper, but Janet seemed to think... well, let's leave that."

He looked down at the sheet of paper in his hand. "There's something you need to see," he said, and offered it to me. "Read it."

It was an erratic hand and hard to decipher.

> *Barnaby,*
> *When you read this I shall be gone.*
> *I can't live like this any longer.*
> *Elizabeth*

"Where did you get this letter?" I asked.

"It fell out of a book lying on my wife's bedside table when I was clearing the room with Kalinga."

"When was that?"

"I found it the day you told me about the Jones' woman's visit to the office." He considered. "That must have been about five days after she died."

I studied his face. Did he realise, I wondered, how odd it would appear that he would produce such a letter only after the circumstances of his wife's death had given rise to speculation?

He answered my unspoken question.

"What purpose would it have served to produce it then? Bravachko said she had died from gastroenteritis. Who was I to question it? And how was she supposed to have killed herself?"

He rubbed his face.

"I turned her room, the bathroom and the house generally upside down without finding a thing she could have taken. All I could think of was the mess there would be if I produced the letter—an inquest, a possible exhumation, a nice, little tit-bit for the bridge tables and bars from one end of the Territory to the other; and I felt that I wouldn't have been the only one involved."

He sat down heavily in one of the chairs, glancing briefly at Janet Frenton.

I remembered that day; the day Mrs. Jones had visited the Boma office; the night of the storm; I remembered that restless pacing up and down the verandah. I regretted that Drayton had not told me about the letter that night; in view of all the circumstances, better then than now.

"I have to tell you, Drayton, and believe me, I hate having to do so—Father Bravachko is now doubting whether his diagnosis in the case of your wife was, in fact, the correct one."

"Why?" asked Drayton, his face suddenly drawn.

We all sat, and I gave them a resume of what the priest had told me that morning.

There was a stunned silence.

I was watching Drayton carefully. Either he was an excellent actor, or he was genuinely astonished by the news.

"I thought he had something on his mind yesterday," Drayton said, "but what possible connection could there be between the deaths of Elizabeth and Maoma?"

His voice was a mixture of conflicting emotions: anger and puzzlement.

"Your guess is as good as mine," I said. "But leaving that for the moment, tell me what's happened this morning to make you produce this letter."

"Janet can tell you that."

The girl's eyes turned to me, their glance guarded.

"I called in at the store yesterday evening, on my way home from here. Martin Prail was there." Her lips thinned. "He wasn't very sober."

"It's all right, Janet," Drayton's voice was hoarse. "We all know he drinks. Let's say he was drunk."

"He was drunk then. He was in a bad temper and was talking away at the top of his voice to Mrs. Jones. So drunk and loud he didn't notice my arrival. He was complaining that having missed his little vacation as he put it, because of Mrs. Drayton's death, it looked as though he would have to postpone it again. He said there would have to be an enquiry; he didn't see what other course the P.C. could take but institute one after the letter Mrs. Prail had written. Mrs. Jones told him to be quiet and he turned and saw me. 'She'll have to know soon enough,' he said and left."

"Did he mention what Mrs. Prail had said in her letter to the P.C.?" I asked.

"No, not specifically, though he may have been quoting when he said, 'it would be in the interests of everybody concerned, if the gossip and speculation were silenced by an enquiry into the death of Mrs. Drayton.'"

"The P.C. said nothing about getting such a letter on the radio this morning," Drayton said. "He surely would have, so it must still be on its way."

"You say this happened yesterday, after you left here?" I turned back to Janet Frenton.

"Yes. I came this morning to find out if Barnaby had heard anything about it. If he knew what was going to happen."

Of course, Janet Frenton could be a suspect as well. Who better to administer a poison to Elizabeth Drayton than the nurse tasked with looking after her? I studied her.

"But it wasn't only what Prail said, was it, that brought you here this morning?" I asked. "There was something on your mind yesterday afternoon. Did anything happen whilst we were out at Chiabele that has any bearing on this?"

There was a query in Drayton's eyes as he looked round at her. She stayed silent, looking down at her hands, and I stirred uneasily.

"Please believe me, Miss Frenton, I am not asking idle questions. Others may have been out for trouble from the word go, but it seems trouble has come from another quarter. To meet it, I have to know all there is to know."

"All right. I'll tell you." Her fingers pushed back the soft, dark hair. "It doesn't amount to much compared with the main issue, but coming on top of the talk there's been since Mrs. Drayton died—"

"What talk?" Drayton interrupted.

"Let Miss Frenton finish," I said. "We'll get round to that in a minute."

He looked as if he was going to argue, but subsided.

"The morning after you left for Chiabele," she resumed, "I got Grace Nelson to stay here with David Young whilst I went down to the hospital. There were one or two patients I was anxious about. After I had seen them I went through to the dispensary to see the orderly and pick up the mail. There was a letter." Her voice shook a little. "It was a sheet of Government notepaper and words cut from a newspaper had been stuck across it. Big capitals all joined to make four words. 'HOW DID SHE DIE?' she stopped, her mouth twisting. "There's been a letter each morning. Why send them to me? I don't know!" Her voice rose and broke on a high note and she jumped up from the chair, knocking it over.

Drayton rose swiftly and, grasping her shoulders, swung

her round to face him. "Stop it, Janet. Stop it! Calm yourself." His hands gripped her arms, compelling, reassuring and slowly the tense figure slackened in his grasp until she slumped against him. For one moment he held her, then stepped back to look down into her face.

"So," he said, "what with the drunken Prail's burblings and anonymous letters, you thought I had—"

"No! Don't say it." She pushed her hand against his mouth. "Don't say it."

Drayton twitched his head away from the restraining hand.

"All right," he said softly, "but I didn't—this I promise you."

They seemed to forget I was there; between them, a pledge unspoken was given and received; then Drayton lightly brushed her cheek with his fingers and released her.

"Let's have a drink," I suggested. "It may do us all good. It's been quite a morning."

"Where are these letters?" Drayton asked, after the drinks had been brought.

"At home."

"You'd better let me have them," I said. "And talking of letters," I flicked the note lying on the table between us, "has anybody, apart from the three of us, seen this note left by Mrs. Drayton?"

"Nobody as far as I know." Drayton regarded the head on the top of his beer with a moody eye.

"So what's set up this particular hare on the station?"

"Not what," Drayton said. "Who? And the answer is Mrs. Prail."

"But on what grounds, if she hasn't seen the letter?" I asked.

"If I could see the one she's supposed to have sent to the P.C. I might be able to answer that." His voice was dry.

"Didn't she say anything the day you saw her in the office?"

"Nothing to suggest that she intended writing to the P.C."

He must have sensed my prevarication.

"Did she suggest anything else?" he asked.

"Yes. That the cause of death as given on the certificate was incorrect." I shrugged. "She gave no reason why, and bearing in mind what you had told me on the previous evening, I felt inclined to discount most of what she said."

"But not all?" Drayton raised an eyebrow.

"Well, no. I must admit, Drayton, that something stuck in my gullet about the whole business. I might add that someone had already rung the office telephone the day before and suggested that I should find out how your wife died. Didn't say anything else and I couldn't tell who it was."

There was a silence. Drayton frowned into space. Janet Frenton watched him. A little colour had come back into her cheeks.

"Well, it's beyond me," Drayton said. He turned back to Janet. "What was this talk you say you've heard?"

"The usual African gossip—it got me down after what happened at the funeral."

"What African gossip?"

"That Mrs. Drayton had died from poisoning."

"I think you're wrong there, Miss Frenton. The story going around the compounds is that Matafwali was responsible for Mrs. Drayton's death; Matafwali, who'd been dead for two weeks before she died; but it was Matafwali's 'magic'."

"No. I'm not wrong," she insisted. "It *is* what they're saying."

"Are you certain you've heard the word poison mentioned?" I persisted.

147

"Absolutely certain! I've heard it at the dispensary and at the hospital; 'ulembe'. There's no mistaking the word in the context in which I've heard it; or rather I've overheard it. The patients forget that I understand more than half of what they say."

"Lancaster's right." Drayton cut in suddenly. "That's not what they were saying to begin with. When did you hear this? Within the last week—two weeks?"

Janet Frenton considered it. "Within the last week," she said.

"But how could it start?"

"Who knows where any of it starts," she said bitterly. "You know better than I. Somebody's cook tells somebody's house servant, who tells somebody's gardener." I had the feeling that there was more in her remark than appeared on the surface. I wondered whether she had heard about Drayton and Elsa Prail.

"Did you overhear how she was supposed to have been poisoned?" Drayton asked.

"In the same way as her monkey," she whispered.

Drayton looked suddenly thoughtful. "The monkey?"

"Mrs. Prail mentioned the monkey's death that day at the office," I said. "She suggested I should find out how it died."

"And did you?" Drayton reached for his glass.

"According to general gossip, the monkey died as your wife died."

The dull flush seeped slowly under the tan. For the first time I saw uncertainty in his eyes; uncertainty and something else, which flickered and vanished so quickly that it barely registered.

"Let's leave it for the moment," I added, getting up. "I'm sorry about this, Drayton, but you do realise there'll have to be an inquest?"

He didn't reply and I left them together.

In my room, I looked again at the letter which I had taken from the table. It was undated.

Suicide? Or murder?

CHAPTER 20

The priest's camp at Feira, above the west bank of the Luangwa, proved to be a daub and wattle affair with a thatched roof, on much the same design as the African villager's house.

Smoke curled slowly upward from a dampened wood fire and a mosquito net, slung from the branch of a tree, enveloped an ancient camp bed. The bedclothes were neatly folded across it. A rickety table of bamboo sticks, thonged together with bark rope, held the simple preparations for an evening meal; a canvas water bag hung from the crutch of the table support.

There was no sign of Father Bravachko and I called. His voice hailed me from the direction of the river.

I found him perched on a rock. His topee, curled and cracked from the weathering of many years, was pushed to the back of his head and his calico kansa was tucked up around his knees. He was fishing with a primitive bamboo rod, string and a bent pin. I squatted beside him.

"It looks as though you were right... I regret to say." I handed him the letter. He read it, his eyes screwed up against the sun. His face was shocked as he handed it back to me. He bent over and wedged the rod into a cleft of jutting rock.

"Suicide?" he said.

"That's what it looks like. I've told Drayton there'll have to be an inquest."

"I thought that perhaps an accident," he said slowly. "Where did you get this letter?"

"Drayton found it in a book on his wife's bedside table."

"But how? What could she have taken?"

"Heaven alone knows. Drayton said he could find nothing; he searched the house."

"When did he find this letter?"

"Five days after her death."

I gave him a brief resume of Drayton's reasons for withholding the letter and he listened in silence, his fingers plucking softly at the wiry beard which flowed over his paunch.

"He hasn't produced it now," I finished, "because of anything you told me this morning. It was the talk on the station which decided him. We've heard that Mrs. Prail has written to the P.C. suggesting an enquiry, though on what grounds I can't begin to imagine."

Bravachko clucked his tongue and started to refill his dead pipe. "It's incredible." he muttered.

"Drayton's explanation?"

"No, no." he interrupted vehemently. "Mr. Drayton's reasons for withholding the letter are credible enough. It was of Mrs. Drayton that I was thinking; thinking of her lying there – dying—knowing—saying nothing—realising what she had done." His voice was angry.

"That's hardly surprising. If she'd decided to end her life, she would hardly defeat her purpose by telling you what she'd done; not unless she'd had second thoughts about it."

I lit a cigarette to discourage the mopani bees which were beginning to collect around our heads.

"And her reasons for doing such a thing?" he asked.

"You knew her. Temporary mental disturbance?" I hazarded.

"Has anyone suggested to you that she was mentally disturbed?" Bravachko looked sideways at me.

"No. But does anyone in a normal frame of mind commit suicide? Did you notice anything out of the ordinary in Mrs. Drayton in her manner, or behaviour, on the night you arrived at Feira? I mean the night before she died?"

"It would be difficult to give a fair opinion on the mental state of a woman who had just recovered from a bad bout of malaria and who, when I saw her, was in acute pain and exhausted with continuous vomiting," the priest said drily.

"True enough, but didn't you tell me the day of the funeral that, on the night before she died, she spoke to you of being bewitched? And before that, on your visits here, you said you got the impression that she was in a nervous state, frightened. Wasn't that so?"

"True." he nodded. "But being nervous and afraid; believing in witchcraft and witches, does not of itself imply a mental instability."

"Such things might point to a degree of mental strain."

"They could." He took up the discarded line and recast it.

"Tell me. What gave you the impression that she was afraid?"

"There was nothing concrete; but I have lived many years—and most of those years have been spent in the Church. I have grown used to listening for the voice of the heart behind the spoken word. With Mrs. Drayton, it was nothing which was said—it was rather what she left unsaid.

At the time, I put it down to the feeling of unrest on the Boma. I may, of course, have been mistaken in my impression."

"And the night before she died? Can you remember what exactly she said about witchcraft?"

"I can recall the general gist of it. She asked me whether I believed in witchcraft and I replied that I certainly believed in spirits of evil. She then asked whether I thought people could be bewitched, despite their disbelief in such powers. I told her that I did not think that possible, but that the surest protection against witchcraft, sorcery, demonology, call it what you will, was an unswerving faith in the power, the goodness and the eternal love of our Creator."

"Why do you think she was speaking of herself?"

Bravachko shrugged. "I felt she was. In my mind I connected what she said with my previous impression of fear."

"Drayton tells me that the Matafwali case had upset his wife. Do you know that Matafwali threatened Drayton's 'house' before he was sent to Lusaka?"

He nodded. "Your colleague, Mr. Young, told me about it."

"Drayton thought that his wife linked her monkey's death with that threat, as she did her own sickness. When she spoke to you that night, wasn't it of this that she must have been thinking?"

Bravachko's face screwed up as he contemplated that. "Possibly."

"Well then; do you think that was a normal state of mind? Don't you agree that the whole affair may have preyed on her mind to a point where she decided to commit suicide?"

"It could well have," he conceded.

"Drayton thinks that one of the servants might have

153

poisoned the monkey. They didn't like it apparently."

The priest hunched his great shoulders and pulled the line in sharply. He began to untangle the weeds which had fouled the pin.

"We're in rather an odd situation here." I went on, handing him his tin of bait. "The ordinance on exhumation says it shouldn't be undertaken unless there's a probability of a satisfactory result. So, in view of what you told me this morning, do you think any purpose will be served by exhuming Mrs. Drayton's body?"

He thought about it for quite a long time, sucking on his pipe which had gone out again.

At last he said: "If the peculiarities of tongue, extremities and pupils common to both Mrs. Drayton and Maoma have any sinister significance, and if Mrs. Drayton ended her life by taking one of the vegetable poisons, by chance hitting on the same one used to get rid of Maoma, then an exhumation is pointless at the present time. The body of Maoma can speak for them both. But even if the pathological report on Maoma is positive, what point would there be in proving beyond a doubt that Mrs. Drayton had died from the same poison?" he hesitated. "One of your English poets once wrote, 'Death hath so many doors to let out life'. Is it important to know which one Mrs. Drayton chose?" His voice was tired and sad.

I didn't like to press the old man, but there was one further thing I had to ask. "From what knowledge you had of Mrs. Drayton, from what you saw of her during the past months and what you could judge of her temperament and make-up, would you say that she was a woman likely to give way under strain and take an easy way out?"

He sat looking across the river, puffing his pipe in silence for a few minutes. "Was she a suicidal type? That's what you're asking?" he replied eventually. "Can one 'type' people, Mr. Lancaster? Over many years, I have found I can't. People have a way of jumping out of these rigid, narrow categories in which we are apt to place them. A man considered to be timid and spineless, can, in a momentary burst of courage, forfeit his life to save a fellow creature; the bravest man can suddenly lose his nerve. Both men acting out of character as far as the world is concerned. I am not expressing myself well, but do you follow me?"

I nodded.

"Human beings are strangely unpredictable," he went on slowly. "The secret impulses, the urges and desires — conscious and unconscious — which make up the man, can depend on so many things; be affected by so many things. If there is one thing of which I have become sure over the years, it is that no man can truly know the mind or heart of another. That is knowledge possessed by our Creator alone." He paused and sighed. "Suicide? I don't know. I shouldn't be prepared to hazard an opinion on Mrs. Drayton or any other fellow creature."

I didn't press him further.

"I'll need you at the inquest, Father Bravachko. Can you stay on? Say two or three days?"

"I shall stay. There is plenty of work in the nearby villages. Mr. Drayton has kindly lent me a bicycle. I shall not be idle."

"I'll keep in touch. The inquest — in fact both of them — will probably be the day after tomorrow. I'll get out to Jatwa Nkwanga tomorrow morning."

I moved off, leaving him sitting by the river. He called to me as I reached the top of the bank.

"Mr. Lancaster."

I turned.

"For people of the Catholic faith, suicide is a mortal sin," he said, and looked back out across the river. "Mrs. Drayton

155

was a Catholic."

When I looked back from the next rise, I saw that he had dropped the rod. He was kneeling, head bent and hands clasped in prayer.

I walked thoughtfully back to the house.

CHAPTER 21

Jatwa Nkwanga was a small village lying about twelve miles north of the Boma. It seemed much further as I cycled there the following day, accompanied by Nyrenda.

After the muscular ease of six months' leave, I was still stiff from the ride to Chiabele and I cursed the non-arrival of the new gear box. The Landrover would have cut down the cycling to three miles.

In normal circumstances, the death of a village headman would not have sent me peddling across country. The D.O. would have been sent out to investigate and report. But these were not normal circumstances; the family connection between Chiabele and the dead man, plus Sikanga's report made it incumbent on me to do the trip myself.

Even so, it was the second feature of Maoma's death which was uppermost in my thoughts. As Drayton had asked: 'What possible connection could there be between the deaths of Elizabeth and Maoma?' Bravachko's conclusions stipulated a common medium; that was the connection; and it was this that worried me.

It was stretching coincidence a little too far to suppose that Maoma had died so conveniently from natural causes; assuming Bravachko to be right, why should Mrs. Drayton, having decided to kill herself, settle on one of the obscure vegetable poisons as the means? Where would she get it? How would she have obtained a knowledge of its properties? And why go to such lengths with a supply of sleeping pills to hand?

I was uneasy. Could the priest have made a mistake? But if he had, what was the purport of the note which Drayton had handed over to me?

I could have wished that the bridge over the Upupulu Stream had held for a few more days. A police officer could have been at Feira within twelve hours. It was not the nature of the affair which I jibbed at particularly, inevitably, murder and suicide were part of our work, but I had no taste for the investigation into the death of a fellow officer's wife.

We branched off the main road to the single-file track through the bush. There had been rain. The fresh, vibrant colours glowed free from dust and, through the sodden compost of dead leaf, thrust the bright heads of bush flowers. Over all hung the oddly nostalgic smell of bone-dry earth stirred into new fertility.

The thin yellow dogs gave tongue as we approached the village and a handful of children scattered and hid behind the grain bins. At that season of the year, mid-morning was not a good time to arrive at a village; the men were out digging gardens and the women planting and weeding.

Two old men sat in the shade of a hut, plaiting grass mats.

An official visit had probably been anticipated; the village was tidy and swept but there was no sign of wariness on the faces of the mat weavers as they came to greet me. The children crept back warily to a little distance from us, eyes round and curious.

Nyrenda went off to fetch the headman from the gardens and I squatted in the shade to wait, questioning the old men in my unoiled vernacular. The smell of drying fish hung in the air.

News had travelled fast. Yes: they had heard that Maoma had died; a sad affair for a man still young and strong, with pleasing wives. No; neither they, nor anyone else in the village had been asked to take food or beer with the headman and his visitors; gossip in the village had not dwelt on his death. No, the village talk was more concerned with who would be next-in-line for the Chieftaincy because of it.

I got nothing from them and my discussions with the headman were not more productive.

Chief Jatwa Nkwanga was a morose looking man, and on that particular day also a very nervous one. The talk bounced gently to and fro; the story never varied. The arrival of Maoma was unexpected; they had eaten early, sharing a communal pot of relish; they had drunk beer from one calabash but in separate gourds; talk had been of tax and village matters; when the noise in the night had aroused him, the women and the messenger were already with Maoma. No, he had not heard Maoma speak after that.

His wife corroborated his account of the evening, in every detail; too closely, I though; it smacked of rehearsal. Only once did she hesitate.

"What did Maoma say to the messenger that night, as he lay sick?" I asked her.

"Nothing!"

"But he spoke to Sikanga while you were there in the hut with Maoma's wives?"

"Yes," she agreed hesitantly.

"But he said 'nothing'?" I pressed.

"I heard nothing."

I did not pursue it.

Corroborating evidence of the shared meal and beer took little time and after instructing the headman and his family to present themselves at Feira for the inquest, I took my leave.

My mind revolved around the matter as the wheels of the cycle took a leisurely course home in the mounting mid-day heat.

I was inclined to agree with Drayton's assessment of this. We'd get nowhere. Communal meal, communal beer pot: man well, man sick, man dead, man buried – finish. I wondered why the headman's wife had lied. She could hardly have expected that Sikanga, a district messenger, would not report that Maoma had mentioned the Chief, even had Maoma's wives stayed silent. Was it only a fear of being involved in a case which might concern the Chief? Or was she scared of witchcraft? Had Jatwa Nkwanga himself warned her to stay silent?

As I left the bush path and turned on to the main dirt road to Feira, I met up with Martin Prail, his great bulk lapping precariously atop a protesting bicycle, white topee gleaming and a long butterfly net balanced on one shoulder.

I thought it an odd hobby for a man like Prail; butterflies. He was on his way to a spot a mile or two further on where, he told me, "just magnificent specimens, yes sir, magnificent specimens of Capys alphaeus, the Protea Scarlet," were to be found. I wished him luck.

I had not seen him since the night of Young's sundowner. The puffed, watering rims, lining the bloodshot eyes, seemed incongruous in the somewhat ascetic and scholarly cast of his face. It must have been quite a bender, I thought.

"Glad to meet up with you, Prail. I intended dropping you a note this afternoon, so you've saved me the trouble. Can you and your wife drop along to the office this afternoon, or tomorrow morning. What time would suit you?"

"Now, I'm real sorry about that, Mr. Lancaster. Elsa's away."

"Away?"

"Yes. She's gone off to spend a few days with the Brackenhursts. You know, the folk who farm up north? Said she wanted a change of air; the heat's been a bit much here and they've had more rain up there. She's taken the Landrover. Hence this!" he indicated the cycle.

"When are you expecting her back?"

"Well, you know the ladies, Mr. Lancaster. I wouldn't just quite know. She said 'a few days'. But what is it? Is it that important?"

"It is, I regret to say. A query has arisen, on whether the cause of death, as given on Mrs. Drayton's death certificate was, in fact, correct."

"Well! Whatdyknow..." The short, sandy lashes flickered.

"I think that perhaps your wife could help me, Prail."

"Now, Mr. Lancaster, I wouldn't be too sure that Elsa could."

"Oh, I think she could, Prail. She's been an interested party to the extent of writing, I understand, to the P.C. and she made one or two remarks in my office the other day."

"In your office? When was that?" he broke in.

"A few days back."

"Oh, yes. Of course," he added quickly. I had the impression that he had not known of his wife's visit to my office. "What did she say?"

"We can't talk about it out here." I interrupted. "Perhaps you could come along to my office tomorrow morning? Say around ten?"

He agreed and we parted company. I glanced back before I turned the next bend in the road. He had not moved. He stood where I had left him, astride the crossbar of his machine, the butterfly net raised like a pennant, head bent, as though studying the ground.

161

CHAPTER 22

I gave Drayton an account of my trip to Jatwa Nkwanga over a late lunch. He was moody and looked as though he had slept little the previous night.

"Sheer bloody waste of time." he commented. "It'll be just one more for the file; 'Death from unknown causes'."

He pushed back his chair and lit a cigarette. "Have you heard, by the way, that Elsa Prail has buzzed off to the Brackenhurst's place? Having got the pot boiling, she's now skipped out."

"I know. I met Prail on the road, knocking hell out of a bicycle chasing butterflies."

"Pity Elsa couldn't take an interest in the damned things." Drayton growled. "She wouldn't have so much time to spare for less innocent pastimes."

"I've told Prail I'll see him in the office tomorrow morning. He'll have to go and fetch his wife. The sooner we get this inquest over, the better. I want her there. I feel she knows more about this business than she's admitted."

"Who else are you calling?" Drayton drew the smoke deeply into his lungs.

"Yourself, Bravachko, Miss Frenton; I think that should cover it, but I'll have to decide finally after I've made a few more enquiries."

"What did Bravachko have to say? You saw him again?"

"It didn't get me much further." I repeated the priest's argument against exhumation.

"Well, he's right, isn't he?" Drayton asked, when I'd finished.

"In many cases, it wouldn't. If it was suicide, I'm curious to know how your wife got hold of one of the local vegetable poisons. Have you any idea?"

I rang the bell for the servants to clear the table and we moved out to the verandah for coffee.

"That's a point," Drayton said. "No. I've no idea."

"Had she ever threatened to take her own life?"

"On more than one occasion, which is partly why I never took her seriously."

"Bravachko told me your wife was a Catholic?"

Above the steaming coffee, his eyes studied my face. "That was the second reason for not paying much attention to such a threat," he said slowly. "Although on my interpretation of the word, Elizabeth was not a religious woman. Superstitious would have described her better. Religion wasn't a great factor in her life. It didn't go deep with her; if it had, she wouldn't have been the person she was."

"In the letter she left, she said: 'I can't live like this any longer.' Do you think she was referring to the general state of affairs between you, as you described it to me, or had something more happened, which might have precipitated this decision to end her life?"

"I don't know. I can't be sure," Drayton said. "When I left on tour at the beginning of October, matters here were worse than usual. Truth be told, I went touring to get away from it; I'd had enough. We had several scenes over my alleged relationship with Janet and there'd been this hysterical nonsense about the monkey dying and Matafwali. It was a

163

relief to get away from the Station. I didn't get back here until two days before she died. I'd cut out part of the tour when I got the P.C.'s minute about my transfer, so the note Young sent to say that Elizabeth had gone down with malaria, didn't catch up with me until I was on my way back. She was over the malaria when I got here. I'd done a lot of thinking out on tour and, as she seemed in a more reasonable state of mind, I broached the subject of a separation, a divorce."

"What was her reaction to that?" I asked Drayton, as he fell silent, seemingly lost in thought.

"She told me she would never agree to bring an action against me and that she'd fight any action I brought with the last breath in her body." He swallowed the rest of his coffee and got up.

"Do you think this could have precipitated a decision on her part?"

"I don't know!" He took a turn or two about the verandah. "She didn't appear to be unduly perturbed about it."

"Did Bravachko tell you that she talked to him about witchcraft the night before she died?"

"No, he didn't." Drayton swung round on his heel, a question in his eyes.

"I suggested to him that it was the Matafwali business she was thinking of. Don't you think it a possibility that this preyed on her mind and, coupled with your domestic difficulties, and her own, low physical state, brought her to a point where she didn't think rationally any more?"

"I don't know," he said again, less vehemently. "It could have been that way, I suppose."

He continued his pacing up and down the verandah.

"Bravachko isn't prepared to give an opinion on her mental state immediately prior to her death. Did you notice anything in her behaviour to indicate that she was in an abnormal state of mind?"

He considered it. "Not that I remember," he said eventually. "Elizabeth was, as always, a neurotic, moody, temperamental and unreasonable woman. Many people might term that abnormal but she was always that way. It wasn't anything new. On the other hand, from what I knew of her, I would have said that in her right mind, she was the last person in the world to commit suicide. She was too..." he cast around for the right word or phrase. "Possessive of all she held, including life. So, perhaps you're right. Perhaps that's the answer: 'Suicide whilst the balance of her mind was disturbed'.

He stopped, stubbing his cigarette thoughtfully into the ashtray, and seemed unsure about whether to continue.

"You were saying?" I prompted.

"Nothing. Let's drop it for the moment."

He was frowning.

After Drayton had returned to his packing, I dropped in to see Young. "How're you feeling?"

"Fine!" The pallor of his face beneath the bandage belied him. "But Father Bravachko won't let me get up. Couldn't you overrule him?"

I was pleased to see his good spirits. "No. He's quite right. Stay where you are. Have you got everything you want?"

"Yes, thanks. I say, sir, is this true about Maoma?"

"Depends what you've heard."

With all the rumours, I was getting extremely sensitive to validating anything without checking first.

"That Maoma's been bumped off by Chiabele?"

"Who told you that?" I dropped into a chair. "My servant

165

was over this morning."

I opted to give him an outline of the facts of the Maoma affair rather than the pastiche his servant may have heard.

"We'll have to wait," I finished, "and see what the Path. Lab. report turns up. I doubt whether the inquest will get us much further. Now, getting away from that for the moment, tell me something Young. What sort of woman was Mrs. Drayton?"

"Why on earth do you ask me that?" He looked startled.

"Never mind my reason for asking. Believe me, it's not a frivolous one. Tell me what you thought of her. What type of woman was she?"

He studied my face anxiously, as though he would read in it the reason behind the question.

"It's difficult to say." He pulled himself up on the pillows. "I didn't know her all that well. She was very much the D.C.'s wife as far as I was concerned. A bit bossy, I suppose."

"Would you say that she was a sociable type? Was she popular?"

"She wasn't a great socialiser, no. And as for popularity, well, she didn't hit it off with the other women all that well. Her tongue was a bit too sharp. You know what women can be like on an outstation, sir. She got on all right with the Prails and Drobinall."

"Was she a moody woman, a temperamental woman?"

He thought that over for a moment. "Yes, I'd say she was. Or at least, she was inconsistent in her manner if you know what I mean."

"When was the last time you saw her?"

"Let me see. I think it must have been the day I dropped the mail here, just before Mr. Drayton came back from tour. That was a few days before she died. She was lying on the settee on the verandah. She looked a bit rough, I must say.

She'd been on mepacrine and I put it down to that. Malaria's bad enough on its own, but those injections." He shuddered.

"Did she seem depressed? Anxious? More moody than usual?"

"I don't think so. It's difficult to remember."

He was beginning to look a bit alarmed at my interrogation.

"Did it ever cross your mind from anything Mrs. Drayton said or did at any time," I paused and leaned forward, "that she was mentally unstable?"

"Never! Why are you asking?"

"It's an unpleasant business," I got up, "but there now seems to be some doubt as to the real cause of her death. Mr. Drayton's turned up a note which suggests she may have committed suicide. There will have to be an inquest."

"Good God!" He sat upright in bed, his face a shade paler even than it had been when I entered.

CHAPTER 23

On the following morning, I walked over to the dispensary to see Janet Frenton. The sun, like a brass balloon, had sailed into a sky as clear and still as a deep mountain lake. The rains seemed to have gone for good and the heat haze veiling the Boma lent a despondent, swaying life to the still air.

I followed the dirt road, little more than a path, branching to the west off the main road. To the right, scrub vegetation stretched up and away to the back of the Nelson's house which stood on a higher level. To the left, a smooth, polished outcrop of rock sloped gradually away for a matter of twenty yards or so, before ending abruptly in a steep drop to the Zambezi. The bank looked unstable, as if we might lose some of it in heavy rains.

A few minutes' walk brought me to the dispensary, backed by the small hospital which overlooked the river.

Stunted scarlet canna lilies fought for space in the beds flanking the narrow path which skirted the buildings. Peering down at me from one of the scrubby trees beside the dispensary, the Boma's resident marsh warbler imitated the trills of a carmine bee-eater today.

The hospital was an ugly building with whitewashed walls and a galvanised iron roof. It was surrounded by huts that had sprung up like mushrooms to house the relatives of the inpatients.

The dispensary was a thatched, oblong building with a split entrance door like a horse's stable. A crowd already besieged the door, awaiting their pills and purges, diarrhoea and cough mixtures. Children played in the dust, some of them scratching at heads grey with ringworm.

I found the nursing sister in the dispensary; the flecked eyes greeted me guardedly above the head of the screaming child whose eyes she was bathing. The starch of the prim cap perched on the dark hair defied the temperature.

"I seem to have arrived at a busy time, Miss Frenton."

"You wouldn't think this so busy if you could see it later in the morning." She released the struggling child and turned away to scrub her hands at the old, marble-topped wash stand.

"Well, I hope I won't have to interrupt your labours too long. I thought it might save time if I came here rather than ask you to come to the office. Is there somewhere less populated," I indicated the battery of curious, dark eyes, "where we could talk?"

She locked the drug cupboard and I followed her out of the dispensary and along the open path which connected it to the hospital. There, to the right of the entrance, she led me into the small, white-washed room which served as an office.

"I thought you might be able to help me, Miss Frenton. Before I hold this inquest on Mrs. Drayton—"

"When will that be?" she interrupted.

"As soon as possible, naturally. But before that, I'd like to get a clearer picture of events in my mind."

She sat on the edge of the desk, one leg swinging nervously.

"I can't believe this is real," she said. "It's the sort of

thing that happens to other people."

"Well, believe me, I don't enjoy worrying you further about it. I would have preferred to shuffle this particular job on to somebody else's plate. I'll try to make it short."

I offered her a cigarette.

"No, I won't smoke, thank you," she said. "What do you want to know?"

"I want to know a little more about the days prior to Mrs. Drayton's death. I want to see whether we can turn up any corroborative evidence of suicide."

The leg stopped swinging. She came to her feet. "You don't believe it was suicide?"

Alarm made her voice shrill.

"I didn't say that, Miss Frenton. But surely you see that the background to an act of suicide is an integral part of my enquiry."

"I'm sorry." She walked over to the window and pushed it open. "What do you want to know?" she repeated.

"Sit down and relax." I pulled a chair forward for her. "I want you to think back. Whilst Mr. Drayton was out on tour in October, his wife had malaria for which you treated her. I presume you saw her daily at that time. Did anything strike you as being out of the ordinary in her behaviour?"

"From the little I knew of her, I would say not. But then, I didn't know her well. I hadn't had a great deal of contact with her before that."

"When did you start the treatment for malaria?"

She got up and took a large ledger from the shelf above the desk. She paged quickly through the book.

"Here it is: 19th October. She sent me a note that morning, I remember, asking me to call. She said she'd been very sick in the night. She was in bed when I got there and running quite a temperature. I gave her aspirins and sponged her down. Elsa Prail turned up at the house and she stayed with Mrs. Drayton whilst I came back here to check her blood smear slide. It was full of parasites and so I started mepacrine injections that morning."

"How did she strike you generally—as a person?"

"I've told you, I didn't know her well, not well enough to form an opinion about her. Elsa Prail could help you more."

She got up from the chair and crossed back to the window, her back towards me.

"So, Mrs. Drayton made no impression on you at all, one way or the other. Excitable or calm, happy or unhappy, accommodating or difficult?"

"No." Janet Frenton spoke without turning. "To me she was just a patient. She was sick, that's all."

I switched away from it. "Isn't mepacrine supposed to be a depressant drug?"

"It has been known to be."

"How did she react to the injections?"

"The fever followed a normal course with no startling symptoms. She complained of nausea but that was to be expected from the combination of malaria and mepacrine."

"I presume she wasn't alone in the house?"

"Elsa Prail had moved into the house to look after things generally. I went up three times a day to see Mrs. Drayton until Barnaby returned."

"And during those visits she never appeared to be unduly depressed? Morbidly inclined?"

"Depressed? Perhaps. But it was quite a severe attack she had so that's not surprising. Morbid? I don't think so."

"She never at any time said anything or did anything, which might throw light on this letter she left?"

"No. My visits were brief and talk was mainly about her health. My calls could hardly have been described as social."

There was bitterness in the girl's voice and I wondered whether the Elizabeth Drayton/Elsa Prail combination had

171

proved a bit too much for her; there had probably been a bit of ganging up to teach the girl her place; in a nice, ladylike, bitchy sort of way of course.

"Tell me what happened on the day Father Bravachko was sent for."

She turned back to the book.

"That was the 30th. Barnaby came to fetch me late that afternoon."

"Had you seen Mrs. Drayton that day?"

"Yes, I'd been up that morning. It was a routine visit only. She'd been over the malaria for three days or more. I only stayed a few minutes. She was still, of course, very weak. But it was nothing out of the ordinary."

"And when you got to the house that afternoon?"

"She was vomiting intermittently and complained of severe abdominal pain and headache; she looked so grey. I asked Barnaby to send for Father Bravachko. I couldn't decide what was wrong with her. I think you must have heard the rest already."

She shut the treatment book and turned back to the window.

"You stayed with her until Bravachko arrived?"

"Of course."

"Did she ask for pen or paper? Did you see her handling a letter?"

"No, but of course I wasn't in the room all the time."

"She said nothing which might have a bearing on the letter which was found?"

"Nothing."

"Sometime that night, Mrs. Drayton spoke to Bravachko about witchcraft. Were you there during that conversation?"

She hadn't been, and neither had Mrs. Drayton ever mentioned the subject to her.

CHAPTER 24

All of which, I thought, as I strolled slowly back to the office, told me little and advanced my actual judgment on the case by nothing.

I stopped on the track below the Nelson's house and walked over the smooth stretch of rock down to the unstable cliff edge. It was a sheer drop down to the Zambezi. Below me the brown water slipped by, sucking and slapping gently at the tangle of weeds lodged against the bank. Across the broad sweep of the river, a lone canoeist paddled towards the far shore.

The nursing sister had added no light or shade to the mental image of Elizabeth Drayton which I was trying to build.

'To me she was just a patient. She was sick, that's all.'

I couldn't quite believe it. Janet Frenton was an alert, sensitive creature. The emotional complications of her being in love with Drayton, and that was no sudden thing, even had she not realised it earlier, would have tended to sharpen her perception I would have thought. Especially where his wife was concerned.

I walked back to the office. Around the flag pole, a somnolent prison working party picked weeds from the lawn.

Prail, waiting for me in the office, wiped the sweat from his face with a large linen handkerchief. I thought that carrying the weight he did, he must find the heat of the station more trying than the rest of us.

"Ah, Mr. Lancaster!" he greeted me. "A lucky day—a most successful day."

"Lucky?"

"Two magnificent specimens—superb specimens of the Protea Scarlet." his voice brimmed with enthusiasm.

"Oh. The butterflies. I wish that was all I had on my mind."

He sobered a little. "Yes. Nasty business for you of course. Any help I can give?"

"I think you can. You can tell me why your wife wrote to the P.C. regarding Mrs. Drayton's death."

The last traces of enthusiasm for Protea Scarlet slipped from his eyes. He blinked.

"It is true that she wrote?" I prompted.

"Well, yes. She did." His fingers flicked nervously at the bottom of his cigarette pack.

"To such an effect that she thought an enquiry would be raised?"

"That's what she had in mind." He licked his lips nervously and lit a cigarette.

"I'm more than curious about this letter, Prail. If your wife had any information which she felt would justify an enquiry, it was her duty to bring it to me."

"Now look, Mr. Lancaster, I'm real sorry about this. I tried to get her to come along to see you before she mailed it, but she just wouldn't."

"Did you see the letter?"

"Sure. She showed it to me."

"She must have had stronger grounds for writing it than the vague suspicions she voiced the last time I saw her in this office. What were they?"

Prail considered for a moment, puffing furiously at his cigarette.

"Now you know the ladies, Mr. Lancaster," he said, after a moment. "Facts don't mean a thing to most of them. Their mental processes seem a peculiar combination of instinct, intuition and guesswork. I suppose Elsa felt you'd refuse to take her seriously on such grounds."

I found it incredible. "You surely can't mean, Prail, that your wife wrote such a letter, raising suspicions about this station with no stronger grounds than this? She was quite right to think I wouldn't take her seriously. It was no more than that the day she came to this office. It wasn't enough."

"Even so, it looks as though she wasn't off the beam after all. Didn't you tell me yesterday that some query had arisen as to the cause of death?" An amused glint flashed into his eyes and was gone.

"The present enquiry is based on something a little more substantial than this much vaunted intuition of the ladies, Prail. Now come on, what reason did your wife have for thinking the certificate was incorrect?"

"But I've told you. That's all there was to it. A hunch. The way she put it to me was that she was just knocked sideways by Elizabeth's death. It was only after the funeral that she started to think; she'd spent most of the morning with Elizabeth that day she was taken sick. Elizabeth was better than she'd been for days; looking more herself. Elsa left the house at noon and promised that we'd call back later for tea as a little celebration. When she left, Elizabeth was looking for a dress and said she thought of getting up for lunch. A matter of sixteen hours later she was dead."

"Did you go to the house that afternoon?"

"Sure we did. We found Elizabeth alone in the bathroom—as sick as a cat. Barnaby had gone to fetch the nursing sister. Elsa got her back to bed. I waited on the verandah and left when Barnaby got back. I thought I'd only get under their feet if I stayed. Elsa didn't come back till pretty late that night. Not until after Bravachko had pitched up. We didn't hear until the next morning that Elizabeth was dead. Elsa went to pieces. It hit her pretty hard. As I said, it was only after the funeral that she got around to thinking more about it. Thinking there was something screwy about it. Then, of course, the talk going the rounds didn't help."

"Talk?"

"You must have heard it, Mr. Lancaster. The whole bang shoot of the Bantu seem to think that Elizabeth was poisoned, like her monkey."

"Hang on a moment, Prail. If you know anything about the Bantu at all, you'll agree that after what Matafwali said before he left Feira, they would automatically connect him with Mrs. Drayton's death. But it wouldn't need poison. For them Matafwali's 'magic' would have been enough."

"Well, as far as I heard, the word poison was mentioned. Anyway, that's the idea Elsa got around to, that Elizabeth had died of poisoning."

"I hear that when the monkey died, Mrs. Drayton and your wife appeared to place some sinister importance on what Matafwali had said, and then again, when Mrs. Drayton fell sick. Do you think this hysterical nonsense might be at the back of your wife's mind?"

"Hell, no. That was a lot of trash. There was something said about it as I remember, but..." he came to a halt.

"Or she may have had the more reasonable idea that perhaps one of Matafwali's adherents had decided to implement the threat?" I said.

"She didn't say so to me."

"So. It went just like that, Prail? Mrs. Drayton had died from poisoning. No question of how or why or who?"

"No. She didn't get as far as that. She just felt, as I've said, that the whole set-up was screwy and she wrote to the P.C. And if it isn't her letter that's started all this, what is it? Something else has turned up?" The pale washed eyes searched my face.

"Quite right; but I don't feel inclined to go into that just now. You must contact your wife and get her to return immediately. I shall need her as a witness at the inquest I propose to hold on Mrs. Drayton."

"Hell! Now what?"

I cut him short. "Nelson's back on the Boma; ask him to let you have his transport."

"So, it looks as though Elsa was right." He heaved his great body from the chair. "I'll get off right away."

I followed him to the door. "Before you go, Prail; how seriously would you say Mrs. Drayton took this business of Matafwali?"

"Well, she was certainly het up about it," he said slowly. "So was Elsa. You know what women are like when they start talking something up."

"What was your opinion of Mrs. Drayton generally?"

He turned back, his glance questioning.

"Elizabeth? She was more of a buddy of Elsa's than mine." He polished his sunglasses thoughtfully. "I guess I'd say she was a woman of class, breeding. Fairly temperamental. A difficult woman, I guess. And as a wife I'd say she was pure hell! Is that what you want?"

"Would you say she was a well-adjusted, happy woman?"

"Well-adjusted?" he repeated. "No. Happy?" He slipped the glasses over his eyes. "Do you know a real happy man or woman? No. To be happy involves a degree of stupidity. Elizabeth wasn't stupid. No, sir."

With a salute of a fat hand he was gone.

177

There would have been little point in his lying to me about his wife's letter, I thought, as I watched him go. If he knew of any concrete reason for her suspicions, he was obviously not prepared to say.

I found it difficult to believe that Elsa Prail had scratched up something which subsequently had turned out to be anything but a mare's nest, without more substantial grounds than she had admitted. But what? Had she seen the note left by Mrs. Drayton? But if she had, why not say so?

CHAPTER 25

"I managed to contact Lusaka on the radio." I told Drayton, later that day.

He looked up intently at me.

"Prail wasn't lying about his wife's letter," I said. "According to the P.C. it was a blend of hysteria and malicious gossip. He'd blamed the time of year and pushed it back in the mail, marked, 'Return to D.C. Feira for information'. He was quite prepared to dismiss it at that. But he's blowing his top over the latest developments. How much of it got over, I don't know. The connection wasn't too good. I've told him we're waiting for Prail to get back with his wife before we can go any further."

Drayton sat hunched on the verandah, his legs aslant the edge of an open tea chest with his surname in stencil painted on the side. Around him lay the debris of straw and paper of the day's packing. On his knees he balanced a box of photographs which he was sorting in an half-hearted fashion.

"Elsa won't delay once she hears the good news," he grunted. "She won't be able to get back quickly enough. They'll be here by lunchtime tomorrow."

"If they are, I'll get on with the inquest in the afternoon. Jatwa Nkwanga has turned up with his family, so I've arranged to hold the inquest on Maoma tomorrow morning; to the point of adjourning it anyway pending a report from the Path. Lab. I don't want to keep Bravachko hanging around longer than necessary."

"I'll wager the pathological report will tell you nothing." He looked up at me speculatively, over the bundle of photographs held in his hand. "What do you expect to get out of Elsa, by the way?"

"Perhaps some corroboratory evidence of suicide." I shrugged. "I've been wondering whether she saw the letter you found, or had some inkling of your wife's intention."

"She must have seen it," he said, frowning. "It's the only possible answer."

"Then why didn't she say so earlier? Why hasn't she mentioned it in her little effort to the P.C.?"

"Does it matter now?" Drayton cut in. "Her aim was that my wife's death would be the subject of a public enquiry. She's managed it. She can't do any more harm. Though I am inclined to agree that her silence about it is puzzling. Then again, that's not the only puzzling thing in this whole affair. There's been something bloody odd going on here."

I glanced at him in some surprise. Was he only just beginning to realise that?

"These things, for instance." He picked up some letters from beside his chair and tossed them onto the table between us.

They were as Janet Frenton had described them; printed letters cut from a newspaper and gummed across a sheet of Government headed notepaper, to read 'HOW DID SHE DIE?'. There were three of them.

"They were in these envelopes." Drayton pushed them over to me. "Somebody on the Boma has got hold of discarded envelopes, originally addressed to 'Medical Officer, i/c, Feira and used them for these letters. They'd been left in the outgoing mail box to be picked up by the orderly who runs around with the circulars and such like. Automatically, they've turned up on Janet's desk."

"Is this the lot?"

"Yes. There've been no more since the balloon went up."

"I'll hang on to them and have a word with the orderly; perhaps he'll remember something about them."

"He doesn't. I've already asked him. I'm damned curious to know who sent these letters, Lancaster. An anonymous, hit-in-the-dark touch, on the same lines as the telephone call you told me about. You'd think Elsa. But why should she? She'd already, she hoped, set the ball rolling with her letter to the P.C. and she didn't bother to keep that quiet." He rubbed his nose and squinted. "No. There's something off key here. And this talk that's been snowballing. Who first mentioned the word poison? Not an African, of that I'm sure."

"There I'm inclined to agree, but let's leave it for the moment, Drayton." I pocketed the letters and got up. "But before we do, there's one thing I would like to say. I do appreciate that all this isn't easy for you and you know what the inquest will be like; poking, prying; question after question; believe me, I'm not finding it easy myself."

"Forget it." he muttered. He retrieved the photographs which had slipped to the floor. "You've got a job to do. I don't imagine for one moment that you're enjoying it."

We picnicked for our meal that night, amid the litter of Drayton's packing and my unpacking—talking shop and avoiding the subject uppermost in our minds. It was with some relief I retired early, leaving Drayton, stripped to his shorts, polishing a pair of old flying boots which he'd found at the bottom of one of his trunks.

It had been an unproductive and irritating day; a day of

work for which I had no stomach.

It was going to get worse. Already, from the outlying villages, the people had started to drift into Feira. By foot and cycle; by bush path and canoe, they had come, the surge of movement breaking up the quiet of the Boma. Speculation and excitement had mounted as the days passed. From mouth to mouth the names had been bandied.

Chiabele. Matafwali. Maoma. Donna D.C.

CHAPTER 26

"If there was half such enthusiasm for attending church," Bravachko muttered from behind his dead pipe.

He leaned back against the deal table which served as the judicial bench, shaking his head as he eyed the crowded court room.

They packed the floor, squatting cheek by jowl; lined the walls where feet could find room to stand and perched in the recesses of the windows; and still they came.

I called for Nyrenda. "Get some of these people out of here. Clear the windows and doors."

I sat back to wait.

The air was already thick with the smell of stale sweat. The protests of the evicted villagers gradually died down and those remaining settled slowly, shuffling and easing themselves into the extra floor space.

The monkey tails of Chiabele's head gear caught my eye. He was there in the corner with the fat Shuwima. They sat on touring stools, raised slightly above the level of the rest of the audience. The Chiefs had reached Feira that morning, as instructed; Chiabele to bring the tax register and fines from Kacinda and Shuwima to pay the courtesy call ordered by Drayton.

I had arranged to see them after the inquest: it would do

them no harm to kick their heels and I had been curious to see whether Chiabele would turn up in the court room. I had no doubt he had already heard reports, garbled or otherwise, of Maoma's accusation. I wondered whether he had yet discovered the loss of the Babenye.

From all sides, eyes swivelled surreptitiously to the corner where the Chiefs sat and the whisper ran from mouth to mouth.

The witnesses from Jatwa Nkwanga sat cross-legged in a quarter circle to one side of the deal table; Sikanga and Maoma's relatives to the other: there was a suggestion of defence and prosecution in the arrangement.

Drayton turned up as the room settled into an expectant quiet and, shaking his head to my suggestion that he join me on the bench, parked his touring chair to the side of the open door.

I took Bravachko as the first witness and led him in evidence over much the same ground as he had covered with me two days earlier.

It was an increasingly restless audience. They had come to hear Sikanga's story; they were not interested in these medical details.

"The messengers will clear the court room if there is any further interruption," I said.

The wave of fidgeting and coughing subsided.

The African witnesses gave their evidence from where they sat. It was a slow laborious process; question, translation: answer, translation; and a quickly developing cramp in my fingers from my efforts to keep my pen abreast of the flow of words.

A stillness settled on the room as Sikanga began his evidence; a sudden, enveloping silence, broken by the occasional, muffled whimper of a child from the constricting folds of its mother's back cloth.

"Think carefully, Sikanga. On the night you stayed at Maoma's village, Maoma came alone to the hut where you were to sleep. What did he say to you?"

In the sea of black faces turned towards Sikanga, the white quarter moons of exposed irises around the dark eyes made a bizarre pattern.

Sikanga spoke clearly: "Maoma said 'if the Chief finds out that I go to see the Bwana D.C. he will kill me. Do you think he will let me live to unseat him?'"

The room seemed to draw breath and hold it.

I glanced towards the Chiefs' corner. Chiabele sat, unmoving. His eyes were fixed on Sikanga's face.

From that point in the evidence, Sikanga's words dropped like stones into a well of silence, which held until he quoted the words spoken by Maoma before he finally slipped into unconsciousness: "'Chiabele has sent the jilombo of Matafwali to creep into my body and destroy me. I must die. This is what Chiabele threatened if I betrayed him.' That is what he said to me, bwana."

A long 'eeee' of expelled breath interrupted Sikanga and, making my gavel heard above the uproar which broke out, I ordered the court room to be cleared.

As the messengers hustled the last grumbling villager from the room, Chiabele approached the bench and requested permission to remain.

I allowed it.

The noise of protest and discussion outside the room gradually died away and questioning continued without further interruption; but no fresh evidence relating to Maoma's death was uncovered.

Jatwa Nkwanga's wife stood by her original statement that she had not heard what Maoma had said that night.

The wives of the dead man confirmed that Sikanga's report was a true one.

There we were stuck and, adjourning the inquest pending the pathologist's report, I dismissed the witnesses.

Chiabele waited until the last of them had left before he came over to the bench. Shuwima hovered in the doorway.

"The mind of my nephew wandered in his last illness," Chiabele said. "I made no threats to Maoma. Why would I threaten him?"

"It is a strange story for a dying man to tell, Chiabele. But as you have heard, it is not yet known what caused Maoma's death. Perhaps time will tell."

"Perhaps." His lips twisted. "When will the Bwana D.C. look at the tax register? I wish to return home."

"You can wait at the office. I'll be over shortly."

Chiabele turned away, his face sullen, and left the court room without further comment. Shuwima fell in behind him, his ragged robe flapping in the dust around his feet.

"That is not a good man." Bravachko stared after him.

Drayton joined us. "Regardless of the possible implication of today's enquiry, I don't think he's going to last much longer as Chief." Drayton turned to me. "Well, Lancaster? I feel a lot of time got you precisely nowhere."

"Pehaps. But even so, I've detailed a messenger to keep watch for any contact between Chiabele and Nkwanga. There could be a tie-up there."

"Will you need me this afternoon?" Bravachko asked as he rose.

"Yes, provided that Mrs. Prail gets back. I'm hoping she will and we can start at 2.30."

They left together and I turned back to finish the inquest report.

Through the open door some time later I saw Nelson's Landrover, followed shortly afterwards by Prail's, turn into the Boma and go uphill.

Good.

I sent a messenger after them with a summons to attend the afternoon's inquest on Elizabeth Drayton.

CHAPTER 27

Drayton and I walked down to the Court House after lunch. The sun hid behind a sultry haze and the expectant stillness promised rain: even the cicadas were quiet, and the gentle suck and smack of water in the reed-clogged inlets of the river sounded too loud in the waiting stillness. Compared with the hard glare of the morning's sun, the Boma seemed shadowed in semi-twilight.

Groups of curious Africans still hung around the Court House door and lounged in the shade of the grass surrounding it.

It was the first time I had seen the Boma residents in force since the night of Young's sundowner. Even the Groblers had come in from the Upupulu bridge.

As at the sundowner, I had the impression of rival groups; Prail, Drobinall and the Nelsons waited in the shade of the thatch, a few feet apart from the Groblers and the Jones who stood with the nursing sister.

Mrs. Jones, looking overheated, watched Janet Frenton with an over-solicitous eye. There was a holiday air about the cotton dress which had replaced the white drill uniform the girl usually wore, and the thick, dark hair, unrestrained by the starched cap, curled softly around the finely moulded face. The shadowed eyes turned to Drayton seemed to seek reassurance.

Nelson, leaning against the wall, watched our arrival with an expressionless face, inclining his head to hear what his wife was whispering to Drobinall, listening with an air of having heard it all many times before. Drobinall hung over Grace Nelson's diminutive figure, his wet mouth twisted in joyless amusement. The glowing, bronze head barely reached his shoulder. He waved a hand in affected salute as we reached the court room.

Of Elsa Prail there was no sign, and I asked where she was.

"Just taking a shower, Mr. Lancaster. Shaking off the dust. She'll be right down, sir."

To be irritated would have meant it was her victory, so I refused to be.

An office orderly had swilled the floor and the smell of carbolic pricked at the throat. A few rickety touring chairs had been produced from somewhere and were scattered around the room.

In the dim closeness, the green of Grace Nelson's dress made a startling splash of colour.

Father Bravachko hurried in and, under the cover of his apology for his late arrival, Elsa Prail slipped into the chair behind Drayton and Janet Frenton. The green eyes flickered over their heads and passed on; behind the dark head of the nursing sister, her smooth knot of hair gleamed a pale gold.

I went through the formalities, as I had to.

"...certain information and evidence which has come to light, there now appears to be some doubt as to the cause of death of Elizabeth Madge Drayton, I convene this Court of Inquest to try to decide by what means she died."

Father Bravachko took the oath amidst a general throat clearing and shuffling of chairs.

He gave his evidence concisely and clearly, covering Mrs.

Drayton's condition on his arrival at Feira, then his diagnosis and treatment, and finally her death.

"Tell me," I asked him, "did you have any doubts at all during the last twelve hours of Mrs. Drayton's life that she was suffering from an attack of viral gastroenteritis?"

"None at all."

"Did you, on her death, doubt that she had died from this condition, following the general exhaustion of malaria."

"No."

"Will you please explain to the Court why you now suspect the accuracy of your diagnosis and of the death certificate which you signed."

The priest repeated in evidence, what he had told me in my office after the post mortem on Maoma.

"These same symptoms," he finished, "together with an identical clinical picture, are common to a body on which I was asked to do a post mortem recently on Maoma. As far as the second death is concerned, the man in question was a strong, healthy man, to whom an attack of gastroenteritis, even an acute one, would not have proved fatal."

"And is it only due to this second death, with its familiar pattern of symptoms, that you now doubt whether your diagnosis in Mrs. Drayton's case was accurate?"

"Yes."

"Did Mrs. Drayton do or say anything, the night before she died, which could possibly be interpreted as an indication that she may have taken something, with the considered intention of ending her own life?"

"No."

"Will you please tell the Court, as far as memory allows, exactly what Mrs. Drayton said to you about witchcraft that night."

He did, occasionally hesitating, sometimes stopping to rearrange his thoughts. One such pause was long enough that I could stop writing. I waited, looking out over the room.

The tip of Grace Nelson's tongue flickered over her lips. Drobinall leaned forward in his chair, hands tightly locked round one raised knee.

My pen moved back to the record as the priest started to speak again.

"And that, I think, is all she said to me," he concluded a few minutes later.

"Did any question of Mrs. Drayton's mental stability ever cross your mind."

"No."

The noise of Bravachko's heavy tread as he returned to his seat accentuated the quiet of the court room.

I called Drayton as the next witness.

"As a result of rumours, and in pursuance of matters relating to your wife's death and the doubts arising as to the cause of it, you handed me a letter. Do you confirm that this is the letter?" I indicated Elizabeth Drayton's note.

He did.

"Will you please tell the Court—" I broke off. There was a stir of movement and I wanted to put down a marker.

"The public will remain quiet or leave the court room."

They subsided.

I turned back to Drayton. "Where did you find this letter?"

"It fell out of a book which I found on the table beside my wife's bed."

"When was that?"

"November 5th."

"Do you realise that this letter should have been produced and investigated earlier?" I didn't look at Drayton.

"Yes."

"Will you please tell the Court why you concealed the

letter."

"It was before any doubts had arisen as to the cause of my wife's death, I did not consider it in the public interest to produce it. She had been dead for five days when I found it."

"Do you confirm that this is your wife's handwriting?"

"I'm sure it is."

I read the letter to a silent room.

"What significance did you attach to this letter?"

"To me it suggested that, despite Father Bravachko's opinion, my wife had killed herself."

"Had your wife ever threatened to commit suicide?"

"On several occasions." Drayton shifted his weight restlessly.

There was more movement. In a brief upward glance, I saw Prail lay a hand on his wife's arm, as though in restraint. She sank slowly back into her chair.

"Did you take such threats seriously, Mr. Drayton?"

"No," he said firmly, but quietly.

"Let's go back to the day Father Bravachko was sent for. Will you please tell the Court what happened that day. What led up to your going to fetch Miss Frenton?"

"I found my wife in the bathroom. She'd been sick."

"What time was that?"

"I'm not sure. It might have been around three o'clock."

"You say that you found her in the bathroom. Had she called out to you?"

"No. I was on the verandah, writing up my tour report; the servants had gone off duty. I heard an unusual sort of noise at the back of the house and I went to see what it was."

"Did she say anything to you?"

"She said she had been sick very suddenly, but that she felt better and would go back to bed."

"So she wasn't up and around the house that afternoon?"

"No. She'd been in bed all day."

"She hadn't been up for lunch?"

"No. She had milk and a boiled egg. The servant took a tray to her room."

"Had you seen your wife that day, previous to finding her in the bathroom?"

"Yes. Before lunch. She was in bed reading."

"She was actually in bed? Not lying on top of the bed, dressed?"

"No. She was actually in bed." Drayton looked at me enquiringly.

"Go on please. After you found her in the bathroom, she went back to bed and you went to find Miss Frenton?"

"No. I suggested going for Miss Frenton, but my wife insisted that it was not necessary as she felt better. I went back to my work. When I looked into her room fifteen minutes or so later, she was asleep. When tea came, I went to ask her whether she would like some sent in. She was again in the bathroom and it was then that I went for Miss Frenton."

"Did your wife suggest that you should?"

"No. I didn't tell her I was going. I thought she might try and veto the idea again."

"Did she appear worried or depressed that day?"

"No."

"You noticed nothing out of the ordinary in her behaviour?"

"Nothing."

"You can think of nothing which might have depressed or worried your wife to a point where she decided to end her life?"

Drayton hesitated for a fraction of a second and then shook his head. "Nothing."

"After the discovery of the letter, did you search her

bedroom and the bathroom for anything which might have had a bearing on this matter: any bottles of unknown content; any boxes of pills; anything of a noxious nature which your wife may have taken?"

"Yes, I did. But I found nothing."

"Before you found the letter, did you for any reason doubt that she had died from natural causes?"

"No."

"Stand down please, Mr. Drayton. Mrs. Prail, will you come and sit here?"

There was something unpleasant in the green, unlit eyes as their glance fell briefly on Drayton as she came forward. It was there for a second and gone as she turned towards me.

She took the oath. In her voice and manner there was a barely concealed excitement and, as I watched her, the sense of uneasiness which had not been a stranger to me for the past days, returned stronger than ever.

"You were friendly with Mrs. Drayton?"

"I surely was."

"Can you confirm that this letter is in her handwriting?"

"Yes, it is."

"Tell me, Mrs. Prail, have you ever seen this letter before?"

"Yes. Once before. It was the day she wrote it. I was with her." There was a dry amusement in her voice.

Somebody in the room coughed in the silence which followed her words.

"Then you..." I began and stopped, warned by the sly anticipation in her eyes. I felt my way more warily. "Tell me under what circumstances Mrs. Drayton wrote this letter."

"She was leaving for a short vacation I guess. Getting away from the house and getting away from Feira."

In the distance came the first reverberating roll of thunder. I glanced over at Drayton. His face was blank as though he had not heard; or if he had heard, was not interested. A muscle twitched in the deepening tinge of his cheek. Janet Frenton's head was bent, the wealth of dark hair falling forward and partially covering her face. The eyes of everyone else in the room were fixed on Elsa Prail. Mrs. Jones raised an uncertain hand towards her mouth. Prail mopped his face. A rat scuttled in the rafters overhead.

"When did she write it?" I asked.

"I guess it was the day before she was due to leave with us for Lusaka. It was the day before she took sick with malaria—we thought—"

I cut across the flow of words. "You were actually with her when she wrote it?"

"I certainly was. She showed it to me. Her cases were packed. She was ready to leave. Early the next morning she sent a servant with a note to say she'd been sick in the night and felt too ill to make it. We postponed the trip when we found out she'd got malaria. I couldn't just up and leave."

"So that must have been 19th October. You say that she was going with you and your husband to Lusaka. Was she intending to stay there?"

"No. She'd got a booking at the Napier Hotel in Mombasa. The three of us were going there. We were going to fly from Lusaka. We all needed a break. Elizabeth was jumpy and nervous. She thought it would do her good to get away from the house for a while."

I stopped her.

"Did you know anything about this, Mr. Drayton?" I called to him.

"This is the first I've heard of it."

"Did you find any cases of your wife's clothes packed, as though she had intended to make a trip?"

"No."

"Because I unpacked them," Elsa Prail said. "Elizabeth

195

changed her mind about going when she heard about the transfer. She asked me to write and cancel the bookings for her. She said if they were being moved there was no point."

"As a letter indicating that she was going off on a trip, it's an oddly worded one, Mrs. Prail."

"I guess she'd just got herself into a state. She said she couldn't stand the house any longer, and that she'd got to get away. As I said, she was jumpy and nervous after the monkey died."

"And the proposed trip seems to have been kept very quiet as far as Mr. Drayton was concerned. Nobody mentioned it to him when he came back from tour."

"Elizabeth asked me not to. Her husband had brought up the question of a divorce. She thought he might light on the idea that she needed a vacation to get her out of the way. I guess she hoped that a new station and out of sight out of mind would get him over—"

"That will do, Mrs. Prail. The presumption of suicide—"

"Suicide!" There was an edge to her voice which accentuated the faint drawl. "That idea never entered her head, not seriously. I'd swear to that."

"That won't be necessary, Mrs. Prail, you are already under oath. Please return to your seat."

Drayton was watching me intently. A deep frown ridged his forehead. He gave the faintest of shrugs.

I called Prail.

"Will you please confirm..."

It was a waste of time. There would have been little point in Elsa Prail lying, I thought. Her story could be too easily checked.

"Thank you, Mr. Prail. Please return to your seat."

The chair creaked under his weight as he subsided and the room drew breath and waited. I shuffled my papers and raised my head to the focused battery of eyes; speculation, bewilderment, excitement and despair. Elsa Prail's were alight with malicious triumph.

I spoke carefully. "At this enquiry, the presumption of suicide raised by the wording of this letter, has not been supported by other evidence, circumstantial or otherwise; and has in fact been rebutted by the sworn testimony of the last two witnesses. Their evidence regarding the letter refutes the suicidal interpretation placed on it. I accordingly adjourn this inquest, pending further investigation.

Back in the stifling heat of my office, I signed an order for the exhumation of Elizabeth Drayton's body and sent a messenger to Bravachko's camp with a request for a post mortem examination. Perhaps Bravachko was right; perhaps it would prove nothing one way or the other; but better that I felt, than wait for decomposition to effect the same dead end, and result in an eternal question mark.

CHAPTER 28

The storm conceived in the sullen heat of the day, sprang into fierce and sudden life from the peaks of the escarpment. Filtered by the mosquito gauze of its hail of leaves and twigs, a strong gust of wind swept through the house, slamming doors and shaking windows. A sheaf of papers on the table fluttered and whirled in a mad helter skelter across the verandah.

I sat and watched the lightning streak viciously in the storm-tossed haze veiling the hills.

It was a prickly situation. In the colonial administration, varied and widespread duties fell to the lot of the District Commissioner. No field of activity in the District was outside his authority or compass. He was an uncrowned king, ruling through the Native Authority. Above all, and paramount to other duties, he was the Law. Legal authority throughout the District was vested in him as magistrate and coroner, defending and prosecuting counsel, judge and jury. And policeman.

The death of Mrs. Drayton under questionable circumstances was now to be the subject of investigations.

I had become friendly with Drayton. He still lived at the D.C.'s house, so we shared the same roof. I liked the man and admired him as a colonial officer, but he was part of the subject of my investigation.

It wasn't only this that exercised my mind. Another aspect of the affair concerned me more: the fact that I had not been surprised by the result of the inquest. It was as though I had, in some measure, anticipated the result as if it followed a pre-ordained pattern. I could not rid myself of the impression that events in Feira, since my arrival, had been shaping themselves to this end.

Not exactly shaping themselves. That was the point: they had been shaped. They had been manoeuvred and, like a donkey enticed by a carrot, I felt I had been following a path which it was intended from the beginning that I should take. I wondered how matters would have been brought to a head had it not been for the circumstance of Maoma's death triggering doubts in Bravachko's mind.

Drayton joined me on the verandah and, helping himself to a whisky soda, stretched out in a chair. He cast a speculative eye at the threatening sky.

"This should cool things down," he muttered. "And thank God for that. Well, Lancaster... quite an afternoon. And where do we go from here?"

"I've asked Bravachko to do a post mortem tomorrow morning. I'll get a working party from the prison on digging, as soon as it's light."

He made no comment and I added, "You'll agree that there's no way of avoiding it, after the Prail woman's evidence this afternoon?"

"None at all." He pulled out his pipe and rammed tobacco into the bowl. "I would take the same line. Perhaps Bravachko is right in saying that a post mortem won't have any positive value at this stage, but you can't afford to just wait for something to turn up to decide one way or the other whether it's going to be helpful. That might be too late."

"Bravachko could, of course, be wrong all down the line.

We can't be sure."

"I don't think he is, Lancaster. He doesn't claim to be a pathologist, but he's a damned good doctor."

Lameck padded in with the lamps and I got myself another drink.

"Well, assuming he's right," I splashed soda into my whisky. "Has it occurred to you what an extraordinary set-up this is? We haven't a scrap of proof that Maoma was poisoned, but the main question about your wife's death has mushroomed from the assumption that he was."

"I'll wager my pension that Maoma would be alive now, if he hadn't been on his way to the Boma to inform against Chiabele," Drayton said. "As we've discussed before, his death, in these circumstances, suggests one of the vegetable poisons. And where will that lead? You know as well as I do that the Path. Report will probably be non-committal. 'Death from unknown causes'. You've seen it happen before."

It was true enough. I had, at one time in my career, had to dismiss a charge of murder against a man because a post mortem failed to show the cause of death, despite the fact that the defendant admitted putting a root powder in the dead woman's food. Variously listed in District returns, as dysentery or malaria, the number of deaths from poisoning in the villages was anybody's guess.

The group of vegetable poisons common to Africa was uncatalogued and of unknown number. Many were undetectable and unknown to European medicine. Africa was a continent where the roots of a particular bush could produce a deadly poison for three months and be harmless for the rest of the year: where a mud and leaf poultice 'cured' a skin cancer on one day and produced gangrene the next; where the witchdoctors lied and prevaricated regarding their remedies, fearing a loss of their powers. Africa was an untapped field for the scientist and the botanist.

"And if Bravachko is right," Drayton was saying, "in suspecting a common agent in the deaths of Maoma and my wife, a like result will apply to her as well. 'Death from unknown causes.' That's a damned fine prospect."

"Isn't that jumping the gun a bit?" I asked.

The wind had dropped and a heavy expectancy hung over the station. The storm held back, waiting with the tensed, alert stillness of a crouching leopard ready to spring.

"You do of course realise, Lancaster, that this affair being practically sub judice, you shouldn't even be talking to me about it?" Drayton stirred restlessly in his chair.

I replied briefly and coarsely and searched my pockets for cigarettes.

He pushed a packet towards me across the table.

"Before this afternoon," he went on, "I inclined to the idea that Elsa Prail had at some time seen Elizabeth's letter; that she had put the same wrong interpretation on it as I had—and was determined that it should be brought to light with as much publicity as possible. It seems that I must have been on the wrong tack. But if it wasn't the letter that had set her off, what was it? Was she just out for trouble and did she, by sheer coincidence, turn up something that produced more fire than smoke. It's not credible."

"I agree, it's puzzling. But she wasn't lying this afternoon, anyway. Prail's confirmed her evidence and the bookings she mentioned are easily checked. Had you no idea at all that your wife had worked herself up about the Matafwali business to a point where she felt she had to get away from the house?"

I caught the matches he threw and lit the cigarette.

"At that time, no. I thought the whole thing had been forgotten until that night I told you about: the night before Elizabeth died—Elsa Prail was going on about it. Elizabeth hadn't mentioned it again, after the first set-to about the monkey's death. But as you know, I was away from the Boma for most of October."

"When did your wife hear of the transfer?"

"Must have been around the 20th. As soon as I'd got the P.C.'s minute which had followed me out on tour, I sent in a runner with a note to say that I'd be cutting the trip short and returning to Feira on 27th October."

He spoke absently, as though weighing up something else in his mind and, for a moment, there was silence between us: then, as though coming to a decision, he leaned towards me.

"This is not intended as a reflection on you," he said, "but I want a police officer sent down from Lusaka. It'll be easier from all points of view."

"I quite agree," I said. "I was going to suggest it myself."

"I've been doing a lot of thinking since the inquest finished this afternoon," he went on, "and I don't like the way things are going. In the first place, natural death is questioned. Secondly, the presumption of suicide arising from the letter I found, has been discredited. What does that leave, Lancaster? Accident?"

"Accident can't be discounted," I said.

"I think it can."

He eyed me curiously from behind the wreath of smoke which curled from his pipe.

"The way this thing has been built up from the beginning is against 'accident'. Listen to my theory on this. Somebody on this Boma has known ever since Elizabeth died that there was something that determined there would have to be an enquiry; everything that's happened on the Boma—the telephone call to you, the letters to Janet, the engineered gossip, has been leading up to that. No, wait a moment, let me finish, Lancaster. Now, irrespective of how such knowledge was acquired, and its possible implication, why was it not made public immediately? Why this underground campaign? To withhold information concerning a felony is to risk being involved as an accessory after the fact. A possible reason for concealing such information is blackmail. But that obviously isn't the motive here. So, whatever this person knew or learnt about my wife's death was kept secret without revealing the identity of the campaigner. Why? The obvious motive—that justice is served—can't be the right one because that could have been accomplished much more easily by a statement to a competent authority, right at the very beginning of the affair. So, what the hell's going on? Something I don't like at all."

"Fear of being involved might be the reason for the secrecy," I said.

"An innocent involvement could have been explained by a statement. On the other hand, if this knowledge held by the mover-behind-the-scenes is a guilty knowledge, why are such pains being taken to now bring it to light? No. It's damned odd."

Drayton had echoed some of my own thoughts but he had taken them further. I sat turning over his theory, sipping the warm whisky in which the ice had already melted. A giant moth crash-dived the lamp, and fell to the floor.

"I feel that even if Maoma hadn't died so conveniently, something else would have turned up to clinch matters." Drayton added, echoing my earlier, unspoken thoughts.

"Why do you presume this knowledge is of such dangerous content?" I asked.

"What point would there be in all this if it were not?" Drayton countered and he went on. "Why has Bravachko rescinded the death certificate? Because he suspects that Elizabeth died of poisoning. Somebody on this Boma knows that she did. That's the only answer. And if the whole purpose of the planning and manoeuvring is to ensure a verdict of accidental death, where's the point. No. Somebody has gone to a lot of trouble about this, with one end in view: a verdict of murder."

The word had an ugly sound and there was silence for some minutes. Drayton got up and pumped life into the dying lamps.

It seemed a tall theory but I found myself agreeing Drayton could be right.

"Have you changed your mind about Mrs. Prail being the prime mover in the matter?" I finished my drink.

"Not completely." He leaned back against the brick pillar dividing the mosquito gauzes. A thin trickle of sweat crept down his temple.

"I'll ask for a police officer to be sent down, if I can make contact with Lusaka tomorrow morning. He can come as far as the Upupulu and we'll get him over by canoe when the spate subsides. Grobler thinks it should be down within a few days and that'll probably be quicker than if he waited for the barge."

The wind, springing into fresh life, had veered fiercely, bringing the storm right over the station. We dragged the chairs and tables towards the shelter of the inner wall as the stinging rain slashed through the mosquito gauze. The lamps spluttered, swaying drunkenly on their steel hooks and I moved them into the sitting room.

I rejoined Drayton on the verandah. The giant cassias bent their gale-tossed branches towards the house; with a deafening roar the storm crashed over the Boma in full fury.

The lightning, illuminating momentarily the darkened verandah, outlined Drayton's head in sharp relief; the face in the unearthly light, was a caricature in black and white; with the strong, springy hair silhouetted against the white distemper of the wall. Drayton suddenly seemed like a stranger: he seemed to be watching me.

A freak playfullness in the battle raging overhead brought an unexpected and momentary lull and, in the silence of the still house, he asked softly.

"Has it ever occurred to you, Lancaster, that you may be talking to a murderer?"

CHAPTER 29

The night's storm transformed the station to a bog of red mud. Even for Africa, it had been a tremendous downpour. The far bank of the Zambezi changed contour overnight, a fifty yard stretch being swallowed in the flood. Lightning had split one of the baobabs in the cemetery to ground level, undoubtedly providing a field day for the local witchdoctor.

Night eventually gave way to a grey morning of fine drizzle, with mists covering the river.

The exhumation of Elizabeth Drayton's body was the only one at which I have ever been present and it was an experience which I hope I shall never need to repeat.

Mud made the task of disinterment as difficult as it was unpleasant and the labour gang from the prison were uneasy. It seemed a long time before their shovels struck solid and the coffin, slipping and sliding in the mud of the hauling ropes, was brought to ground level. It was taken to the shelter of a grass screen which had been erected earlier that morning. Bravachko had suggested that it would be easier to do what had to be done on site, rather than have the coffin carried down to the Court House.

The solid coffin and heavy clay soil had kept the body in a fair state of preservation, except for the brain which had completely deteriorated. It was a shocking business and, not staying a second longer than the letter of the law demanded, I moved away from the grass screen to fresh air, and was then forced to combat the smell with a cigarette.

I had finished my fourth cigarette before Bravachko signalled me. Concealed beneath a strip of mutton cloth, the jars which Bravachko had brought with him had been placed to one side. He was reclosing the coffin.

"These jars must be taken to the Court House," he said, "the sooner, the better."

Elizabeth Drayton's coffin was reburied within the hour.

It was a relief to return to the shadowed relative coolness of the office and the dry, dusty files, after the work of the early morning. I had thankfully left the priest at the Court House, to finish what he still had to do.

In absent-minded and mechanical fashion, I cleared the in-basket of its pyramid of files and checked through the outgoing mail. It was a full bag for the P.C.: the trouble at Kacinda; assault on the D.O.; the theft and recovery of the Babenye; inquest reports from the previous day.

So much for being boring in my communications.

I signed the last item—a request for a pathological report.

The labelled jars relating to Maoma waited with the straw beside the empty crate. The curt descriptions of the specimens being sent forward for analysis seemed little to do with the living man: kidney, wall of stomach, sections of heart, lung and liver. There was something unnatural in the juxtaposition of the name he had born in life, to these remaining pieces of what had once been a perfect machine and was now not just broken but dismantled.

The barge already waited at the landing stage to take them upstream to Chirundu and on to Lusaka. From there they would be sent to the Government Pathologist to start the rounds of the pathological laboratory—the spectroscope, the bunsen burners—the endless tests; I wondered with what result. And as with Maoma, so with Elizabeth Drayton.

My mind went back to my conversation with Drayton on the previous evening.

There were plenty of counter arguments to these theories. If there was a murderer, had that person being using the Matafwali affair as a smokescreen? Drayton's take was based on the elimination of alternatives. Mine on that and the impression of having been manoeuvred somehow.

Would any adherents of Matafwali have gone for so subtle an approach? And would any have attempted to implement the threat to Drayton? I didn't believe so. The ringleaders of the ritual killings had been hanged with Matafwali. The hangers-on deemed closest to him had been gaoled. And the rank and file members of the secret cult living around Feira would be naive enough to expect Matafwali to carry out his threat without physical aid from them.

There was another factor which appeared to exclude any Africans. There had been no doubt in their minds at the beginning, why Elizabeth Drayton and her monkey had died: Matafwali had threatened, and so it had happened. I had heard the story within days of my arrival at Feira. It was only later that the word poison had been mentioned. By whom? And when? It had cropped up before Bravachko had even voiced his suspicions.

Janet Frenton had described the gossip circuit: 'somebody's cook tells somebody's house servant who tells

208

somebody's garden servant.'

No. That hadn't been the compound gossip. At least, not originally. But it wouldn't have been too difficult, I thought, for a European to have dropped the hint which had later given rise to the suggestion of poison.

The letters to Janet Frenton and the telephone call pointed to a European: the most likely source of any of the vegetable poisons was an African. How did they fit together?

The questions revolved in my mind.

Was a common poison the only connection between the deaths of Maoma and Elizabeth Drayton? Was the connection merely a coincidence? And where had the poison come from, if poison it had been, which had caused Mrs. Drayton's death?

Eventually, I pushed the jotted notes into a drawer and turned back to the mail, wondering whether the crate would be large enough to take the jars which still had to come from the court house.

As Father Bravachko had predicted, so it turned out for the first step of the medical investigation: it was impossible to determine what had caused the death of Mrs. Drayton.

The priest looked exhausted.

"As in the case of Maoma," he reported to me, "the liver and kidneys show a gross degeneration. The heart muscles are flabby and there is the same discolouration of the stomach lining with an appreciable reddening, as far as I can judge at this stage, of the gut. There is no sign of other abnormality nor indication as to the cause of death. It could have been a gastroenteritis, as I first diagnosed, but I am not a pathologist."

"Speaking unofficially, and not as a pathologist, give me

your frank opinion."

"As a man and a doctor, I do have an opinion but it is one not based on fact: it is based on conjecture and surmise. As a priest, I would prefer not to voice an opinion." He shrugged his great shoulders. "Let somebody better qualified to judge, determine the matter. I must be off, Mr. Lancaster, but I want to go up to the house before I leave to see Mr. Young. Could you organise another barge to drop me off at the Kapoche Mission landing?"

"I'll arrange it."

He stopped as he reached the door and stood outlined against the light, his face shadowed, the wiry beard skirting the paunch.

"If need arises and I can help, send for me," he said.

I watched him make his way slowly uphill to the house, then I attached a copy of his report to the inquest proceedings and added a postscript to the covering minute.

"It will be apparent that the necessity for Drayton to appear as a witness at the resumed inquest, precludes his leaving on transfer as instructed."

I went down to the barge later and slipped the last mail into the bag. The sun had broken through the mists of the early morning. The rain had stopped.

Two messengers squatted aft, in charge of the mail and the crated jars.

The paddlers pushed off. Travelling upstream and impeded by the revitalised flow of the river, it would take them two weeks to reach Chirundu. The paddlers' chant, nostalgic and harmonious came back to me across the water as they reached the first bend in the river.

I walked tiredly back to the wireless room, where I contacted the P.C. and made an official request that a police officer be sent down to Feira.

CHAPTER 30

After the departure of the barge, the Boma settled into quiet. An uneasy, watchful quiet, and during the following days, life slipped back into a semblance of normality. The pressure of routine work was a welcome aid to this end, even if below the mechanical round of everyday duties, one sensed the brooding. It was as though somebody on the Boma marked time. At night the mysterious drum had fallen silent, as if it too, was waiting.

The light, steady rains had set in. Day followed day of grey skies and high humidity.

David Young, up and about again, had moved back to his own house. Despite the freckles standing out against the underlying pallor, he seemed reasonably fit but I vetoed his idea of getting down to district touring. Village to village touring in the rains could be a hard slog. I would have much preferred getting out into the district myself: the touring schedule for the quarter would be sadly lagging by year's end and the onset of the heavy rains in the new year would make travelling difficult, if not impossible, in some parts. But I had to stay on the station until the issues were resolved.

I saw little of Drayton at the Boma office and at the house, I had the impression that he avoided me.

On the occasions on which routine duties brought Janet Frenton to the office, she was withdrawn and uncommunicative. The question of her transfer to another station seemed to have been forgotten.

I found Nelson waiting in my office one morning. His Landrover and trailer, standing ready to move off, was piled high with touring kit.

"I'm off this morning." he greeted me. "Here's a copy of my proposed route. One of the game guards has sent word that elephant are moving into the new cleared strip here..." He laid out a map and went into details.

He seemed ill at ease, I thought, compared with my previous impression of him.

"It's a shortish trip, isn't it?" I asked.

"I worked it that way. What with one thing and another, my wife's got the jitters. She's nervous of being left here." He waited, as though to allow me to take up the point. "I'll be back at the Boma within the week," he added, "and if things are quiet here, I'll push on to the south strip within a day or so."

"Why doesn't your wife go with you if she's nervous of being alone?" I deliberately ignored the obvious question.

"She doesn't care for touring."

She wasn't a bush type, I found myself thinking, calling up mental picture of her arranged, doll-like prettiness.

"Have you asked for a messenger to sleep at your house whilst you're away?" I asked. "If not, you'd better see Young before you leave. He's got the duty roster and can lay it on."

It was a common practice for a district messenger to sleep in the kitchen or on the verandah when station officers were on tour.

"Yes. My wife doesn't like having a messenger sleep at the house when I'm on tour, but now, I've insisted she has one."

Again, I forbore to pursue it.

"Well, I'll get off." He moved towards the door. "Oh, by the way," he turned back, his voice casual, "there seem to be a few errors in the Ivory Register."

"Oh?" I waited.

"Young showed me the Register. I've just been checking through it."

I should have warned Young.

"What sort of errors?" I asked.

"Weights, numbers, sizes of tusks," he said slowly. "Just here and there the figures disagree with the Game Camp records. I wondered..." he paused. "Perhaps I could take the Register out with me. I could check at the Game Camps on the way."

"Afraid not, Nelson. Registers can't leave the Boma." I pretended to think about it. "How do you think the mistakes have occurred?"

"Difficult to say. Clerical errors? Mistakes in weighing?"

"All right. See me about it when you get back. That'll be time enough."

"I suppose so."

"Tell your wife to contact me if she needs help on anything."

"I'll do that." He left.

I wondered why he had raised the subject. Had he really thought he would be allowed to take the Register, or had he been sounding the ground to find out whether Drayton had voiced his suspicions to me? Or was it that, if an eventual enquiry were raised, he could say that he had been the first to draw attention to the discrepancies?

Prail called for me in his Landrover shortly after Nelson had gone. I had arranged to go out with him to Baluti, the quarantine station. Drobinall had reported five suspected fly-struck cattle.

"When are you coming out to see my little place?" Prail asked as he swung the nose of the Landrover round.

"I can make it now that most of the routine stuff's off my plate. Sometime tomorrow afternoon, if that suits you? How's your wife?"

"Can't wait to get back to the States. She's had a bellyfull of this place. Elsa's a restless type. I guess there's not much for a woman like her in a place like this."

Privately I agreed with him.

"It takes all sorts," I said. "There are women who like this sort of life—touring, gardening, running the house. They seem to find enough to keep them occupied and reasonably content."

"Elsa's idea is that to really go for bush life, a woman has to be a vegetable and get really bogged down in the domestic rut."

"Surely it depends on the woman? I think she can get bogged down, as you put it, just as easily in London as she can in the bush. Or New York."

"Not much risk for Elsa, wherever she is!" Prail said drily and went on to talk of life in Java and the results of a recent survey there.

Baluti lay eight miles to the north east of Feira. In some parts the flooding of the Luangwa had reduced the road to a sea of mud, in other parts, pot-holes and erosion had narrowed it to a mere strip. It was a typical bush road in the rains and conversation became spasmodic and disjointed.

It was a grey morning but, even so, Prail's eyes were hidden behind sun glasses. I wondered how he had come to be married to Elsa Prail. The leonine head and scholarly face were magnificently cast and still handsome, despite the red-veined onslaught of alcohol but there was something repellent in the grossness of the body stuffed awkwardly behind the wheel.

"This your first trip to Baluti, Mr. Lancaster?" he asked suddenly.

He seemed amused to hear that it was.

"I guess you're in for a little surprise then." He started to laugh.

The Landrover, skirting a deep subsidence in the road, bumped and crashed through the skirting bush.

"What's so funny about Baluti?" I asked when he'd got us back on the road.

"It's nothing, I guess," he said and went on laughing, his amusement agitating the folds of skin, bulging above his collar.

It was another half an hour before we reached Baluti. The station was set up on a raised plateau above flood level, a mile or so from the banks of the Luangwa. The narrow dirt road spiralling upwards brought us in sight of the bush-pole paddocks and the sea of moving cattle within them. Crush pens and dip tanks lined and sealed a narrow path, coming up from the river and joining the main road. The grass of the pens, close cropped by the cattle, laid an even floor, sparse and brown against the green fecundity of the bush, which hung like a stage back drop in the distance. Water furrows ran between the pens.

"Where does the water come from?" I asked Prail.

"There's a small tributary of the Luangwa close by," he said. "The water's run off that."

The actual station of Baluti was a mile or so farther than the cattle pens. It was a collection of pole and thatch huts with the inevitable spread of the labourers compound looming in the background. It was not until the Landrover had skirted the first huts that Drobinall's house became visible.

Prail braked. "Isn't that just something?" He waved a

hand.

It certainly was.

The brick-built bungalow with its roof of thatch, stood on a higher level of ground, removed from the administration huts. A lawn, green and velvety as a bowling green, sloped gently towards us, edged in a half circle by a neat, gravelled drive which led to and from the bungalow. Orange fingers of golden shower twined through scarlet sprays of bougainvillaea and matted in a thick screen, completely veiling the west wall and stretching in brilliant streaks of colour across the thatch of the roof. Terraced beds of roses edged the outer circle of the drive and dropped away into miniature rockeries.

"Drobinall must be quite a gardener." I murmured as we skidded round the wet, gravelled drive.

"This is his hobby. His 'baby' you might say." Prail laughed.

Drobinall met us at the door of the bungalow, wearing bright blue denim shorts and single-thonged sandals. He was cultivating a beard, I noticed, and wondered how long the half inch of fuzz had been nurtured.

"Time for a cuppa," he said. "Will you join me?" He half bowed us into the bungalow. The room into which we walked was startling. I realised what had been amusing Prail on the journey. On the white-washed walls, painted nymphs and satyrs chased Rubenesque females through ethereal glades and dark caverns: a crescent of moon and a sprinkling of stars glittered tropically in the blue haze of the ceiling. The vivid cretonne of the frilled curtains draping the windows, matched the covers of the plump cushions arranged neatly on the chairs.

It was a grotesque room. It put me in mind of an unhappy mixture of a third rate night club and the waiting room of a quack doctor. I wondered how long it had taken

Drobinall to achieve that careful disarray in the fan of London journals lying on the table.

"Let me welcome you to Baluti." he said formally, in his fluting voice.

"You're by way of being an artist." I indicated the walls. It would have been difficult to ignore them.

"I dabble in this and that." He cast a glance at me. "How do you like your tea?" He hovered over the wooden trolley which had been polished to a shade of dark plum velvet: sugar loaf, lemon and an ornate silver tea service; nothing was missing. It seemed a deal of trouble for mid-morning 'cuppa', as he called it.

"Milk, thanks." I could feel Prail's eyes on my face and avoided catching his glance. "I wanted to get out earlier but it's been a little difficult. I hear you've got a batch of suspects in the last cattle through."

"Five. I've put them in the segregation pens. I'm almost sure it's sleeping sickness. We'll go along when we've finished tea."

The conversation which followed, dealing as it did with the incidence of tsetse fly, tick borne typhus, blood sliding and cattle generally, seemed slightly incongruous in that setting of domestic pride and an uninhibited artistic flair.

I found myself speculating on Drobinall's background. As I had thought when I first met him, he was an unusual type to find in the bush and an unusual type of livestock officer. I hadn't realised just how unusual.

He picked up the silver flask holding a solitary rose, standing in isolated perfection on an antique writing desk. He brought it over to me.

"Exquisite, don't you think?" he asked.

I could do no more than agree. In Africa, where the open bud of the morning is full-blown and fading by the evening, it certainly was exquisite, even down to the perfume, which was often something lacking in roses grown in the Territory.

"It depends on a nice choice of time for cutting," Drobinall was saying. "I find the evening is best."

He was a nauseating little tick, I thought.

In the background, Prail smirked. I was glad to get back out into the fresh air after tea, away from the cloying atmosphere of the room and Drobinall's posturing.

We walked down to the segregation pens, Prail bringing up the rear with the blood-sliding equipment for the suspect cattle.

The pens, two of a block, were built in the shape of a 'T' behind the labour compound.

"They're all screened." Drobinall said. "With a healthy herd so near, I feel it's running a bit of a risk to leave them open."

There was a different air about him, away from the house. He was more animated about his job and much less annoying.

CHAPTER 31

We took samples from the cattle and Prail returned to the Landrover with the slides while Drobinall showed me round the rest of the station. It was a fairish size and the tour took over an hour.

"How big a herd do you get through at a time?" I asked as we strolled back towards the house. Prail had not re-appeared.

"Well, the last time it was a smallish one. Usually it's about four to five thousand at a go. It's been falling off lately."

"Where do they cross?"

"Over by the shallows below the Gorge. It's quite an easy crossing."

"When Prail goes, as he soon will, what are you going to do about blood-sliding?"

"Spencer used to be quite helpful. He's the permanent medical superintendent that Janet Frenton is standing in for. He'll be back soon, but until then, I suppose Janet Frenton could do them."

"Permanent?" I questioned. "How does it happen that Spencer is permanently here? Bit unusual."

"He wangled that. His name's not Spencer, of course: it's Maravko or something similar. He's a Pole. He practised medicine in Poland before the war. He's not allowed to practise here until he's taken his examinations again in English, so Feira suits him in more ways than one at the moment: nice chap, terribly clever. It's a pity he wasn't here when..." he stopped.

We walked in silence for some minutes.

"What do you think the result will be of the lab report on Mrs. Drayton?" he asked suddenly.

"I haven't any idea," I answered shortly.

"I've heard that these bush poisons are untraceable." There was a question in his voice.

"There's no proof at the moment that Mrs. Drayton died from a bush poison."

"But, speaking generally, is it true that they're untraceable?" he persisted.

"It's true enough I suppose, that most of the African vegetable poisons are untraceable, even given a lead on what's being looked for." We had reached the Landrover.

"A lead on what?" Prail asked, coming round from the back of the vehicle.

"Mr. Lancaster was saying that some of the bush poisons are impossible to trace." Drobinall answered.

"Why? You're not telling me you think these cattle were poisoned?" Prail looked bewildered.

"No. We weren't talking about the cattle." I cut in before Drobinall could answer. "Are you ready, Prail? I must get back."

"I guess so. I'll let you know what I find in the slides, Drobinall." Prail heaved his bulk into the Landrover.

I was not sorry to leave Baluti and Drobinall.

"He's an odd type," Prail said as the Landrover rattled over the pot-holes. "But amusing."

"Depends on one's sense of humour," I muttered.

"No. You don't get me. He's got quite a wit. He can be

quite amusing, if malicious. Elizabeth used to find him entertaining. She used to say that to hear Drobinall giving his version of the latest gossip from Lusaka, was as good as going to the theatre."

"Was Drobinall a frequent visitor at the Drayton house?"

"Well, I guess I wouldn't put it quite that way: but he used to change Elizabeth's library books at Lusaka and call round with them. He gets to Lusaka more frequently than most of us. He keeps out of Barnaby's way. They're not exactly buddies, I guess, but he certainly could make Elizabeth laugh. In fact, all the ladies seem to enjoy listening to Drobinall's patter. He goes out of his way to amuse them. I suppose it compensates him in some way. I mean, you couldn't call him a handsome man." Prail's face changed suddenly and he raised his voice. "Chez Baluti, we call it. You must come over and see my little place."

Drobinall himself might have been sitting in the car: the mimicry was excellent.

Prail laughed and went on. "I remember Elizabeth saying the day before she took so sick, that to listen to Drobinall made her feel good. She'd got up for the afternoon and Elsa and I were over having tea. Drobinall dropped in. He'd just got back from Lusaka, and as usual, he was just full of it. It was a pantomime to watch him."

There was a curious note in Prail's voice which caught my ear. It might have been envy.

Then he fell silent and nothing was said for the rest of the journey.

CHAPTER 32

Drayton was on the last lap of his packing and the house looked a mess. Everyday noises had begun to echo through the rooms and footsteps sounded loud on bare concrete floors.

Tea chests, sealed and wired, lined the inner wall of the verandah, awaiting transport to the Boma store: others, in various stages of completion, spewed straw and paper, with the inevitable space, waiting like an incomplete jigsaw for a suitably shaped tenant. There was the typical, last-minute crate into which would eventually be crammed an uncatalogued confusion of kit which turned up too late to fit neatly elsewhere. Katundu we called it, using the Bantu word.

Patterns in unbleached distemper stood out in glowing relief against their faded surrounds on the stripped walls. As Drayton's effects had gradually disappeared into the crates, the house had appeared to grow larger and in the illusion of slowly increasing space, the basic furniture of the house shrank and lost stature; its years of service became more pronounced. Stripped of Drayton's personal effects, one noticed as though for the first time, the ingrained red polish of the years, dyeing the feet of beds and chairs; the discoloured rings and cigarette burns scarring the table tops;

the sliver of wood propping the legs of the bookcase; the holes in the thonged seats of cushionless chairs.

It was a common practice in those days for the incoming officer to unpack as the occasion called for it, slowly replacing for use in the house, the china and glass, cutlery and cooking pots, linen and lamps, as these were crated by his predecessor. Drayton and I had been working to this routine and the changeover had gone smoothly.

It was the day following my visit to Baluti that I took the morning off from the office to catch up with my unpacking: the stage had been reached where most of my katundu could come out of the crates without being in Drayton's way. He had taken advantage of a rainless day to get some of his crates down to the store and I had the house to myself.

It was not until early afternoon, after a sandwich lunch, that I went to the Boma, leaving Lameck to clear the mess of unpacking and watch the temperamental flickering of the paraffin fridge.

The rivers flowed slowly and silently in the hot, still afternoon and a crocodile sunned himself on a still-visible sandbank. The spate from the heavier rains up-country had slowly subsided.

I found Drayton in the office, sitting cross-legged on the floor in front of the stationery cupboard, leafing through books and files from the bottom shelf. I hadn't seen him since the earlier part of the morning.

"Did you get something to eat?" I asked him. "There are sandwiches at the house; all we could raise today."

"I haven't bothered—thought I'd get this stuff out of your way—I'm almost ready to pack it anyway."

"Lameck's bringing tea later. He could bring you some."

"Not to worry. I'm almost through here."

"I've one or two things to see to here, then I'm off to Prail's place."

"For any particular reason?" He stopped sorting books and turned to look at me.

"No. Just to have a look around. I haven't been over there yet. I can check on those slides he took at Baluti whilst I'm there."

Drayton grunted and turned back to the cupboard.

"It might be an idea to go through these whilst you're here." I pulled out the desk drawers. "You may have left something behind."

I turned out the drawers, working automatically, in turn, sorting, discarding and replacing. They held the customary miscellaneous collection: labels and envelopes; pencils and nibs; screwed carbons; outdated pamphlets; ancient petrol caps; a roll of perished insulating tape; sealing wax; a ball of string, and...

I leaned over and retrieved the thing I had just dropped into the waste-paper basket.

It was an envelope which had been lying folded on top of the stationery in the right hand drawer. It held an inch or so of coarse white powder. There was something in it. I picked it out of the powder and shook it free. It was a ball of black fuzz, the size of a good dandelion head, mounted on a cork. It was a stopper.

I knew what it was in the moment of looking at it and in the same instant, I realised in one of those odd flash backs of memory what nebulous query had teased my mind on an earlier afternoon, which seemed so long ago—when I had stood looking down at the collection taken from Matafwali and decided to burn most of it.

I slipped the stopper back into the envelope and pushed it into the pocket of my bush jacket. Unlocking the safe, I took out the Court file and paged through it until I found what I wanted.

There it was: listed towards the end of the exhibits

recorded in the Preliminary Enquiry on Matafwali.

'Rhino horn—hollowed: stoppered with cork/human
hair: Contents—white crystalline powder'

But I remembered clearly that afternoon, the horn had
been empty and the envelope holding the powder and
stopper had certainly not been in the desk drawer. The
empty horn itself still lay on the shelf above the trestle table,
along with all the other items not disposed of in the bonfire.

Drayton still sat with his back towards me, paging
through journals. He showed no interest. I mechanically
went through the motions of tidying the remaining drawers.
For some obscure motive which I did not trouble to define, I
said nothing to him. I wanted to think.

After he had left, I locked the door against interruption
and, taking the envelope from my pocket, I shook some of
the powder on to a sheet of paper. Then I scratched with my
penknife at the residue of powder in the bottom of the rhino
horn. There was just sufficient to make a comparison: as far
as I could see, they were identical.

I sat for a time looking at the powder, the questions
slowly turning in my mind. Why the powder had been put
in the drawer was easy enough to answer: it had deliberately
been put there for me to find.

As before, I had the feeling of the carrot dangled in front
of my nose.

When? Within the last two days, I thought.

But answers to the other questions were more difficult.
When had the powder been removed from the horn? By
whom? For what purpose? And why would it be left for me
to find now?

It was the possible answer to the last question which I
didn't like.

Was it because enquiries were now afoot as to the cause of Elizabeth Drayton's death?

Sealing the horn and the dregs scraped from it in one large envelope and the stopper and powder found in the desk in another, I locked both in the safe.

I had two options.

I could send them off with a couple of messengers to try to overtake the barge and include it with the crates going to Lusaka. Then the Pathological Laboratory could sort it out at the same time as their analyses of the organs.

Alternatively, the envelopes could await the arrival of the police officer, and he could decide what to do. I still didn't know when a police officer would arrive. I'd heard nothing back on the radio.

The gentle knock on the door brought me back to earth with a start. It was Lameck with the tea tray.

Whilst I sat drinking the strong, dark tea I began to have second thoughts. Was I letting my imagination run riot? Had the powder been lying in the drawer all along? Was the coincidence of finding it, measured against the background of recent events, attaching to it an importance which it didn't merit? I felt suddenly unsure.

An idea presented itself and I unlocked the safe. From the powder I had found in the desk, I took a little, shaking it into a fresh envelope, which I slipped into my pocket.

CHAPTER 33

The house allocated to the Prails for their use during their stay in Feira lay on the far side of the nursing sister's house, which in its turn lay just beyond the dispensary. I walked there that afternoon.

It was one of the old type houses, condemned years before, Drayton had told me, but reprieved and put into some sort of habitable condition for the Prails, it being the only housing available at the time. Built on the uncomplicated and somewhat primitive design of most old, out-station houses, it was much like the one I was taking over from Drayton.

Around the house, which was somewhat cut off from the rest of the Boma proper, the bush had crept back. Low brick walls crumbled gently around ancient terraced flower beds, and still showed in a distorted pattern evidence of their former glory, though pushed out and over by the passage of years and the ever-increasing perennials. Dahlias and rudbeckia, slashed down by the rains, buried their heads in the caked mud, their choked roots fighting a losing battle with the tough, smothering couch grass. Spreading like a colourful spider web through the branches of the frangipani, brilliant coral creeper twined itself around its own dead growth of previous years. At the side of the house, a young

227

African swung a slasher blade at the coarse grass in a lazy rhythm.

Beyond the house lay the Nissen huts used by Prail as offices and it was in the first of these, at the end of a brick rubble path, that I found him. Down on his hands and knees, his enormous behind grotesquely aloft, he was sprinkling ant powder from a canister along the cracks where the metal fitments interlocked.

"Hi there," he said over his shoulder. "Serowe!" He waved me to a chair. "I'm mighty scared of these things. We've been battling all day. I don't care for them around with the guinea pigs just next door."

The thin red-brown trickle of carnivorous ants spread as the powder hit them and I moved back to the door.

"Hot ash is as good as anything," I said, "but the surest way to spread them all over the place is to go for them haphazardly with anything."

Prail jumped up suddenly and started to slap and pinch at his trouser legs, cursing as they bit into him.

"See what I mean?"

He fled, throwing the canister to the floor. "I'll be right back," he shouted as he lumbered off. "Make yourself at home."

I felt that my visit would be more easily accomplished out of reach of the pincer jaws of the Serowe and I wandered over to the next Nissen hut. There was no sign of ant invasion there, so I went in.

I could see what Prail meant about the guinea pigs. Their hutches covered one side of the office. He had had the sense to put the feet of the hutches into tins of water, I noticed, but even so, it wasn't unknown for the Serowe to make a living bridge across water to reach their prey. There were a dozen or more of the pigs. They wouldn't last more than a couple of hours if a stream of Serowe found them, but I could see no sign of the ants.

I fingered through the books on the circular metal shelf. He had a catholic taste in reading, I thought. I wondered what he used the pigs for.

On a table, several huge butterflies lay beneath a gauze cover, amidst the paraphernalia of mounting.

I was idly looking through a copy of the New Yorker when he returned. "Sorry to leave you like that. Had to strip right down before I could get rid of them. We lost a few chickens the night before last with the bastards, but rather them than the pigs."

"What do you use the guinea pigs for?"

"Wouldn't that be telling? Perhaps I've a notion that one of these days, Martin S. Prail might come up with a new slant on sleeping sickness. Now wouldn't that be something?" He looked amused. "Anyway, they're useful in lots of ways. Not so much in the line of the official survey, more from a hobby point of view. Spare time research, let's say."

He leant over the table. "Aren't they beautiful?" He indicated the butterflies lying there.

"They certainly are. They'll take a lot of careful packing when you leave, if you've got a big collection."

"This is the least of them. I'll show you the best of the collection over at the house later."

"You mentioned the other evening that you'd probably be moving off shortly. Have you heard any more?"

"Yeah. The Lower Andes it is. We're due to pull out from here in six weeks. I'll be right sorry. I've enjoyed it here, but on the other hand..." he stopped, then went on: "Anyway, the job will be finished as far as we can take it by that time. We'll have to wait and see what the back-room boys make of the data collected by the various teams."

For the next half hour, we talked shop: incidence of tsetse

229

fly in the District; methods of checking; the breeding and feeding habits of the tsetse. Prail had the subject at his finger tips and was not without a few new ideas on it. It was an interesting discussion.

"You'll be getting a copy of my final report," he grinned, "in quadruplicate, at the end of the month and I'll let you have a copy of that fly incidence map that we've made up. The people out in the District with the Game Guards are being brought in next week and they'll be paid off. Then it's just a matter of tying up loose ends and we're off. We're flying from Mombasa to the States where we'll stay awhile. We need a break. Our kit can go by sea."

"That's looking a bit ahead," I said. "I'd like to hear a little more about these ideas of yours before you go, especially as far as the feeding habits are concerned. It could open up an entirely new approach to the problem. When do you think the final report of the survey will be published?"

"That's mighty hard to say. Could be anything up to six months, but let's say a year."

He flicked a fat finger against one of a row of jars lining the near shelf. A big, brown fly flew from the leafy shade at the bottom and smacked itself against the clear glass.

"By which time," he added, "we'll be well into the next survey: another home, another camp, another continent, another bug."

He looked thoughtful and hesitated. Then: "Tell me," he said slowly, "we're supposed to be off in six weeks. Will there be any hitch do you think to prevent it?"

"Let's hope not." I knew what he meant. If the enquiry was still running I could require them to stay.

"It's the one thing I'd sure like to see before we pull up stakes finally," he said, "and that's some light on this business of Mrs. Drayton."

"Don't we all?" I did not think it necessary to point out

that the departure of the Prails would in all probability depend on his wish being granted.

"It's a mighty sad business. I'm real sorry for Barnaby and the girl. It's damned unpleasant." He stopped and shrugged. "Hell, let's go get ourselves a drink." He moved towards the door.

"Just a second, Prail. There's something you can do for me, if you will. I'd like this tested, provided you don't mind risking one of the guinea pigs."

I gave him the envelope from my pocket.

He opened it and peered into it. "What is it?"

"I don't know. That's why I'm asking you to test it. Can you do that for me?"

Prail put his nose to the envelope and withdrawing it, reached a finger to dip into it.

"I wouldn't do that," I said quickly. "At least not until you've tried out its effect. And there's one more point. I'd like this matter treated as confidential for the moment."

He looked at me sharply. The grey eyes flickered and a slightly conspiratorial look crept into them.

He shook the envelope in his hand and peered into it again as though there he might find the answers to the questions he would like to ask me.

"Hmmph. It looks like salt." He stopped abruptly.

"What looks like salt?" Elsa Prail's voice came from the doorway. She stood there, leaning against the lintel, the setting sun behind her burnishing the aureole of blond hair hanging loosely over her shoulders. Released from the severe style in which she usually wore it, it curled softly and sensuously around her face. The long legs were encased in tight, olive-green slacks and a black tailored blouse provocatively revealed the lines of her figure.

"Salt, of course, honey," Prail said smoothly and tucked the envelope into his shirt pocket. "The Bantu out at the

Mvuu Swamps are making quite an industry out of it."

She might not have heard him. The lambent eyes were on me, green and questioning.

"Hello there," she said shortly. "I'd no idea you were visiting us."

"Good evening, Mrs. Prail. Thought I'd look in on your husband for a chat."

She looked quickly from one to the other.

"Interesting?"

"Not to you, Elsa. All about tsetse!" Prail laughed.

"The rye's on the rocks," she said to him and, turning to me, "come and have a drink."

There was a challenge in her voice.

"I was just suggesting that very thing," Prail said.

"I guess it'll be a welcome change to see a new face over the rim of a glass." She turned to go. "Nobody seems to go anywhere any more."

"Now look, honey." Prail raised a hand, but she was already gone. "Women," he muttered quietly as we followed her to the house.

The long, low verandah of the house was set out with up-to-the-minute garden furniture—lengths of tubular steel and gaily coloured canvas. Elsa was lounging in a swing settee when we reached there.

"Help yourself." She waved a hand towards the metal trolley.

The furniture was obviously non-Government issue but despite, or perhaps because of, its holiday style, there was a feeling of impermanence about the house, as if they were just camping there. The walls were bare and patterned here and there with discoloured streaks like dirty icicles, where rain had leaked through from the roof.

"Do you carry all this furniture about with you?" I had to ask Prail as I poured myself a whisky.

"Yeah, it's collapsible mostly. Doesn't take up a lot of room. In most of the places we go to, we need to be independent of houses and furniture; we camp out. Here at Feira, we've been lucky."

"Lucky?" His wife's voice from the settee was mocking.

"Now, Elsa." Prail turned towards her.

"Why shouldn't I talk about it? It's the thing everyone's thinking about!" Her eyes, angry and hostile, swung away from him and fixed on me.

"What's going to happen?" she asked.

"As a matter of conjecture, Mrs. Prail, your guess is as good as mine, but it surely depends on what has already happened and that still has to be decided. The Pathological Laboratory will report on Mrs. Drayton and, in the meantime, a police officer is being sent to Feira."

I squirted soda into my glass in the silence.

Prail cleared his throat in embarrassment. His wife leaned carefully back against the cushions and sipped her drink, rocking herself gently in the swing. The swiftly failing light drained the greenness from her eyes.

"Poor Elizabeth," Prail muttered at last and, taking my arm he drew me towards the side verandah. "Come and take a look at these."

"Poor Barnaby," Elsa said behind us. Her voice was vicious.

CHAPTER 34

The nursing sister visited me at the office two mornings later. She was worried: with the Upupulu Bridge out of commission, drugs and general dispensary supplies were running low. From behind a hedge of professional reserve, she touched on patients, their rations and the general matters like leaks in the dispensary roof.

I found myself agreeing with Prail: I was sorry for the girl. Below the crisp rustle of starch and calm efficiency, there was a hint of strain. It showed in the grip of the long hands on the files and the rigid set of the slim shoulders.

"I'm having to turn out-patients away," she said.

"Well, try and hang on a bit. If I can manage to get Lusaka on the radio this morning, I'll see what the chances are of getting supplies down to the Upupulu. From there, they can be ferried over, conditions permitting. I'm going up there later this morning to see how the bridge is coming along. I've heard nothing from Grobler."

She stopped by the door and turned. "What's going to happen?" she asked, echoing Elsa Prail's question.

I knew she wasn't referring to the drug supplies and I replied on much the same lines as I had answered Elsa Prail.

"But this waiting," she said, "it's unbearable!"

She came back to the desk and leaned on it.

"You don't know Barnaby as I do. He's not a poisoner." She got the word out with difficulty. "How could anyone poison her?"

"Now wait, Miss Frenton. Don't go jumping the gun like that. No one has yet suggested that Mrs. Drayton was deliberately poisoned, or that Barnaby Drayton was responsible. In fact it's not even proved it was poison."

"Everyone believes it. You can see it's what they're thinking." The violet eyes in the shadowed face were full of tears.

"Let's wait and see. Don't you realise the whole business may turn out to be a complete mare's nest?"

"I wish I could think so. Do you really think it will?" she asked and, without waiting for an answer, turned quickly and left the office.

Did I think so? No, I didn't. Like Miss Frenton, I wished I could. Instead, I pushed it out of mind and settled down to work.

Prail came in later.

"What was that stuff in the envelope?" He flung his great weight into the chair opposite the desk. The sun glasses hanging from a cord around his neck, tipped at an angle on his paunch.

"I told you, I don't know. What was the reaction?"

"One guinea pig dead and one dying." His mouth pursed speculatively but the question in his eyes remained unframed.

Though I had been prepared for his answer, it still came in the nature of a shock to hear it put so bluntly.

"I hope you've no more tests you want done. Or if you have, it's with something a little less lethal," he went on, eyeing me curiously.

"Nothing more, thanks. Perhaps I could have the dead guinea pigs, in formaldehyde."

"Can do. I'll have them sent over." He got up. "I'm off to the Portuguese side. Those five animals of Drobinalls were heavily infected. First batch we've had through for months from that particular route. I want to get over there and check on it. I think they must be taking a short cut somewhere." He went over and traced a finger down the map. "Through here. I think that's where they're picking up the tsetse fly. I'll take the small barge if that's OK with you, those canoes just don't come in my size."

"Help yourself, and thanks for the use of your Landrover this morning. I'm only going as far as the Upupulu, I'll be back by dusk."

"Any time. No trouble at all. I'll put the jars in it and leave it by the landing stage." He raised a hand in a vague salute and left.

Reception on the radio that morning was good.

The P.C.'s voice came through loud and clear:

"Lusaka calling Feira, Lusaka calling Feira, over."

"Feira calling Lusaka. Receiving you strength nine, over."

"Lusaka to Feira: Chief Inspector Blake despatched. ETA Upupulu River Thursday midday. What chances of ferrying him over? How long is the bridge likely to be out of commission? Spare parts Boma Landrover also being sent with Blake. Tentative contact already made with Minister on question of His Excellency's withdrawal of recognition from Chiabele. Any further developments in Feira? Over."

"Feira to Lusaka: Understand ETA Blake Thursday midday. Will arrange transport. Inspecting Upupulu bridge this day, will advise further tomorrow. Request send monthly quota routine dispensary drugs with Landrover parts. Also, exhibits, repeat, exhibits with possible bearing on Drayton/Maoma investigation, being sent with messenger via Upupulu this day. Covering minutes explain. No further developments. Over."

"Lusaka to Feira: message understood. Contact me tomorrow. Over."

"Feira to Lusaka: Roger: Wilco: Out."

I was glad it was Blake being sent down: I'd met him and he was a good policeman. Thursday evening should see him in Feira, the Upupulu River allowing. I had only two days to wait.

Nelson's Landrover drew in to the Boma as I left the wireless shed.

It came to a halt.

"False alarm," he called to me as he got out. "There's no sign of jumbo near the eastern strip."

He followed me into the office. "What's this I hear about the police coming?"

"And you only just back? News gets around fast."

"I dropped the katundu off at the house. Grace mentioned it."

"Well, she's quite right. Chief Inspector Blake will be here in a couple of days with any luck. Apart from not finding elephant, how did your trip go?"

"Fine. Road's not too bad..." he launched into details.

There was nervousness behind the casual air, I thought, as I listened to him. The secretive eyes were restless in the thin, tanned face.

"I'm off again tomorrow to the south strip," he went on, his eyes sweeping across my shelves. "Though I'm hoping jumbo hasn't moved that way: it would mean..."

I made a mental note to see that the Ivory Register was put under lock and key.

CHAPTER 35

It was a sticky trip to the Upupulu. The rain started before I left Feira and continued for most of the journey. Without the four-wheel drive, I would never have made it. Even so, I was glad to get away from the station for a spell.

The bridge lay sixty miles north and the road was new to me. Nyrenda and a junior messenger, squashed beside me in the Landrover, cushioned the bumps as we skidded and bounced over the pot holes and mud lakes of the road. Twenty miles brought us to a point where we started to run parallel to the new road strip on which Grobler had been working before the bridge over the Upupulu had collapsed. Piles of gravel and ballast poles lay in sodden heaps, sinking into a quicksand of mud.

The 'Road Work Ahead' notice was just visible.

Not until the rains had finished, I thought. We'd seen all the work we were going to, until April. From now till then, it would be a matter of keeping the old road open and propping up bridges as they collapsed over the swollen streams.

After fifty miles we passed the Brackenhursts' turn-off from the main road: time and weather permitting, I thought I might call in on them on the way back.

Five miles from the crossing, the sky lightened and it was

in the hot, bright sunshine of mid-afternoon that we reached the Groblers' camp, by the bridge.

Their caravan stood in a cleared camping site to the side of the road. A line of washing was strung between the trees and skinny, native-bred chickens scattered in squawking confusion as I brought the Landrover to a halt. A tawny ridge-back dog, launching himself from the shade, stopped barking and instead bared his teeth as I climbed down.

Mrs. Grobler was washing her hair over a tin bowl set on a touring table of bush poles. She was squinting her eyes up under the dripping hair at the sound of the intrusion.

"Ag, Mr. Lancaster, the time you pick to turn up! Down, Bunjy man, down!"

"I'm sorry to butt in at such an inconvenient time, Mrs. Grobler. I'm looking for your husband. I suppose he's down at the bridge. Don't worry about me. I'll find him."

She grabbed at the towel as the suds slipped towards her eyes.

"Ja. You'll find Lou down there. Give me five minutes. Have you had some scoff? I'll get you something. Plenty here."

Her voice followed me down to the bridge as did Bunjy, the snarling, suspicious dog.

I found Grobler waist deep in water driving home a dowel in the last pole of the line which stretched across the narrow stream. A tangle of drift wood and general debris marked the level from which the stream had slowly receded. It had dropped a good six feet. He waved a hand as he caught sight of me and shouting instructions to the labourers in a rapid stream of Bemba, he waded back to the bank where I waited.

"What's the road like?" he asked.

I commented briefly and rudely and he grinned. "What

brings you, Mr. Lancaster?"

"Wanted to find out how long this job's going to take."

He dragged himself up the bank and stripped off his waders to tip out the muddy water from them.

"Another week if the weather holds. It's been a killer. Have you had anything to eat? We'll fix you something. Let's get up to the camp, man." He waved at the workers. "They can carry on a bit now. I'll get out of these clothes. How about a cold beer?"

It was two beers later and over egg and bacon sandwiches, that I said to Grobler, "I want the messenger I'm leaving here ferried across to the far bank when a Landrover arrives there on Thursday midday. The Landrover's bringing a police officer who's to be brought over the stream with his kit and sent on to Feira in your vehicle. The messenger needs to go back to Lusaka in the police Landrover with these things." I nodded at the parcelled jars which Nyrenda had unloaded.

Grobler's great hand pulled at the thick, grizzled eyebrows. A slight smear of mud still clung to the hair. He looked at me shrewdly.

"Easy enough if the rains keep off and the stream stays at this level."

"Mail and dispensary supplies will probably be on the same vehicle. Look after them."

"What's happening back there?" He jerked his head in the general direction of Feira.

"Nothing," I replied.

Which wasn't true, as it turned out. Something must have been happening at the time I was speaking to Grobler. Something which led up to the final events of that day.

CHAPTER 36

The jumping lights of hurricane lamps around the Boma office and the pin point flash of torches winking in the darkness of the surrounding bush, caught at my tired eyes as we drew up to the house back at Feira. It was after ten at night, and one puncture and two mud drifts later than I had anticipated.

I was caked in mud, hungry and bad tempered. The rain still fell in a steady downpour, veering with the erratic gusts of wind.

"What the hell?" I said. "Hang on, Nyrenda. I'll just get a bath and meal organised and then we'll get down there and see what's happening."

But the house was silent and deserted. Of Lameck or Drayton's servants, there was no sign. I pumped the single pressure lamp on the verandah. The rest of the house was in darkness. I went back to the Landrover. Voices on the night air rose and died away.

"What the hell?" I said again and let in the clutch.

I found Drayton outside the Boma office, the centre of a group of messengers and labourers. The rain ran in rivulets from his hair and streamed from his saturated bush jacket.

"It's Elsa Prail," he said shortly. "She can't be found."

He turned to the nearest messenger. "All right, Lazaro.

Take these four men. Join up with Mwendapole and his group. Work from the left bank across." He swept his hand graphically.

"Since when?" I asked.

"Difficult to say. Prail says he left her in the house, taking a shower—around seven this evening. He was out in the Nissen hut messing around with his butterflies. When he went back into the house later, there was no sign of her. He didn't think anything of it. Thought she might have gone back to the Nelson's to collect something she'd forgotten. She'd been over there in the afternoon. But it started to rain again and he walked over to take her mackintosh. They hadn't seen her. Nobody else has either. She can't have left the station, unless she went on a bicycle which is hardly likely. We're just starting to beat through the Boma. Messengers and labourers are working from east to west. Prail, Nelson, Drobinall and Young are working down the west side with the servants."

Janet Frenton came from the darkness of the road, her raincoat buttoned high.

"Any news?" she asked. "Oh. It's you, Mr. Lancaster." She turned to Drayton. "Have you found anything?"

He shook his head.

"I can't stay," she turned back. "There's been a difficult confinement case this evening."

Drayton watched her go and spoke to me. "What about you and I taking the east side and working upwards with the rest of these labourers and Nyrenda?"

"Good idea. Let's go."

Midnight passed. The station had been covered by lines of beaters in all directions. Every house, office, store and both compounds had been searched, and we had not found her.

The rain had stopped and a lambent moon peered intermittently through the drifts of soft, grey mist. From the far banks of the Zambezi came the scream of baboon, shrill and clear above the roar of the rising water.

We gathered at the Boma office around one in the morning, where Janet Frenton had laid on drinks and sandwiches.

Prail looked on the edge of collapse.

"Here, drink this." Drayton pushed a half glass of neat brandy into his hand and the glass rattled against his teeth as he drained it.

Nelson drank his beer, leaning against the wall, eyes closed.

Drobinall stood next to him, fingers beating a nervous tattoo on his glass, eyes flickering from one to the other of us, questioning and uncertain.

"Well, Lancaster?" Drayton blew the froth from his glass. "What do you think?"

"One more beat through after this break," I said. "A single reinforced line. If that produces nothing, we'll have to give up until morning."

"Where is she?" Prail asked in a dull, shocked voice. "There's no place else to look, except..." his voice trailed off.

The rivers. The thought must have been in everybody's mind. If she was in the rivers there would be nothing we could do, and little likelihood we'd ever find her body.

"Let's go," I said to Drayton. "I'll take the left flank this time, you take the right. The rest of you disperse yourselves along the line between the messengers. We'll work up the west slope and down the east. You'd better stay here, Prail."

He didn't appear to hear me. His eyes were fixed on the empty glass in his shaking hand.

We left him, and worked slowly uphill, beating every bush, clambering through every gully and storm drain. The

243

hurricane lamps, interspersed along the straggling line of beaters, weaved and twisted in a slow, macabre dance, as of giant fireflies.

It was Nyrenda who really found her. We had reached the path which forked to the dispensary, off the main, uphill road. The right flank of the path stretched through the thick undergrowth which overhung the path, reaching the higher ridge where Nelson's house stood. To the left, the smooth, polished rocks sloped gradually away, to drop steeply to the river.

In the darkness I heard Nyrenda grunt.

"What is it, Nyrenda?"

The slim, pencil torch which he had picked up from the coarse, bushy tufts at the side of the dirt track was not the usual heavy type used in the bush. It was a delicate affair; a woman's torch, the sort she'd keep in a handbag. In the fading light of my own batteries, the stamp on the bottom was just visible. 'Made in Chicago U.S.A.' I flicked the switch and the thin beam split the darkness across the rocks to the river.

"Wait here, Nyrenda!"

I made my way cautiously across the smooth slopes towards the edge and, leaning over, played the beam downwards into the darkness below.

The crumpled figure lay on a mud bank thirty feet down and within two feet of the rising river.

I shouted, and in the darkness behind me I heard an answering echo, taken up and re-echoed along the line of beaters.

"You find the Donna?" Nyrenda's voice asked from behind me.

"I can see her," I answered.

I let the torch play round the depths below. From where I lay atop the ridge, it was a steep drop; too steep to climb down without a rope. Along to the left of the ridge, the downward slope was more gradual. That might be managed and there was little time.

I pointed. "I'm going down that way, Nyrenda. Tell the labourers to hold their lamps over the side to give me as much light as possible. Find Bwana Drayton. Tell him we want ropes, the Landrover, the stretcher canvas and the Donna nursing sister."

I went towards the edge, farther along the ridge.

"And a rifle." I yelled after Nyrenda. "These lights will attract the crocs."

It wasn't a difficult descent—merely a slow, careful one. As I worked my way down and across, the labourers appeared along the edge of the ridge, their lamps throwing a pale light down the cliff side.

Above me came the noise of an engine and David Young's voice shouting instructions. The lights of the approaching Landrover crept down the rocky slope towards the cliff edge.

"Hold it! Hold it!" That was Young shouting.

The headlamps were like the eyes of a crouching animal, their light angled and shining onto the river.

Down. Down. In the spreading outer radiance of the light, my eyes were on the bank where the still figure lay. Nearer. Nearer. Not far now. Careful.

If we hadn't found her on this pass, we shouldn't have found her at all, I thought. The bank which held her was an earth bank, collapsed from higher up the cliff side, and the rising river gnawed greedily at its edges.

"Young," I shouted. "Get that canvas on the end of a rope and lower it. Hurry it up!"

Above me came a mingled babble of voices: in some way they seemed distant and disembodied. Someone yelled and there came the crash of a rifle; a heavy one. Nelson's voice rose in triumph from the cliff edge and below me, the river erupted in a violent churning, fifteen yards away from the bank where Elsa Prail lay.

It would be useless to hurry it, I told myself. The rocks were too slippery. But I felt a rising sense of urgency. I hoped one dead or wounded croc would keep any others busy for a time. The quickly disintegrating edge of the bank worried me more. It wouldn't hold much longer.

As I reached her, I saw Drayton swing himself over the cliff edge where I had started, and begin the slow descent.

"Watch it, Drayton," I yelled, "It's as slippery as hell."

She lay curled on one side, as if asleep, one arm bent at a curious angle beneath her. I turned her gently. She was still alive but in quite a mess.

"Let down that rifle, Nelson," I called up. "We're a bit too near the water here for comfort."

I released the canvas stretcher from the end of the hanging rope and spread it beside her. The blond hair was matted in a dark tangle of mud and blood across her face. I pushed it back. Her eyelids flickered and opened.

"Why, hello there," she said and her eyes closed again.

"Mrs. Prail." I leaned over and touched her shoulder gently.

She opened her eyes again and tried to raise her head. "Why's there salt on Elizabeth's table?"

Her voice died.

"What happened, Mrs. Prail?"

"Walking from the house... something hit me." She raised a hand to her head. "No. No." she whispered.

"What hit you? Who hit you? Did you see?"

But she didn't hear me. Her hand fell back to her side, limp and yielding.

"Is she alive?" Drayton's voice asked behind me. He clambered over from the near rock.

"Yes. We'd better get her out of here though. This bank's going to collapse at any moment."

We rolled her on to the canvas.

Prail's voice rose above the others. "Elsa! Elsa!" he screamed. "Are you all right, honey?"

"Shall I come down? Do you need me?" Janet Frenton shouted.

"Stay there Janet, there's no time," Drayton called up. "You too, Prail. Your wife is alive, we'll get her up."

We passed the edge of the canvas across the limp body and tied her in securely.

"Did I hear you talking to her as I came down?" Drayton asked.

"Yes," I said. Guarding my words was becoming a habit. "I thought for a moment she was conscious, but it must have been a trick of the light."

He didn't appear to be listening.

"I think we can get the ropes pulled straight up from here," he said. "It'll be easier and quicker than trying to get her back the way we came."

"We need a second set of ropes to keep hold down here and stop her from banging against the cliff."

He nodded agreement and I shouted instructions to Young.

Drayton's eyes were scanning the rising waters behind us as we waited for the extra ropes to be let down.

"With the river coming up like this," he said, "another fifteen minutes would have seen her gone. That or the crocs."

On the wind, Prail's voice floated down. "Elsa, honey. Elsa, honey." He sounded as though he were crying.

CHAPTER 37

It seemed like hours, but it could only have been twenty minutes and Elsa Prail was being taken carefully to the hospital while Drayton and I climbed tiredly up the way we'd come down.

I wanted Bravachko back at Feira quickly and Nelson offered to fetch him.

He sat in his Landrover with a messenger in the passenger seat, looking like an ebony statue.

Nelson switched on the engine and the headlights lit up the front of the dispensary, reflecting back onto his lean, secretive face.

"Take it easy," I said. "The road's washed out at the ten mile point. I was stuck there. With luck, you'll find Bravachko at the mission and you can get back with him by tomorrow morning."

"Depends what the road's like after the Kapoche Mission turn-off. It's not up to much at the best of times and they've been getting the same rains."

"It's the best we can do." I interrupted, eager for him to be on his way. "The bridge at Upupulu won't be usable for a week or so. Even were it feasible to take her to Lusaka by road in the state she's in."

"How do you think she came to go over the side there?"

He let in the clutch. I grunted non-committally.

"What was she doing, wandering along there in the dark, I wonder?" His voice was speculative, rather than questioning.

The Landrover moved forward and I watched the rear lights disappear round the bend in the road.

'If you need me, send for me' Bravachko had said. Was this what he had had in mind? Violence breeding violence? For of one thing, I was convinced: someone had tried to kill Elsa Prail.

Behind me in the dispensary, the same questions voiced by Nelson were being raised. Prail's voice came in shrill anger.

"How the hell could she have fallen down there? She knew the path!"

"I was only suggesting she might have fallen." David Young's voice was placating.

"Why was she out in the dark at all? Out there, by the cliff? It's odd." That was Drobinall.

"Not any more odd than a lot of bloody things that have been happening on this Boma," Drayton cut in. "Even without a torch, there's slope enough to warn anyone that they're off the track, and would she have been out there without one?"

"How in hell's name should I know?" The anger had gone from Prail's voice. He sounded tired.

"No. She'd hardly be out there without a torch." Young said.

No, she wouldn't, I thought, and she hadn't been. I fingered the torch in the pocket of my bush jacket. I decided I wasn't going to offer any information about this evening at all. I wanted to listen, just listen, and hear what people said.

Perhaps someone would give themselves away.

I walked quietly along the covered porch that connected

the dispensary to the hospital block, to the open door of the Labour Room.

Janet Frenton looked up at me across the figure on the bed. Her dark hair hung damply around a face set in lines of fatigue. Her fingers rolled the last inch of bandage around the swathed head.

I shut the door behind me.

"Well?" I asked. "And keep your voice down, please."

"One arm broken. One ankle dislocated or broken—difficult to tell without an X-ray. Multiple bruises and abrasions." Her voice was cool and professional. "The wound at the side of the head is bad enough but it doesn't look as dangerous as the one at the base of the skull—pressure bandage is the best thing I can do." She pinned the end of the bandage in place and added. "She's obviously badly concussed. Her pupils are unequal. Her pulse is very slow. Shock and exposure, didn't help of course."

"Quite enough to go on with, I should say. Has she come round at all?"

"No."

"And you must see that she doesn't." I said softly.

There was amazement, and fear, in the violet eyes which flashed up to meet mine, above the still figure.

"What on earth do you mean?" she whispered.

"Look, Miss Frenton, I have to trust you."

"Have to?" Her voice was icy.

"All right." I said wearily. "That was badly put. I want to trust you. You see, someone tried to murder Mrs. Prail."

Janet Frenton made an inarticulate sound.

"If that somebody thinks that she's not going to recover, it might forestall another attempt. If she remains unconscious, I think she'll be safer, for the present at any rate."

She sank down on the chair beside the bed, her hands

shaking. The eyes fixed on my face had widened in horror.

"Now brace up, Miss Frenton." I needed to get through to her. "Janet. Brace up. I'm relying on you. We must play for time, so as far as the Boma's concerned, Elsa Prail is dying. Do you understand?"

"As she may well be," she whispered.

"In which case, the murderer will succeed," I said brutally. "If not, any chance she's got of pulling through this may depend on people thinking that no such chance exists. We'll move her to your house. It's the nearest, and she'll be less vulnerable, there. We don't want it to be too obvious that she's under guard; that would spoil the impression we're trying to make. We'll say she can't be left here—"

It was going to take me some time to come up with the right subterfuge. I didn't need to.

"Because it would be too disturbed in the morning. She's a dying woman," Janet said. Her hands stopped shaking, and a new resolve showed in her eyes.

"Coupled with what's happened on the Boma lately, it's bound to be thought odd that Mrs. Prail would be found at the bottom of a cliff, but there are only three people who know for certain, that it was an attempt at murder. You, me and the murderer. It must stay that way."

"And why are you so certain that it was?" she asked. She had taken swabs from the bowl and was cleaning off the blood and dirt from the broken arm.

She was much steadier when she was being a nurse.

"Because Mrs. Prail told me," I said. "She regained consciousness briefly when I got down to her. If it becomes known that she's recovered consciousness sufficiently to speak, even once, someone might suspect she'll do it again, and might consider that too dangerous a risk."

"That someone might be me. How do you know it's not?"

"I'm counting on the fact that you were dealing with a

difficult birth this evening. The night orderly says the woman arrived at five. The birth was at nine thirty—it's in the records. You didn't leave the woman until she was back in the wards, some time after ten. I've checked it."

"For these small mercies," she muttered, without raising her head from her task.

"What chance do you think Mrs. Prail has?"

"I don't know. There may be internal injuries, apart from everything else."

"When you've finished, we'll move her, but I don't want a sound out of her whilst we're doing that. And nobody else is to be left alone with her. Nobody."

"I don't think there's much chance of her coming round yet."

"Is there any way of making sure?" I asked.

She left the room and returned within minutes with an hypodermic syringe, containing half an inch of colourless fluid. She bent over Elsa Prail.

As she cleaned the forearm, preparatory to thrusting the bright needle under the skin, I felt the sweat break out on my forehead: if my judgement were at fault, if the night orderly had told less than the truth for whatever reason, I could be watching a murder.

CHAPTER 38

For what was left of the night, I stayed on the verandah of Janet Frenton's house, at intervals walking quietly along the corridor to the room where Elsa Prail lay.

The paraffin pixie lamp, set on a shelf over the head of her bed, barely outlined the squat shapes of the furniture in the room.

On each occasion, at the sound of my step, Janet Frenton would start up from the camp bed in the corner of the room.

"How do you think she's doing?" I asked. It was my fourth visit.

"There's a slight improvement, I think. Her pulse is up to sixty five and respiration's better."

"Why don't you try and sleep. I'll stay here and watch her. You'll be played out tomorrow."

"I can't sleep," she whispered.

"I'll wake Lameck and get him to send you some coffee." I'd got Lameck to sleep at the back door as an extra protection.

I started to leave, and turned, trying to keep my voice casual.

"Funny how these details keep popping up in my mind. Think back to the day Mrs. Drayton died. Can you remember if there was a salt cellar on Mrs. Drayton's bedside table?"

"There wasn't. I would have noticed it," she said. "Why? Is it important?"

"Just an idea I had. Something someone said. Can you remember what was on her table?"

We had moved out of the room to the dimly lighted passage. She pushed the thick, dark hair away from her face, considering the question.

"Drinking water," she said at last, "and a glass half full of milk. On the shelf underneath there were two or three books. I think that's all."

"Let me know if you remember anything else that was there."

I went to the back of the house to rouse Lameck.

Dawn flared over the Zambezi as I sat drinking the steaming coffee. My eyelids pricked with fatigue.

The ever changing outlines of colour shimmered against the purple hills, drenching the bush in a bronze glow. The river ran silver through the early mists, reflecting every shade. There was no sign of rain. It was going to be a scorcher.

Prail would turn up soon. I had persuaded him in the early hours to go off and rest at his own house, promising him word would be sent if he were needed. He had gone reluctantly, taking Drobinall with him. They had all gone eventually—even Drayton, with an unspoken question in his eyes.

"I think a couple of messengers should stay on duty here," he'd said before he left.

"I've already arranged it," I replied.

I could see his mind working, but he made no further comments.

The verandah settled into a grey shadow of vague outlines. As I sat and watched the sunrise, I wondered what the coming day would bring.

Probably someone I would speak to today was a murderer. I would have to lie to them all, innocent and guilty, in order to catch him. Or her.

A little later, Janet Frenton went to bath and change, and I took over the guarding of Elsa Prail.

Except for the occasional, involuntary muscular twitching, there was no movement from her still form in the bed and beneath the bandage, the face was grey and drawn. It didn't look like the face of Elsa Prail as I remembered it.

"I've ordered your breakfast," Janet Frenton said when she returned. "I'll have mine here, on a tray."

"Thanks. With any luck Bravachko will be here this morning. That will ease things, but in the meantime, please remember, there's no sign of rallying. Her condition's deteriorated, if anything. She mustn't be disturbed for any reason, by anybody. Make it clear those are medical orders with my full backing."

She nodded.

"What chances are there of her regaining consciousness this morning?"

"Slim."

She went back in and presently, my breakfast arrived on a tray.

I sat on the verandah. Prail arrived at the house whilst I was eating. He looked as though he hadn't slept. His eyes were red and puffy.

"How is she?" he asked abruptly and looked as though he feared to hear the answer.

"Much the same, I'm afraid." My conscience pricked me to deceive him so cruelly but I turned a deaf ear. It would be unwise to encourage him with hope for all the Boma to see.

He lumbered off, quietly enough for a man of his size, towards the bedroom.

Janet Frenton stopped him at the door, and allowed him only to stand in the doorway.

I heard her voice, low and shaky, then the door closed and he returned.

He was trembling so much and I had to hold a match to his cigarette.

"Sit down and have some coffee, Prail."

"I hope you're watching her," he whispered.

"Of course. Both Miss Frenton and I."

"It's her I'm talking about," he hissed. "Janet Frenton! How do you know she didn't push Elsa over the cliff. I want a guard on Elsa." His bleared eyes were truculent.

"I think I've taken adequate steps to see that your wife is well looked after. We're doing our best. But tell me why you think someone pushed Mrs. Prail over the cliff. There's no evidence she was."

"Evidence? Evidence?" His voice rose and fell when I held up a hand. "Do you have to see her being pushed over that edge before you'll believe it wasn't an accident?"

"What do you think she was doing out near the cliff?"

"I can't imagine." He shrugged his great shoulders.

"Suppose you tell me what happened yesterday evening. I've heard nothing apart from the few details Mr. Drayton gave me when I got back from the Upupulu. I understand you last saw your wife in the house. When?"

"That's right!. She was about to take a shower. That was around seven. She'd just got back from the Nelsons' place. I'd left her there."

"What do you mean exactly when you say that you left her there?" I interrupted.

"At the Nelson's. She was having tea with Grace when I got there. I dropped around when I got back from the

Portuguese side. I wanted to check with Nelson on this possibility of the tsetse fly spreading from the north east bank. You know the query there was on the routing of the last batch of cattle coming over."

He took the cup of steaming coffee I held out to him. "By chance Drobinall was there and we thrashed it out between us, then I left. Elsa said she'd be along later."

"So Drobinall was there." I'd wondered how he'd come to be in on the search parties last night. "What was he doing on the Boma?"

"He found three more suspect cattle in that last herd. He came in to see me and Nelson about it."

"So she was there with the Nelsons and Drobinall, and then she came back later. What time was that?"

"It was getting dark. It must have been a quarter to seven. We had a drink and she went off to shower. She was undressing when I went to ask her where the store keys were because Drobinall had turned up to borrow some gin. Seems the Nelsons had run out. That was the last time I saw her before..."

"What time did you return to the house? I understand you were out in the Nissen hut."

"It must have been nearly eight. I'm not sure. Drobinall might remember."

"Drobinall was still there? He didn't go back with the gin?"

"Yes. He walked over to the Nissen hut with me to see the butterflies I'd picked up on the Portuguese side. One thing led to another. You know, we just started talking. He didn't go until I came back to the house."

"And your wife wasn't there?" I prompted as he fell silent.

"No." He roused himself. "I didn't think anything of it. Not right away. I asked the servants where she'd gone but they didn't know. I thought she might have gone back to the Nelsons' place to get something she'd left behind."

"Was it usual for her to go out alone after dark?"

"As far as the Nelsons', yes! Though she'd usually take the Landrover, but you'd got that."

"What time did you go to fetch her, as you thought?"

"When the rain started again. I thought I'd walk over with her raincoat and rubber boots. It must have been half past eight, or thereabouts."

"Was there anything unusual in your wife's manner last evening?"

"Not that I noticed."

"And you can't venture a guess as to what took her out of the house?"

"Not unless she'd left something at the Nelsons' which she needed like the store keys."

"But it couldn't have been the keys."

"No. She gave them to me to get the gin for Drobinall."

"Well, leaving that for the moment, let's get back to your theory that what happened to your wife was no accident and that somebody tried to kill her. Why would anyone want to kill her?"

He leaned towards me, the scholarly face thrust forward. The stubble stood out on his chin.

"I've been wondering about just that, ever since you found her," he said softly. "Do you really think that Elsa going over the cliff so soon after Elizabeth's death could be a coincidence? Like hell it is. There must be some tie-up, I guess. And what could that be?"

He dropped his voice lower. "Suppose, just suppose, that Elsa knows something that somebody doesn't want known about Elizabeth's death?"

"But you told me yourself that Mrs. Prail was working on what you call a hunch. No, wait a minute, Prail. Let me finish. If she did after all, have some knowledge about Mrs. Drayton's death, that she didn't disclose at the time, why would it suddenly become dangerous now?"

"I certainly think she was following a hunch, originally. I said so, didn't I?" Prail lifted his bulk from the chair and towered over me. "But couldn't she have discovered something recently? Say in the last day or so?"

"But she didn't mention anything to you?"

"If she had, she might not have gone over the cliff."

"Any further ideas on it, Prail?"

"No. Except that someone found out what she'd discovered?"

"All right." I pushed back my chair and got up. "Let's assume Mrs. Prail did discover something. Some knowledge dangerous to X. How would X know she'd decided to walk along that track after dark? Unless," I hesitated, then added slowly, "she'd arranged to meet somebody."

"Who would Elsa be meeting?" he asked, a dull flush seeping up his face. "And without my knowing it? Are you suggesting she was having—"

"I'm not suggesting anything. This is your theory and I'm merely pointing out that it's ludicrous to think that anybody would sit out there in the dark, hoping your wife would happen to come along."

We stood looking at each other in silence.

Prail lowered his eyes and rubbed hands over his face. "I'm sorry," he said, his voice muffled. "I guess I'm a bit on edge. The whole thing's beyond me. It's been going round and round in my head since you found her. I'm sorry for what I said about Janet."

"And what did you say about Janet?" Drayton's voice came from behind us, cold and threatening. He let the verandah door swing to behind him.

"Now look, Barnaby, I've already apologised. Just

something said in the heat of the moment."

"Watch it, Prail." Drayton turned on his heel and headed to the corridor leading to the room where Elsa Prail lay. Prail watched him go.

"Look after Elsa," he muttered to me. "I'll be at the house if there's anything."

"If Drobinall's still there, ask him to drop over here in an hour?"

Janet Frenton repelled Drayton as efficiently as she had Prail. He was back on the verandah while Prail was still walking slowly down the drive.

"What was he saying about Janet that called for an apology?"

"Let it go. He's overwrought." I was going to add, 'you would be in his shoes', but I decided against it.

Drayton leaned back against the gauze and blew a smoke ring towards the ceiling.

"Elsa Prail came to the house looking for you," he said abruptly. "Yesterday afternoon. She wouldn't tell me why she wanted to see you."

"What time was that?"

"A little before four, perhaps."

Immediately before she went to the Nelsons', I thought.

"Aren't you going to ask me where I was between the times of four and seven?" He flicked a dead match at a fly sitting on the mosquito gauze. "I was at the house alone. Nobody saw me. Nobody spoke to me. The servants were in the kitchen. I had an ideal opportunity to slip out in the dark and push her over."

I played it along in the same vein. "How would you know she was out there, waiting to be pushed?" I asked.

"I could have arranged to meet her there when she came to the house in the afternoon." He raised a sardonic eyebrow. "Easy, my dear Watson." He left, slamming the door behind him.

I sent a note to Grace Nelson, asking her to come over to the nursing sister's house.

CHAPTER 39

"Yes," Grace Nelson said. "Elsa did come over to our place yesterday afternoon. She stayed to tea."

She perched on the edge of the chair, diminutive and fragile and I had a swift vision of her trying to lift Elsa Prail. Impossible. Could she have dragged her? Perhaps.

"When did she arrive at your house?"

"Sometime around four, I would say."

"Had she arranged to come, or did she just drop in?"

"She just dropped in. She said she'd got a fit of the blues, that Feira was getting her down."

"Did anything unusual happen whilst she was there? Anything out of the ordinary, that you can remember?"

"I don't think so," she said slowly, her brows pursed in a V of concentration. "Drobinall turned up. We just sat around drinking tea, until Martin arrived. He wanted to talk to Larry about the re-routing of the cattle coming over."

"What were you talking about before Prail arrived? Anything in particular?"

"I can't remember. I don't think there could have been."

I didn't think Grace Nelson was lying, but I knew there had to be some clue, somewhere, in all the talking that had precipitated last night's events. I didn't think Grace Nelson had attempted to murder Elsa Prail, but it was possible she'd heard something, and I didn't believe they'd talked for a couple of hours about nothing.

"You didn't, for instance, talk about the recent events on the Boma such as Mrs. Drayton's death?"

"No. You know, I remember it struck me as odd. It's the subject uppermost in people's minds and it has been for weeks, but no-one mentioned it."

"Not at all?"

"Well, I think someone did say something about the police officer coming down to Feira, but just in passing."

"Did Mrs. Prail have anything to say about that?"

Grace Nelson hesitated, the varnished nails beating a restless tattoo against her handbag. "I don't think she did," she answered doubtfully, at last.

"Was she her usual self? Nothing odd strike you about her?"

"Perhaps Elsa wasn't as talkative as usual. She seemed a bit jumpy. A bit on edge."

"So you'd say nothing out of the ordinary cropped up in the conversation? Nothing unusual happened whilst she was at your house?" I was leaning forward in my frustration and forced myself to relax. Doing that triggered the thought of a slightly different approach. "Nothing that might have been usual for you, but someone else like me would have though unusual?"

"Well, unless bickering with Drobinall could be called unusual. I suppose you wouldn't find it usual, but they were always at it."

"What were they bickering about yesterday?"

"Drobinall's taste for gossip."

"How do you mean they were always at it? I thought the women on the Boma found Drobinall's gossip quite amusing?"

"I suppose we do. So does Elsa, but between her and

Drobinall there's always something. I don't know how to describe it. She's always a little contemptuous of him. He retaliates by teasing. You know the sort of thing I mean: little digs. One's never sure whether there's another meaning to lots of the things he says. He's like that with everybody, but more so with Elsa than the rest of us."

"What started the argument yesterday?" She took out a cigarette and I leaned forward to light it.

"I don't know. I went out to the kitchen. The servant hadn't brought enough cups. They were well into it when I came back. But don't misunderstand me, you really couldn't call it an argument. It's not as if they were quarrelling."

"Can you remember what was said?"

"Not much of it." she hesitated, then: "I remember that Elsa told Drobinall that he was a 'bit of an old woman'. Those were the words she used. She said that he invented most of the gossip he dined out on, and that if he did get hold of two cents worth of truth, he embroidered it until it was unrecognisable. Then she said if he didn't watch his tongue, it might land him in trouble."

Grace Nelson stopped suddenly and bit her lip. "I know how that sounds, saying it to you," she hurried on. "It sounds as though they were quarrelling, but they weren't. It was all quite light. They weren't angry with each other. Drobinall even laughed when she said that to him. He made some remark about being able to ring up on a few sixty-four dollar questions, any time."

It certainly didn't sound as if Elsa Prail had whipped Drobinall into a rage, but I kept prompting her. What she'd described wouldn't have taken up much time.

"Did it finish there?" I asked.

"Not quite. Drobinall said that he didn't have to rely on feminine intuition anyway. I can't remember quite how he put it," she stopped and looked down, frowning again in concentration.

I waited.

"He must have been getting a dig at Elsa about this business of Elizabeth," she said slowly. "I'd forgotten about that."

I stayed silent, trying not to distract her.

"Now what was it Elsa said? It was something about catching someone's tail. I can't remember exactly. She obviously thought it was funny. She was grinning, but Drobinall didn't seem to think it was funny. He looked quite oddly at her. I remember he asked her what was so amusing about it. She told him to wait and see. And I think it finished there because my husband called Drobinall over."

"Were they not sitting together?"

"No. Martin and Larry were over at the end of the verandah. They were looking at a map which Martin had brought over with him. Something to do with the tsetse fly and that's what they talked about for the rest of the time they were there." Grace Nelson's voice reflected the boredom with which she must have listened to the conversation of the previous afternoon.

"Who left first?"

"Martin. He said he had some work to clear up. Elsa said she'd walk home later. Drobinall was staying on to a meal with us."

"What time did Mrs. Prail leave?"

"It must have been nearly six-thirty. She said she'd better get back before dark. I'm not sure of the time but I remember the servant bringing the lamps just after she went."

"Can you remember at what time Drobinall went over to the Prails' to fetch the gin?"

"Not long after Elsa left. It can't have been even seven."

"And he came back when?"

"Let me see. It must have been nearly eight o'clock when

265

I got back to the verandah. I'd bathed and changed."

"And your husband was there on the verandah? Had he been there all the time?"

Fright came to sit in the blue eyes. The insistence of my questioning was clearly not routine.

"He was there when I went to bathe," she said. "And he was there when I came back. We were having dinner when Martin came looking for Elsa."

"Thank you, Mrs. Nelson. You've been most helpful. Sorry I have to worry you with these questions."

She walked to the door and turned to ask abruptly. "Do you think Elsa fell over the edge?"

"What I think is not important," I replied. "But failing any statement from Mrs. Prail herself, I must certainly try to find out how she came to go over the cliff."

"How is she this morning?"

I just looked down and shook my head.

CHAPTER 40

I got little more from Drobinall.

Yes, he agreed that Mrs. Nelson's account was more or less correct. No, he'd noticed nothing unusual in Elsa's manner the previous day. He couldn't remember what had started the argument, but there was nothing unusual about that. He and Elsa often argued. She always rose to the hook and he'd been teasing her. It didn't mean a thing.

He was nervous, fidgety. His eyes were increasingly unable to hold mine as I kept asking more and more questions.

Yes, she had said something about salting something's tail. Or someone's tail? He hadn't understood the reference.

"An old children's fable about how to catch a bird," I said. "You have to put salt on its tail."

It was also used as a metaphor for catching someone like a criminal. But Drobinall professed not to know it.

I took him through more of what he'd done.

The Landrover had been left at the office so he had walked over to borrow the gin. Yes, it had been he who had wanted the gin. He found whisky a little heavy and he didn't drink a lot of beer. Prail had got him the gin from the drinks cabinet, and then they'd gone outside and stayed in the Nissen hut. He hadn't gone back in the house afterwards. He'd seen nobody and nothing on the way back. The Nelsons had been on the verandah when he returned, and they'd had dinner shortly afterwards.

I let him ramble on a bit.

Such a pity about Elsa. Such an attractive woman. How was she? Too, too dreadful.

He was scared, I thought, as I watched him saunter with exaggerated nonchalance down the drive, his topee tilted at a rakish angle. Scared, but was he guilty?

I glanced through the notes I'd made. Had Nelson stayed on the verandah whilst his wife was dressing and Drobinall had been over at the Prails' house? Had Mrs. Nelson been bathing and dressing from seven to eight, as she said. Had Elsa Prail followed Drobinall back along the road for some reason? He said he'd seen nobody on the road.

My eyes tracked the notes back, to where I'd drawn underlined the word salt. It was an odd remark of Elsa Prail's to Drobinall, about salting someone's tail.

Had it meant something to Drobinall, despite his denial?

'Looks like salt' Prail had said of the powdered poison from the witchdoctor's collection.

'Why's there salt on Elizabeth's table?' Elsa Prail had asked me before sliding back into unconsciousness.

But what if I was seeing to much? She'd taken a severe knock to the head. Some obscure joke at Drobinall mixed up with her grief over her friend's death?

The morning wore on, with the heat on the verandah mounting steadily. Elsa Prail maintained the slight improvement of the night hours but showed no sign of returning consciousness.

Young turned up at the house with several queries from the office, and we worked through them.

"Do you think Mrs. Prail's going to be all right, sir?" he asked as he turned to go.

"I don't know," I answered. "Perhaps Bravachko will be able to give us an idea when he arrives." I looked at my watch. "Any time now."

"You know what they're saying?" he said slowly. "That Mrs. Prail was pushed over the cliff."

"Well, let's hope Mrs. Prail herself will soon be able to tell us how she came to be down there on the bank." I said it, knowing it was the sort of thing he would expect me to say.

"Do you know she was looking for you at the Boma, yesterday?" he asked.

"No. I didn't. Did she say what she wanted?"

"She wouldn't. She asked when you'd be back from Upupulu. I told her I thought it would be some time later in the afternoon."

"When was she at the Boma?"

"Just after you left."

We were lucky. Nelson made it through to the mission hospital, found Bravachko and made it back. He'd had difficulties with the roads and it had taken double the expected time, but we were still lucky – the road could easily have been impassable in this weather.

Janet Fenton and I brought Bravachko quickly into the picture as he checked on Elsa Prail.

His face got more sombre as we progressed.

"It isn't necessary for me to lie," he said at the end. "Mrs. Prail is nearer to death than life, at present."

With that, he ushered us out.

It was with some measure of relief that I left Janet Fenton's house, partly because I felt I had unloaded some of the burden of responsibility.

My thoughts turned to Nelson, as I walked down the path. He had confirmed the outlines of his wife's account of

Elsa Prail's visit, whilst being less definite about times. He had not heard the end of the argument between her and Drobinall. He'd been looking over the tsetse fly map with Prail.

"And who suggested that Drobinall should go for the gin?" I had asked him. Drobinall had, he thought: it was he who had particularly wanted gin.

I came to the point in the path where Nyrenda had found the torch. There was no mistaking it. The ground around was a mud cast, dried hard in the hot sun. Here there were the smudged impressions of naked feet, there the deep imprints of Wellington boots. Over to the left, the ruts made by the Landrover, leading to the rocky incline. I quickly realised that, even had there been anything to find before the ground had been ploughed and furrowed, there wouldn't be now.

I walked across to the edge and looked over carefully. The mud bank she'd lain on had gone; in its place there was only the seething, brown scum of the river, sucking at the rocks. The collapse of the earth bank from the higher level had been lucky for Elsa Prail.

Nyrenda spotting her torch had been just as lucky. If he hadn't seen it that last sweep, and we'd resumed in daylight, she would have been long gone.

I wondered who had switched off the torch which Nyrenda had found. Mrs. Prail? Had she stood there in the darkness talking to somebody? But then, she surely would have known to whom she was talking? That wasn't the impression her response to me had give.

'Walking from the house... something hit me,' she'd said.

Did that imply the torch had been switched on?

So if she hadn't been talking to whoever hit her, why would she have switched the torch off?

She heard someone coming and didn't want to be seen?

Why?

Perhaps she heard something and suspected her attacker was there. Perhaps she hadn't been quick enough to turn the torch off and he, or she, knew where Elsa Prail was standing.

But then surely the attacker would have thought of retrieving the torch? Unless he, or she, didn't realise Mrs. Prail had dropped it on the path. They thought it had fallen down to the bank with her.

I walked on down to the Boma, one tired thought lumbering after another, and never quite catching up. Could I build other scenarios that would fit the scant facts I had?

The station was deserted and quiet in the afternoon heat. I left word with the duty messenger for the guard to be changed at the nursing sister's house and walked on again, despite the heat.

Mad dogs and Englishmen, I though idly, but it was easier than sitting in a chair, fighting an irresistible desire to close my eyes. Also I needed some more tobacco. I walked on to the store.

CHAPTER 41

The narrow, bush road running above the west bank of the Luangwa river led only to the store run by the Jones. It was a store catering mostly for African trade. The Jones' house, built on a higher level above the river, was removed from the store proper.

On the thatched stoep of the store which faced the river, the bare, broad foot of the African tailor, worked the treadle of the heavy sewing machine. There was always a tailor, I thought, always a machine, always the row of brightly coloured dresses of indeterminate design and poor material, always that pile of khaki shorts and kansas steadily mounting beside him.

It felt cooler beneath the thatched roof but, even so, Mrs. Jones sat beside the counter fanning herself. The knitting lay neglected on her lap.

"This heat," she said. "My goodness, you look tired. It's silly to be walking in this sun at this time of the year." She walked into the dark recesses of the store and I heard the slam of a fridge door. She was still talking as she came back.

"I don't know what's worse, continual rain or this humidity. There." She placed the glass of orangeade on the counter. "Drink that."

She was as fussy as a mother hen, I thought, but it made

me smile. The faded blue eyes watched me anxiously as I drank.

"Now, isn't that better?" she asked when I finished.

"It certainly went down well, thank you."

"And now," she said, "how is Mrs. Prail?"

"It's difficult to say yet. Father Bravachko is with her now."

"The poor thing. I know I was cross with her about this business of Janet, but I wouldn't wish her harm. I keep thinking of that river and the crocs." she shuddered dramatically.

I nodded.

"And Janet," she went on. "She was up all night too, she must be tired. Isn't there something I could do up there to help, Mr. Lancaster. I could sit in for Janet. I could always do that if it would help."

"That's very kind of you Mrs. Jones. I'll let you know if there's anything."

"I only heard about it this morning," she said. "Mr. Drobinall came in and told us. Mr Jones and I went over to the store at Chiteto yesterday and we couldn't get back last night. That rain made the road impossible in the dark. We gave it up and waited for daylight. How did she come to go over that cliff? She knew that path well enough."

"Again that's difficult to say. Perhaps Mrs. Prail can help us, if..." I left it hanging.

"You don't mean she's that bad?" she asked in a shocked voice.

"She's certainly not in a good way at present."

"The poor thing," she muttered. She turned away and groped for her knitting.

"I suppose you don't keep this brand?" I showed her my empty tobacco tin.

"No. But I've got one or two other brands I get in." She

led me over to the shelves at the far side of the store, the knitting tucked under her arm, and pulled back the glass shutter to give me access.

"And to think it was only yesterday she was in here talking to me," she said. "I was just shutting up shop. Mr. Jones wanted lunch early so that we could get off to Chiteto."

"What time was that?" I turned over the packets of tobacco. They felt dry and brittle. "Nothing in tins, Mrs. Jones?"

"It must have been getting on for twelve, I would think. She said she was running low on a few things, given there haven't been any stores coming in since the bridge washed out."

She peered into the back of the shelf and moved a couple of items.

"No. We've nothing in tins, I'm sorry."

She was almost talking to herself as she rearranged the stock on the shelves. "She'd got to have this and she'd got to have that. Nothing else would do. And you know, even then she forgot to send the servant back for them." She pointed to the brown, paper bags sitting off to one side. "One minute she's chopping and changing about what she wants, as though I'd got all the time in the world, and I hadn't, and the next she's off and forgets it all."

Was it on her way back from the store, that she had called at the Boma, looking for me?

It seemed to fit the time. But then, she had to pass the Boma on her way to the store. Why not then?

"Don't know why she didn't take the things with her," Mrs. Jones was saying. "They're small enough parcels, but all at once she's in a terrible hurry as though she's forgotten something. Maybe she'd left a cake in the oven?"

Or remembered something?

274

"Standing right there, she was, as I stood here, talking one second, and the next staring into space over my head and then suddenly, 'I'll send the servant for them,' she says and off she goes. Almost running." Mrs. Jones chattered on.

Standing right where I stood, staring into space. There were only the shelves in front of my eyes, dusty shelves with their mixed assortment of goods. My eyes flicked over them: coffee, tea, soap, marmalade, toilet rolls, packets of cornflour... I worked my way down. It was on the third shelf that I saw them.

As they caught my eye, they seemed to take a step forward, until I could see nothing else on the shelf. There were three of them in a row. In my mind's eye, I saw Drayton as I had seen him so often. This was what Elsa Prail had seen. This was what had sent her running out of the store to look for me.

"...a terrible business for Mr. Prail, the poor man." Mrs. Jones' voice seemed a long way off as I, too, stood and stared at the shelf.

"I'll take one of those." I cut across her chatter.

"Well, I suppose Mr. Drayton won't be wanting them now—we've always stocked this line for him."

"Wrap it, please, Mrs. Jones."

Drayton wasn't at the house when I got back and I did what I wanted to do without interruption. It took little time.

Yes. It could have been. It was possible. But had it happened that way?

I had to see Janet Frenton. I wondered whether Elsa Prail had seen it in the same light? How had she interpreted it? Would she have been so anxious so see me, if she had been thinking along the same lines? I didn't know.

I took my purchase with me to the nursing sister's house,

but I found Father Bravachko alone in Elsa Prail's room.

"I've sent Miss Frenton to get some sleep," he said. "You too, should rest." He sat beside the bed, his legs propped on a stool.

"How is she?" I nodded towards the bed.

"Too soon to say."

I sat on the camp bed and unwrapped the parcel I had brought with me. I talked quietly.

The old man's shrewd, grey eyes hardened as I talked.

"It's monstrous," he said softly. "But who?"

I couldn't answer the last question and it circled around in my tired brain as I sank into sleep on the settee in Janet Frenton's sitting room.

The room was dark when I awoke. The house rested in silence. I started up much as Janet Frenton had in the shadows of Elsa Prail's bedroom and looked at my watch. I'd been asleep for seven hours.

I threw back the blanket that someone had put over me and went swiftly through the lighted verandah and down the passage to the bedroom.

There was no change in Elsa Prail.

I asked Janet Frenton about my purchase after I'd sent the priest off to bed.

"Yes," she said. "Everyone knew. It became a standing joke on the Boma. Once a messenger had to go thirty miles with them once, because they'd been forgotten."

A standing joke, I thought, which had led to murder.

CHAPTER 42

"So you think Mrs. Drayton's death was an accident?" Tony Blake asked.

"You might call it that."

He faced me across the office desk. It was the evening of the following day and the shadows were swiftly lengthening across the Boma lawn. I had been talking for more than an hour.

"Can't think why you bothered to send for me, Jim." He smiled. "You don't seem to be doing badly at all, no, not badly at all, old boy."

He still wore the mud-bespattered and crumpled uniform in which he had arrived on Grobler's truck: his cap, baton and belt had been tossed aside. His capacity for beer hadn't changed much, I though, watching him down his second, and neither had he. The hair was a little thinner, perhaps. It had been six years, seven years? Was it that long since Barotse days? I could hardly credit it. I pushed another bottle nearer his hand.

"But even so, assuming you're right about this," he was saying, "it doesn't alter the case. It's still murder."

"True enough."

"But," he went on, "the important point of this excellent clarification of the circumstances surrounding Mrs.

Drayton's death, if it's correct, is that it's a useful pointer to this affair of Mrs. Prail." He stubbed out his cigarette. "That's the case which looks more promising. Not so much water under the bridge. It's fresh. And it's a spur of the moment affair. They all forget something when they're in a hurry." He looked up at the ceiling for a moment. "Can you rely on this girl, Frenton?"

"I'd say so." I outlined my reasons. "Then there's Bravachko and two messengers permanently posted at her house."

"Fair enough."

I handed over the sheaf of notes which I had written during the hours I'd spent on Janet Frenton's verandah.

"These outline, in a little more detail, what I've already told you." I grimaced. "But now, as I say, I'm stuck."

"And do you know why you're stuck?" Blake slapped at the fly which buzzed drowsily round his head. "I'll tell you why. You amateur policemen are all the same. You overlook the obvious just because it is obvious. You plump for the complicated rather than the simple explanation which is under your nose." The smile on his face took the bite from his words. "Now, for instance..." he thumbed through the notes and, finding what he wanted, scored two lines and pushed them back at me.

"There," he said. "Why take that statement for granted? Because it appeared to be the truth. You didn't try to confirm it, because you accepted it. And right there, I think, is a promising lead, because if that statement is untrue then the whole perspective changes, especially in relation to the one puzzling factor in which you saw some significance, but later ignored."

He drained his beer and got up.

"But why—" I began.

"Think it over," he interrupted. "I'm for a bath, change,

278

meal and sleep. This canoe and bush bashing is a bit out of my line now. I'll tell you tomorrow, if you haven't tumbled to it before then. I'll take these notes of yours and go through them again."

I stared down at the page he had scored.

"I don't get it." I said. And I didn't. I couldn't see what he meant.

"Because you're looking at it from the wrong angle. Perhaps you've been thinking too much about it." He scratched thoughtfully at one bushy eyebrow. "Are you sure that nobody knows about that?" He motioned towards the purchase I had made at the store.

"Not in its context, they don't, I'm sure. Except Bravachko and Janet Fenton, of course, and I

warned them to say nothing."

"Better make sure he doesn't. It could be important."

"I've put you at the house with Drayton." I handed Blake the notes again. "I'll take you along and get you installed, then I'll get back to Janet Frenton's place and relieve Bravachko. We've been doing turn and turn about."

Blake stretched and gave a mighty yawn, his lean six foot two towering above the desk in the gathering gloom.

"We'll get down to it tomorrow. It's wonderful how a night's rest will sort your ideas out for you," he said.

"Don't tell me you have to wait until tomorrow before you can turn up the answers." I muttered. "I thought you'd got it all buttoned up. Just like that!" I clicked my fingers at him.

Blake chuckled. "It's only an idea I've got. Just an idea, that's all."

"Do you think we should speak to Drayton tonight?"

"No. Let it lie. Tomorrow will see what it will see."

There was a lightening of Father Bravachko's face when I got back to the nursing sister's house.

"A definite improvement," he said. "Only slight, but it's there."

"And glad I am to hear it." I stopped him before he left. "Remember that only the three of us must know about this for the time being. It mustn't become common knowledge. Don't even tell her husband."

"That seems cruel." The priest's clear eyes searched my face. "How long will this go on?"

"Not long now, I hope. What are her chances of regaining consciousness over the next twenty-four hours?"

He shrugged. "She may intermittently, but not for very long periods. She'll be in no condition to make a statement. You don't want it known if she recovers sufficiently to speak. On the other hand, I do not wish to keep her under too heavy a sedation now. I've therefore told Miss Frenton that she is to have no visitors for the present."

"Fine. But I must be there if she does start talking, even if incoherently. I'll tell Miss Frenton."

The priest went off to rest on the understanding that I would call him at two in the morning.

The evening passed slowly. Prail turned up and sat playing patience on the verandah, for an hour or so. He said little. His face was grey with fatigue and nervous fingers plucked endlessly at the edges of the cards. He had aged overnight.

"If I could just know that she's going to make it," he said more than once. He left around eleven with Nelson who had dropped in to ask about Mrs. Prail's progress. I heard Nelson suggest a drink and a game of bridge as they walked off together down the drive.

And, as the hours passed, I tried to fathom what Blake had been getting at. The week-old newspaper which he had brought down with him from Lusaka held little of interest and lay neglected on my knees.

I gave it up eventually, and searched the bookshelf for something to keep my mind off its insistent, fruitless circling. I found an old paperback by Ngaio Marsh and settled down to read, fortified by the thermos of strong, black coffee which Janet Frenton had thoughtfully provided. In the quiet recesses of the house, I heard the messenger coughing.

It was much later, as I followed the intricate reasoning of the polished Superintendent Alleyn in the concluding pages of the book, my mind suddenly produced the answer. I tossed down the book.

So that was what Blake meant. Good God. Yes, of course. He'd got it, he had it exactly right. That one puzzling factor which I hadn't followed up was the key. But even so, there was a second factor on which Blake himself would stick because he didn't know. The thought made me feel smug.

It was past three in the morning when I called Bravachko and Janet Frenton was sent to bed. I settled back to finish the book.

CHAPTER 43

Blake joined me for breakfast early the following morning.

"How's Mrs. Prail doing?" he asked.

I told him.

"Good, but watch her carefully today. The 'No Visitors' arrangement might arouse suspicion."

His grey eyes were appraising over the rim of the coffee cup. "You look pleased with yourself this morning. I take it you've tumbled to what I was getting at?"

"I think so. But what I don't see is how you caught on to it so quickly."

"Motive, and the nasty, suspicious mind peculiar to policemen." He pushed away the cup and glanced at his watch. "I'd better get weaving."

"What are your plans?"

"I'll stick to the routine drill. Questioning may turn up something useful in the way of corroboratory evidence, though I'll have to tread carefully here and there. We don't want to raise any suspicion that we're on to this yet. I'm starting with Drayton. I've asked him to come down to the Boma around seven. I'll use your office if I may."

"Help yourself."

"And if I could have a couple of messengers to run around, fetching people in?"

"Nyrenda, the Head Messenger, he'll look after you."

"Drobinall's still on the station, I take it?"

"Yes, he's staying with Prail."

"Good, that'll save a trip out. Here," he returned the notes which I'd given him the previous evening. "I won't be needing these any more. I'll get off now."

If he hadn't sounded so damn cock-sure, I might have told him then.

Instead I said maliciously, "At some time today, Chief Inspector, let me quote you, you'll overlook the obvious just because it is obvious. When that happens just come back and see me."

He turned back from the door to regard me suspiciously, one eyebrow raised in question.

"What the hell's that supposed to mean?"

"Think it over." I mimicked his tone of the previous evening.

Muttering something unintelligible, he went off down the drive. Watching him go, I thought it wouldn't do him any harm to sweat over it a bit when he got to it.

The morning seemed endless. There was little I could do except wait.

Prail and Drobinall called at the house on their way to the Boma, Drobinall sporting a maroon coloured beret.

"We've been summoned to the presence," he said. His eyes belied the nonchalance in his voice. He was nervous.

Prail had disappeared down the corridor leading to the bedroom and I heard him talking to Bravachko. The tone of the priest's voice was persuasive and reassuring and he was patting Prail's arm gently, as they returned to the verandah.

"It won't be long now, I hope," he was saying, "before I can give you more definite news about your wife, but head injuries are tricky."

"I guess you're doing all you can," Prail muttered as he went through the door.

"This is inhuman," Bravachko said softly as we watched them go. "If you would just let me give him some encouragement."

"Won't be long now, I hope." I found myself repeating the priest's own phrase and patting his arm reassuringly, in much the same way as he had done with Prail.

Later I saw Drobinall pass along the road, returning from the Boma. He walked swiftly as though on an errand, his eyes turned towards the ground.

The messenger's light tap at the door roused me from a half sleep. My legs, straddled across a chair were stiff. He brought a note from Blake, asking to see the nursing sister and I sent her down.

I paced the verandah to drive away the insidious urge to settle into sleep.

Janet Frenton returned within the hour with the message that Blake would not be back for lunch, and I sent sandwiches and coffee down to the Boma office.

In mid-afternoon, from the end of the verandah, I caught a glimpse of his tall figure, walking slowly along the path at the back of the hospital, going north.

Finally, I gave in and snatched a couple of hours' sleep on the sitting room settee. Blake woke me when he came back to the house. He was hot, tired and cross. It was nearly five.

"All right" he said. "You've had your fun. Let's have it. How was it done?"

I told him and he started to laugh softly.

"Touché—couldn't be more obvious. Now let me see the clothes she was wearing when you found her."

"Miss Frenton will show you those. They're still in the

room."

I called to Lameck to bring tea.

"It's all very well," Blake said, when he returned to the verandah. "But I can't see how we're going to prove it even now. You feel pretty sure that she didn't see who hit her?"

"I don't think she did. Not from the sense of what she said."

"It's more than likely she didn't. I think he came from behind a bloody, great bush on Nelson's side of the road. If she recovers, he'll bluff it out and say that the knock on the head has muddled her mind."

He refused the tea and lapsed into silence, his long frame stretching back in the chair, his face hidden behind the wreaths of smoke from his pipe.

Presently he said, as though thinking aloud: "There's just a chance that he wouldn't risk it though. I wonder..."

He was pacing the verandah when I came back with the beer from the fridge. "Are you sure he doesn't know that Mrs. Prail spoke to you when you reached her?" he asked.

"He may suspect it but he can't be sure."

"Hmmph. It might work at that." He swallowed the beer without stopping to take breath. "Thirsty work—police work." He refilled the glass.

It was ten minutes before he spoke again and then he said. "There are a helluva lot of ifs and buts about this, but I'm sure we're right even though we've got damned all to go on. What I'm going to suggest is highly irregular and if it doesn't work out, I'll be for the high jump, but I think it's worth a try."

CHAPTER 44

Later that evening I watched from behind the curtained door which led from the lighted verandah to the sitting room. With the room in darkness, I could see and not be seen. I turned the key in the lock. It wouldn't do to have anyone barge in for extra chairs or ash trays.

The whole thing smacked of melodrama to me, but when Blake had asked if I could think of any other way, I had to admit that I could not.

He was waiting on the verandah, leafing through his notebook. I was curious to see him in action.

Finally, the lighted eyes of torches danced in the darkness of the drive.

"Here we go," Blake muttered.

The Nelsons arrived with Prail and Drobinall.

"Sorry to drag you along here like this." Blake ushered them to chairs. "But I thought it might be easier to sort out a few points here, rather than have another singles session down at the Boma tomorrow."

Drayton came through the verandah door and let it slam behind him.

"What's all this about, Blake? Haven't we had enough for today?" He sounded angry.

"Just one or two loose ends to tie up. Won't take long Mr.

286

Drayton. Come and sit down. Who are we waiting for? Ah, Young, there you are. Find yourself a chair."

Janet Frenton came from the corridor leading from Elsa Prail's room and shut the intervening door.

"How's Elsa?" Prail asked.

She replied so quietly, I couldn't hear her reply.

"Come and sit down, Miss Frenton." Blake said.

As before, they seemed to split into rival camps: the Nelsons, Drobinall and Prail to Blake's left and Drayton, Young and the nursing sister on the right.

They were all a little jumpy, except Drayton who sat, seemingly unmoved and uncaring. Drobinall gnawed gently at his inner lip. Grace Nelson took another cigarette, leaving the first, half-smoked burning on the edge of the ashtray.

Whatever Janet Frenton had said to Prail, had not erased the haggard mask of worry from his face. It was obvious to me that he had cut down on his brandy intake over the previous two days and was feeling the effect of it. He passed his hand over his mouth and chin in an endless finger massage.

Nelson's expression was that of an adult, reluctantly joining a children's party game.

And they all watched Blake as though he were a conjurer about to produce a rabbit out of the hat.

Well, let's hope he can, I thought.

"As you all know, I was sent down here to investigate the circumstances of Mrs. Drayton's death," Blake said. "What I intend to say about that is only conjecture. At this point, it can't be more than that. If the pathological report is negative, such conjecture will be pure, unsupported theory, based only on the notes handed to me by Mr. Lancaster and what I've heard since I arrived on the Boma. Was Mrs. Drayton poisoned? Father Bravachko thinks that she was; that she died from the same type of poison as was used on Chiabele's

287

nephew Maoma, who was brought in from Jatwa Nkwanga. Can it be proved? Perhaps not. Some of the African poisons defy identification."

Blake's voice was casual. He perched on the edge of the verandah table. "But," he went on, "proof or not, there's no doubt at all in my mind that Mrs. Drayton was murdered."

In the following silence, somebody coughed. Blake's eyes moved lazily round the half circle of faces, resting momentarily on each.

"I think it was because Mrs. Prail knew this that she went over the cliff," Blake said softly. "Someone here now pushed her."

It was as though the tension had been increased by the turn of a dial. Glances locked and broke free only to return to Blake's face.

"What I've said right along," Prail muttered. His bottom lip shook.

"There's a pattern that I've seen before: one murder leading to another," Blake said. "After the first time, it comes more easily. You can only hang once. And as confirmation that an attempt was made to murder Mrs. Prail, we have her own words. She was attacked as she walked along the path that night. She told Mr. Lancaster when he reached the bank where she lay. For obvious reasons, Mr. Lancaster kept quiet about this, and unfortunately, Mrs. Prail has not since then recovered consciousness. So we are left with that one statement; but that statement is enough for a working hypothesis."

"I knew it was no accident. I told Lancaster." Prail half rose from his chair. Blake's hand waved him back.

"On the day in question," he went on, "the day Mrs. Prail went over the cliff, she had been trying to contact Mr. Lancaster. She called at the Boma around lunch time but he'd already left for the Upupulu bridge. From the fact that she made a special visit to his house in the afternoon to see if he had returned, we may assume that her reason for wanting to see him was important and that there was some degree of urgency involved. In fact, it's more than an assumption: Mr. Lancaster discovered within the next twenty four hours why she had wanted to see him. It was both important and urgent. It had a bearing on Mrs. Drayton's death. And such knowledge almost cost Mrs. Prail her life. So we conclude that the rumour and gossip rampant on the station, did in fact, have a sound basis. Mrs. Drayton was poisoned. We may assume that the person responsible for that was also responsible for the attack on Mrs. Prail. So we have homicide and attempted homicide. As far as the first is concerned, any one of you could be guilty, but a strict cross-check of the time element has narrowed the field for the second. Only two people here had the opportunity."

Amongst his listeners, in the ensuing silence, the heightened tension was a tangible thing.

"Let's go back a little," Blake continued. "Remembering, as I've said, that this is conjecture only. I think it actually started with Matafwali, the witchdoctor who was hanged for the murders in the Chiabele country. It was what he threatened in Mr. Drayton's court that gave birth to the idea for the first homicide. If Mrs. Drayton died from the effects of an African vegetable poison, and even if it were discovered, wouldn't the blame appear to lie with the Bantu? The African has easy access to bush poisons. Perhaps one of Matafwali's followers had decided to revenge himself on Drayton? Was that how it was meant to look? But for such a plan, a bush poison was needed and a European would find this well nigh impossible to come by. You might ask why I suggest that it was a European who had this idea. One of the main reasons is, as Mr. Lancaster has always contended, that any African suspects would be confident enough to leave matters to Matafwali. They would believe that, dead or alive, Matafwali wouldn't need their help to carry out his threats. So, now... an African bush poison was needed, and there in the Boma office lay Matafwali's rhino horn, referred to during the Preliminary Enquiry, as 'The Horn of the White Sleep'. It contained a powder of unknown properties. There again the evidence points to a European. No followers of Matafwali would have dared to touch his rhino horn and the powder it contained. No, it was a European who took the powder and tried it out. We even know how it was tried out: the monkey died."

He paused.

"And then Mrs. Drayton died. A viral gastroenteritis following malaria. No questions asked. There it would have ended, with no necessity to fall back on the revenge motive, had not tongues started to wag. But our murderer was ready, and he had an even cleverer idea than his original one. So there was an anonymous voice on the telephone, anonymous letters, the gossip which was deliberately encouraged by a word dropped here and there. The pot was brought to the boil, and at that point, following the death of Maoma, Bravachko questioned his own death certificate. Now that was a stroke of luck for the murderer, and just the right moment to produce the letter from Mrs. Drayton, suggesting she'd been contemplating suicide. The timing was excellent. You knew quite well, didn't you, Mr. Drayton, that your wife hadn't committed suicide?"

"You must be out of your mind, Blake," Drayton said icily. He leaned forward in his chair, an expression half anger, half disbelief in the face he turned towards Blake.

Janet Frenton made an involuntary movement of her hands.

"I don't think I am." Blake's eyes were fixed on Drayton—watchful, calculating. "I'm pretty sure that on general lines, that's the way you planned it. When the first question was raised, you saw how it could be turned to your advantage, if the revenge motive didn't work out—by clever manoeuvring and stirring up of suspicion, it could be made to appear that you were being victimised. That somebody was out to get you accused of the murder of your wife. Quite clever really."

Drayton knocked out his pipe. "Try proving that," he said between clenched teeth.

"If the pathological report on your wife is positive, we might do just that with Mrs. Prail's help."

"What possible motive?" Drayton's lip curled contemptuously.

"Your wife wouldn't agree to a divorce; she was a Catholic. You wanted your freedom."

"Which I was determined to get." Drayton cut in. "I'd already contacted my lawyer on the possibility. I didn't need to resort to murder."

"And then there's the trust fund which now comes to you, failing issue of your marriage to Mrs. Drayton. I had a talk to the P.C. before I left Lusaka. These things get around you know. What about that for motive?" Blake asked softly.

"I don't need that. I've sufficient private means of my own. This is a pack of bloody lies."

But for the first time there was an edge of uncertainty in Drayton's voice.

"You had motive, opportunity and an easy access to means," Blake went on. "None knew better than you, the possible properties of the powder in the horn, and the difficulties the chemical examiner meets in trying to isolate and identify these vegetable poisons."

"Anyone could have taken the powder from the horn," Drayton said angrily.

"But I'm pretty sure it was you," Blake interrupted. "You

must have considered yourself pretty safe on the victimisation angle, if the revenge theory fell through. Drobinall and Nelson hate your guts. Young's jealous of you. Mrs. Prail was after your blood and we needn't go into the reasons for that now. If the worst happened and it was proved that your wife had died of poisoning, you'd manoeuvre it so that it would appear that one of these people had deliberately planned to get you accused of her murder. Wasn't that the plan?"

"You're crazy!" Drayton spat the words at Blake.

Janet Frenton sat rigid in her chair, her face a frozen mask of misery. Young leaned over and whispered something to her and she shook her head in a swift sign of negation.

In the slanting rays of the lamplight, I could see the beads of sweat gleaming on Young's forehead.

"I think that's how it happened," Blake was saying, "and I'll tell you why I think so. We'll jump ahead a little, to the attempted murder of Mrs. Prail. As I've said, there are only two people here who could have been responsible for this: the time element narrows it down to Mr. Drayton and Mr. Young."

David Young's hand jerked.

"I'm not sitting here to listen to this!" Drayton rose swiftly. "And I'll see you broken for this pantomime, Blake."

"You'd better sit down, Mr. Drayton." Blake eyed him coldly. "If necessary, I'll use force to keep you here."

Something in his tone and bearing prevailed and Drayton sank slowly back into his chair.

"At seven o'clock," Blake began, "Mr. Prail and Drobinall walked over to the Nissen hut, leaving Mrs. Prail, who was about to take a bath. The servant confirms that the bath water was used and that the towels and bath mat were damp, so she took her bath. Allowing half an hour as an average time for her to bath and dress, would bring us to seven-thirty as the earliest time she could have left the house. Mr. Prail says he returned to the house around eight—but, fortunately, we can get the time more accurately than that. Drobinall, having left Mr. Prail on the drive, arrived back at the Nelsons' just as the bell went for dinner, which, as we'll see later, was at five minutes past eight. His statement that he returned direct to the Nelsons' after leaving Mr. Prail, is confirmed by the Prails' kitchen servant. He went to borrow cornflour from the Nelsons' cook and he followed the light of Drobinall's torch to the Nelsons' house. Drobinall said that he hurried because he was afraid he'd be late for dinner. At the quickest pace, the walk from house to house can't be done in less than ten minutes, so we can conclude that it was not later than 7.55 when Drobinall left Mr. Prail. We may assume therefore, that Mrs. Prail left the house between 7.30 and 7.55 as she had already gone when Mr. Prail went back inside. It started to rain at 8.30 and Mr. Prail went over to the Nelsons' to take his wife's mackintosh—only to find that she hadn't, as he had supposed, returned there. Mrs. Nelson has pinpointed the time at which Mr. Prail arrived there: she recalls that her husband said, when suggestions were being made as to Mrs. Prail's possible whereabouts 'But it's twenty to nine! Where the hell could she be at this time?' There are indications that the attack on Mrs. Prail took place on the dirt road, running along the cliff edge, above the point where she was found. It must have taken place not earlier than 7.30. That would allow her twenty-five minutes for bathing and dressing and five minutes to get to the spot, and not later than 8.45 when the alarm was raised and the whole Boma started to buzz."

Blake's glance embraced the verandah. "I apologise for this tedious time check, but it's important." he said. "Let's take the Nelsons first..."

It was airless in the shut-in darkness of the sitting room. I

293

studied Blake's audience. Their interest could not have been more apparent.

The wet redness of Drobinall's mouth caught and held the light. The knuckles of his hands, nursing one casually cocked knee, gleamed bone-white.

From behind half-closed lids, Nelson's eyes fixed unwaveringly on Blake. Beside him, his wife's fingers were on the chair arm, thrust out as though she were drying her nail varnish.

In the manner in which Young inclined towards Janet Frenton, there was something protective, but she seemed unaware of him. Her attention was focused on Blake. They were all watching Blake—all except Prail. He was staring at Drayton and behind his eyes a red bubble of anger had started to glow.

"...and I believe Mrs. Nelson." Blake was saying. "Their cook is certain that it was ten minutes to eight when she went to the kitchen to delay dinner by five minutes only if Drobinall had not returned. Their dinner was usually served at eight. Leaving the kitchen she rejoined her husband on the verandah. It isn't conceivable that in the twenty minutes between 7.30 and 7.50, she could have got down by the back path to the road, attacked Mrs. Prail, rolled or dragged her to the cliff edge, returned to the house, bathed and changed as she would necessarily have had to do, and appeared in the kitchen at ten minutes to eight . She couldn't have managed it, and neither could Mr. Nelson. He didn't leave the verandah. The servant started to set the dinner table at 7.30, which was the usual time. He could see Mr. Nelson through the open doors of the dining room. He was sitting on the verandah, reading. As the servant finished setting the table, Mrs. Nelson passed on her way from the kitchen to the verandah. That was 7.50. It would have been impossible at that point for the Nelsons, either one or both, to have left the verandah, gone down the back path to the road, and returned to the house, without meeting Drobinall at some point, or returning after him."

Blake paused and lit a cigarette and in the short silence, Grace Nelson's fingers slowly relaxed.

"Now, to Mr. Prail." Blake went on. "Within five minutes of his return to the house from the Nissen hut, he and the servant were sprinkling DDT to discourage the Serowe ants which were invading the house. The servant confirms that Mr. Prail left the house when 'it began to rain'. That was at 8.30. Mr. Prail had no time to do other than walk from A to B in order to have reached the Nelson's house at 8.40."

"Miss Frenton, as hospital records and the medical orderly confirms, was at the hospital from five until some time after ten. Which leaves us with Mr. Drayton and Mr. Young. Young had ample opportunity to be down there on the road that night, but the motive for the attack on Mrs. Prail lies in the death of Mrs. Drayton. Young had no motive for the murderous assault on Mrs. Prail, unless he had been responsible for Mrs. Drayton's death. He was away touring for three days prior to her death and he was also away when the monkey was poisoned. And that brings us to Mr. Drayton."

"I didn't leave the house that night until Prail and Nelson turned up." Drayton's voice was cold with anger. "You can't prove that I did."

"Perhaps we won't need to," Blake interjected. "I think we've enough to go on without that." He leafed through his notebook. "Let me quote to you, the exact words spoken by Mrs. Prail to Mr. Lancaster, when he reached the bank where she lay. They were: 'Why's salt on Elizabeth's table?' and then 'Walking from the house... something hit me'. At that time, the reference to salt made no sense to Mr. Lancaster. It wasn't until he heard of a remark made by Mrs. Prail to

295

Drobinall that afternoon, about 'salting someone's tail', that he began to wonder whether there was anything significant in those few muttered words. Whether perhaps, the subject uppermost in her mind when she spoke to him, was the subject which had made her seek him out twice that day. It was a chance conversation with Mrs. Jones at the store that uncovered what Mrs. Prail had meant. It was something that Mrs. Prail had seen in the store."

Blake removed the wrapping from the parcel which had been lying on the table behind him. The battery of eyes switched from his face to the bottle of health salts which I had bought at the store that day.

"This, I think, is what she saw." Blake stood the bottle on the table beside him. "What significance she attached to it we don't know yet. But it was important enough to send her hurrying back to the Boma to find Mr. Lancaster. Not salt. Salts. Did Mrs. Prail suddenly remember that the bottle, such as this, which she'd seen on Mrs. Drayton's bedside table, had never once been mentioned? That no-one had suggested that Mrs. Drayton had taken anything but a boiled egg and milk on the day she became so ill?"

"What the hell are you talking about, Blake?" Drayton broke in loudly. "I told you this morning, she remembered seeing the bottle on Elizabeth's table and it was what she wanted to see Lancaster about. That's what she said to me that afternoon."

"I suggest that you only gave me your own version of what Mrs. Prail said to you that afternoon," Blake cut in. "And for this reason: up to the time that Mrs. Prail came looking for Mr. Lancaster that afternoon, the salts had not been mentioned in evidence. They were an ideal medium for the introduction of the powder from the rhino horn. In texture and appearance, there isn't the slightest difference between them. Your wife could have been persuaded quite easily that the salts would alleviate the nausea she complained of following the malaria and the mepacrine. It was careless of you to have left the bottle on your wife's table when you left the house to fetch Miss Frenton, though. Mrs. Prail, arriving there, whilst you were gone, saw them, and later, her memory jogged by seeing the supply the store kept for you, she remembered. You could always claim, of course, that you had forgotten about the salts, but I suggest that a better idea presented itself to you, an idea that would lend weight to the victimisation theory that you'd carefully been building up. Everybody on the Boma knew that you took this stuff regularly. You, not your wife. It had become a standing joke after the famous occasion when a messenger travelled thirty miles because the bottle had been left out of your touring box and the store kept them in stock, specially for you. I think that when Mrs. Prail, with her unwelcome and inconvenient memory, came to the house that afternoon, looking for Mr. Lancaster, she said enough to make you realise that she had seen the bottle standing on your wife's table. It's difficult to do more than guess at what she said to you, without knowing exactly what significance she placed on the information she had for Mr. Lancaster, but whatever she said was enough to put you on your guard. At the same time, you saw a way in which the pattern of events could be turned to your advantage. If Mrs. Prail were to die before she could disclose this information, wouldn't it appear that she had been killed to prevent her from doing just that? But by a singular stroke of good fortune, of course, she had already told you about the salts that afternoon. How did you put it to me, when we were talking at the Boma, this morning, Mr. Drayton? 'I've just remembered,' you said, 'Mrs. Prail told me that she'd seen a bottle of health salts on Elizabeth's table that last day'. At last we get the picture clear. These salts were a habit with you. It was you who drank them regularly. It was you who would have died, not your wife. And Mrs. Prail had been silenced before she could tell Mr. Lancaster. What luck she had mentioned it to you that afternoon. Here was another pointer that you were the target. The original plan had been to poison you but it had misfired. It was succeeded by the plan to get you accused of your wife's murder."

"That's the first sensible thing you've said, Blake," Drayton snapped, but the hand with which he plugged his pipe was unsteady.

"You probably told her to keep quiet about it until she'd seen Mr. Lancaster, that the knowledge might be dangerous. Is that how you worked it, Mr. Drayton? Then, did you suggest that she come back later, say seven-thirty and that Mr. Lancaster would have returned by then? Seven-thirty would have been a good time to choose. It was dark by then and Boma residents would be getting ready for dinner, or having a sundowner. There'd be less chance of them being abroad. It was you who waited on the road, wasn't it Mr. Drayton? You knew she'd have to walk. You knew approximately at what time she'd be coming along there. It was you who came out of the darkness and hit her over the head, then carried her to the cliff edge and dropped her over. What a pity that you didn't think of shining the torch down to make sure she'd gone into the river. But no, it all had to be done in the dark, didn't it? You couldn't risk shining a torch around there."

"You bastard!" Prail screamed and lurched across the verandah towards Drayton. Blake stepped between them as Drayton came up from his chair.

"All right, Prail. Back to your seat." Blake thrust a restraining arm against Prail's upraised fist.

"Try proving it, Blake!" Drayton glared.

"We'll certainly be able to, I think," Blake said softly.

"We may not be able to prove anything about your wife's death, but you'll hang for murder, if Mrs. Prail dies."

God! That was my cue and I'd nearly missed it. I snatched the bush jacket and torch from the table and, slipping out of the sitting room and through the kitchen, I sped on silent feet around the back of the house and through to the drive and the front verandah.

"...the button must have fallen off as Lancaster and I rolled her in the canvas, that's why you found it caught in her dress," Drayton was shouting as I came through the door. I threw Drayton's bush jacket across to Blake.

"Left breast pocket," I said.

Blake placed the button, with its backing of torn cloth, which he had been holding in his upraised hand, against the jacket pocket. It fitted exactly into the jagged, inch-wide tear.

I handed Blake Elsa Prail's torch: the torch made in Chicago, USA.

"Can you identify this torch as your wife's?" Blake asked Prail.

He stumbled forward and took it. "Yes. That's Elsa's." His voice was that of a broken man.

"Where did you find it?" Blake turned to me.

"Lying on the desk at the house. It wasn't hidden actually."

"Of course it wasn't hidden, you bloody crazy bastards," Drayton shouted. "I found that torch this evening on the path below the Nelsons' house."

"Mr. Lancaster went over the place. He didn't find any torch lying there."

"It had rolled under a bush. I did find it there, I tell you." Drayton was flushed with rage.

"And why didn't you bring it to me?" Blake asked coldly.

"Because I forgot," Drayton said savagely. "You'll never prove..." He stopped speaking and swung a fist instead.

Blake caught his fist in an iron grip and Nelson came at Drayton from behind.

Drayton shook himself free and backed away.

"Try proving it, Blake," he said again. His voice was bleak.

"I trust we'll have some help there. Mrs. Prail, I am very pleased to report, has made some progress. There's a chance she may pull through this all right. In the meantime, Drayton, you're under arrest." Blake pulled the warrant from his pocket.

Drayton's face was sculptured in stone as the warrant was read out. The pallor set in deep circles around his temples and streaked his jaw line.

CHAPTER 45

Cramp was gripping my leg but I dared not move too much. In the hot darkness, I silently stretched my legs, one after the other. I wondered whether the plan would work. As Blake had so rightly pointed out, if he didn't panic, he'd see through it all right—there were enough holes in the case to make a good prosecutor throw his hand in, before he started.

Would he take the bait?

Through the chink between the curtains of the bush wardrobe, which made a triangular section of the bedroom corner, I could see the bed. The still figure, the bandaged head, were barely outlined in the dim glow of the small lamp above the bed.

The voices from the verandah had gradually stilled. The Nelsons had gone long since with Drobinall. Janet Frenton had been given sleeping pills and sent to bed by Bravachko.

"Try to sleep, my dear, you need the rest," he had said. "It doesn't need two of us here now."

I had heard the departure of Prail.

Young had been the last to go. "Shouldn't I stay, sir?" I had heard him ask the priest.

"No, my son. I can manage quite well alone." Bravachko had sent him off.

The house had slowly settled. Noises from the kitchen

had ceased. Darkness and quiet took over; a quiet overlaying the myriad noises of an old house at night. From a distance, on the still night air came the surge of the river. It sounded like the throb of a muffled engine.

An hour passed with nothing. My eyelids pricked with fatigue and in the enveloping closeness of the curtained recess, I could feel the rivulets of sweat trickling down my armpits. He'd smelt a rat. Where had we gone wrong, I wondered? Perhaps we'd laid it on too thick. If Elsa Prail recovered, he'd bluff it out. Perhaps it was—

I froze and stopped breathing. From somewhere in the house had come the faintest whisper of movement. Somewhere near.

A rat scurried in the roof, and there was silence again. Then a faint creak, alien and not entirely lost beneath the protest of ancient furniture in the night coolness. On the verandah, the priest coughed lightly and near me someone caught breath. Was he here already, in the room?

It came again, the merest sensation of movement.

Wait. Wait. Mustn't be too quick, I thought, but on the other hand, not too late. Pray that Blake was right.

If he chose some other way and not the pillow, what then? I felt the blood pounding in my ears as I watched. An indeterminate shadow that made no sound hesitated, bent over, got up again and moved on more quickly now. The arms were thrust forward like a sleepwalker. In the hands was the white blob of the pillow taken from the camp bed.

Wait. Don't rush it. Now!

I leaped as the beam of the torch cut across the darkness and the still figure on the bed exploded into swift life.

"Hello there, Prail. Thought you'd drop in!" Blake's voice said, and the next moment, the three of us went down in a tangle of arms and legs. The torch smacked against the wall and went out.

For all his fat, he fought with strength to match the pair of us. His elbow cracked into my jaw and I heard Blake grunt in the dimness as a knee caught him.

"The two-timing bitch," Martin Prail spat the words out and then he was gone. It hadn't taken more than thirty seconds.

The slap of his bare feet on the concrete floors came from the corridor. He was fleeing the way he'd come in, from the back verandah.

"Where's the bloody torch?" Blake swore in the semi-darkness as Bravachko came down the corridor from the front verandah with a Tilley lamp.

"So it worked," he shook his head sadly. "The poor, wretched creature."

"The murdering bastard," Blake responded. He retrieved his torch in the light of the lamp and we ran through the house.

But before we'd even reached the door, I knew we were too late. I knew what Prail intended to do.

The thin scream carried on the night air above the muffled call of the river.

I caught Blake's arm. "Careful. Waste of time. He's gone over the cliff and there's no mud bank tonight if you fall."

"Did you catch him?" Drayton's voice came from the darkness. He ran up to join us.

"He caught himself," I said.

And from the hills came the throb of a solitary drum. It was the last time I heard it at Feira.

CHAPTER 46

"If he'd stuck to the truth, he might have got away with it," Blake said. "It's highly unlikely that she saw him."

The light from the spluttering lamp was a sickly yellow in the shadowed greyness of the approaching day. Was it the third or the fourth dawn in the last week that I'd seen shoot up from behind the hills? I'd lost count, and I was exhausted.

We sat on the verandah, drinking cold beer. For the first time in weeks, Drayton looked completely relaxed.

"His mistake was to lie about the time," Blake was saying. "Why didn't he simply say that she'd never returned from the Nelsons' house? There are two possible reasons of course. One, that he wanted to cover himself for the time she was supposed to have disappeared, and two, he may have been forced to delay the search for her, because he'd seen that she'd fallen on the bank and had to make sure the river had time to complete the job for him."

"Your briefing before the charade last night was too short," Drayton complained. "I couldn't follow all of it. I thought Elsa was at the house when Drobinall went over to borrow the gin."

"Drobinall didn't see her. He only heard her voice, or thought he did. Prail worked the same thing with the

304

servants. They were prepared to swear that Mrs. Prail returned to the house that evening, and that she was there when Prail went over to the Nissen hut with Drobinall. But start with the torch. There it was on the road, obviously dropped at the time of the attack. It was switched off. Now what does that suggest? As I asked Jim. What was the simplest explanation for the torch being switched off? The answer was that she didn't need it. And when do you carry a torch without using it? Walking in the dusk. That was around the time that Mrs. Prail would have been returning from the Nelsons' house. So perhaps Prail was lying. A second point which lent colour to the theory was that when she was found, she was still wearing the dress she had worn that afternoon, as Grace Nelson described it, which meant she hadn't changed after her bath. Now that seemed unlikely. Prail left the Nelsons' house before his wife and waited for her on the road. It was barely light. He came up behind her. He didn't see her drop the torch. He hit her on the head and threw her over the cliff edge. Imagine him running along that back path behind the hospital. No one must see him going home at that time. No one did. Once back at the house, it wasn't hard for him to create the illusion that she had also returned. Prepare two drinks and leave a lighted cigarette burning on the ashtray beside one of them. Call out as though she were in the bedroom, just as the servant was bringing the ice to the verandah. Arrange the bathroom: dampen the towels and the bath mat, turn on the taps, leave the soap in the bath, talk in the bedroom and bathroom so that the servants could hear. And at that moment, Drobinall turned up. 'Gin? Of course, old boy... I'll get the keys from Elsa... she's gone off to bath'. He'd go through the bedroom calling out 'The Nelsons want to borrow some gin, where are the keys?' Then into the bathroom and turn off the taps, back would come her voice:

'In my handbag'. Drobinall heard her voice."

"Of course," Drayton said. "Prail was an excellent mimic. Regular marsh warbler."

"So Jim told me, eventually." Blake snorted. "He'd had a demonstration of it, the day he went out to Baluti with Prail. So, there we are at the house. Prail had created a complete illusion. The servants and Drobinall were convinced that she was in the house. I made a small bet with myself that Prail had seen to it that he hadn't been left alone for more than a minute or two at a time, after Drobinall left and he re-entered the house. And so it turned out. The servant was told to bring the DDT because the Serowe ants were invading the front verandah. On one pretext or another, Prail made sure he had company, until he left for the Nelsons' house, ostensibly to fetch his wife. I plumped for Prail, and if Prail had sent his wife over the cliff because she knew something she intended to make public about Mrs. Drayton's death, then that knowledge must have constituted a danger to Prail, which, in turn, implied that Prail knew more than he should about your wife's death. Substitute Prail for yourself, and I think that what I said last night about the beginning of the affair, was actually accurate. It was Jim's theory entirely, I might add. When the monkey died from the effects of the powder which Prail had taken from the horn, it wouldn't have been difficult for him to plant the idea in his wife's mind that there was a relationship between the monkey's death and Matafwali's threat. She, in turn, influenced Mrs. Drayton towards the theory. He was helped of course by the gossip from the compounds. They were all abuzz with it. Then all he had to do was to find an opportunity to substitute some of the powder for the salts in one of your bottles and wait. But the wrong person died. He must have got an almighty shock when he arrived at your house that afternoon, the day you wife became ill, and saw the salts beside the bed. He realised then that she'd taken the stuff he'd left for you."

"But I don't remember seeing the salts on Elizabeth's table that day." Drayton reached over and turned out the lamp as the light increased.

"They weren't there to be seen when you came back with Miss Frenton," Blake stifled a yawn, "because Prail had removed them. They could have been there earlier though, without your noticing."

"Isn't it possible," I cut in, "that Mrs. Drayton took the salts after you left to fetch Miss Frenton? It's possible that the previous vomiting was in fact due to a normal reaction of the liver to the malaria and the mepacrine. Your wife had complained frequently to Miss Frenton of nausea. That might explain why you didn't see the salts: your wife didn't take them until after you'd gone. Where were they usually kept?"

"At that time, I used to keep them in my bedroom. The bathroom cabinet was too small to cope with more than Elizabeth's creams and things."

"But your wife would have known where to find them, I suppose. Did you notice that a bottle went missing, around the time your wife died?"

"I can't say that I did, but then I might not. I invariably took a new bottle on tour, leaving behind the one in use. There might quite easily have been one or two bottles, with a little in each in the bedroom cupboard."

"Well, I would think," Blake said, "that the bottle you left behind the last time you went on tour, was the one that Prail had tampered with. When you returned, by lucky chance, you continued to use the one you brought back from tour with you. Not so lucky for Mrs. Drayton though."

"But I never knew Elizabeth to touch these salts. She was very much against taking this sort of thing. She never made any secret of the fact that she thought it a fad and a waste of time."

"And there you are. Prail must have considered it a fairly safe bet that you'd get the dose he'd prepared for you. Your wife must have taken them just that once. Maybe as Jim's suggested. Once your wife died, Prail changed his plan. If he hadn't got you one way, he'd get you another, for the murder of your wife. It was he who instigated the talk that started, of course. It really would only need a word dropped here and there, with the compounds already humming, then the rest: the telephone call; anonymous letters; plant suspicion in his wife's mind and keep it going. The letter you found, of course, couldn't have been better adapted for his plan. That was a stroke of luck for him. But there was one thing he hadn't realised, and that was the elusive quality of some of these bush drugs. That was why he left the remainder of the powder in the desk drawer, where it would be found after he'd heard the discussion between Jim and Drobinall that morning in Baluti."

"But how did Prail get on to the fact that his wife had remembered seeing the salts on Elizabeth's table?" Drayton asked.

"Perhaps Mrs. Prail can tell us that when she recovers. In the meantime, I'll make a guess. She could have said something to her husband when he joined her at the Nelsons' house that afternoon. He could have told her to keep quiet about it until she'd seen Jim. Or he could have read danger in the remark he overheard her making to Drobinall about salting someone's tail. One thing's certain: he did realise that she had remembered seeing the salts that day. Perhaps up to that point, he'd been under the impression that she hadn't noticed them at all. From there it was one step to the realisation that it might be only a matter of time before she worked out that the trap had been set for you and that Prail himself had a strong motive if he knew about the affair. Or, perhaps he feared that she might suddenly remember that though the salts were on the table when she arrived that afternoon, they had disappeared before you returned with Miss Frenton, and only Prail could have taken them."

"How did you get on to this business about the salts?" Drayton asked.

"Jim did. He had it all buttoned up before I arrived."

"Sheer fluke," I said, "and the need for tobacco. Mrs. Jones told me that Elsa Prail had been at the store that morning acting a little oddly. Bearing in mind what she said to me the night we found her and that peculiar reference she made to Drobinall about salting someone's tail, Mrs. Jones' chatter led me right to it. Three bottles of your health salts, sitting on the shelf. I'd seen you drinking the stuff dozens of times. This was what had sent her hurrying to the Boma to find me. Not salt but salts. That's what she'd been trying to say. I wondered whether your wife's death had been an accident, whether in fact, it should have been you who died, and when that plan misfired, the campaign was started to get you accused of her murder. You were quite right about that part of it, Drayton. Whether Elsa Prail attached the same significance to the salts, is open to question. I'm inclined to doubt it. But the knowledge that the salts had been the medium for the poison was dangerous, in that it indicated that you had been the target, not your wife. Of all the people on the Boma, Prail had the strongest motive for hating you, because of the old affair between you and Mrs. Prail. Prail's awareness of the affair, must have been known to somebody else on the Boma. Perhaps it was Drobinall with his penchant for gossip, who'd told Prail. You might have known that the affair couldn't have gone unremarked on a Boma this size. So, if it came to light that the poison had been meant for you, Prail felt that he would automatically come under suspicion. He probably considered that other peoples' motives wouldn't measure up to his own: Young's jealousy of you; Drobinall's fear and loathing. It's unlikely that he knew of Nelson's fear of you as far as the ivory poaching is concerned."

"But what could we have charged him with?" Blake asked slowly. "Perhaps nothing, if he'd kept his head. The path report on Mrs. Drayton will lead most likely to a verdict of death from unknown causes and we couldn't have got him on that. What proof had we that he had attempted to murder his wife? Damned little. He could have bluffed it out about the time, if she'd recovered from the head wound. But no, he couldn't resist that one chance he saw. There was Drayton, parcelled and tied, he thought. This was what he had planned, if only Elsa didn't recover to raise awkward questions. There was another point, of course, although it was highly unlikely: Prail couldn't be certain she hadn't recognised him when he attacked her. He decided to avoid the one and make certain of the other. And the pillow, as I told you, Jim, was the answer. No questions raised. A case of heart failure following the head injuries."

"You still might have told me a little more about it before I went into my act last night." Drayton said.

"Would have spoiled the effect, old boy, but I must say I'm damned glad I don't have to justify to the powers that be that pantomime we staged last night."

EPILOGUE

Copy of Semi-Official Minute addressed to the Provincial Commissioner, Lusaka.

Feira, December, 1948.

Dear Sir

I have forwarded under cover of the official minute, copies of the proceedings in the adjourned inquests on Mrs. Drayton and Maoma Makusi and I take this opportunity of writing you this semi-official letter on various aspects of recent events in Feira.

In view of the negative report from the chemical examiner, I think you will agree, that a verdict of "Death from Unknown Causes" was the only possible one. Although laboratory experiments on the powder found in the rhino horn, indicate that death can be induced in circumstances similar to both cases, this fact constitutes no proof in law. The powder, to date, remains unclassified.

The unsatisfactory conclusion of the inquest on Mrs.

Drayton will undoubtedly give rise to considerable speculation, and the potential injustice [to Drayton in particular and other Boma residents in general] inherent in such speculation, is obvious.

I hope that it will however, to a great extent be counteracted, by the result of the hearing into the death of Martin Prail. With this in mind, I have, as you will see from the copy of the proceedings sent under cover of my official minute, allowed evidence to stand, the quality of which may strain the precepts of admissibility, even for an inquest. An inference of Prail's guilt emerges quite clearly. The rap over the knuckles which I shall most certainly receive from the Chief Justice, when he reviews the record, will no doubt be heard from one end of the Territory to the other. I am prepared for that. From a legal point of view, it is all highly unsatisfactory but it was the best we could do. I feel that all in all, justice has been better served by this attempt to remove suspicion from innocent parties.

To date, Prail's body has not been recovered and in view of the lapse of time, I think it unlikely that any trace of it will ever be found.

Mrs. Prail's physical condition, though greatly improved, does not allow for her to be informed, at this stage, of the true facts surrounding her husband's death. I am arranging for her transport to Lusaka Central Hospital. Miss Frenton will accompany her on the journey. I must leave it to medical opinion and your own discretion to decide when she should be told the full story.

May I prevail on your kind offices in the matter of Miss Frenton? The last weeks have been trying for her, both emotionally and physically. Moreover, the knowledge that it was Drayton's affair with Mrs. Prail [ephemeral though it may have been] which precipitated the whole tragic business, has upset and confused her. She will not be returning to Feira as Spencer, for whom she was deputising, is due back any day now. I feel she needs time to sort herself out. This will be more easily achieved in Lusaka than on any small rural Boma, where she might be subjected to unpleasant and quite unwarranted speculation: what the bush telegraph will make of recent events here, is anybody's guess. Drayton, I know, is going to Kalomaloma: I think that a word from you in the right quarter, will keep Miss Frenton at Lusaka and obviate the slight possibility that she might be posted to the same place. I do not think that either Drayton or Miss Frenton would wish for that at the present moment. Drayton's leave comes up in six months, and by then, I think, she may see things in a different light. It will then be up to Drayton.

He leaves on transfer, as instructed, within the next three days and will, of course be calling at Lusaka on his way through. No doubt, he will be able to fill in any gaps for you.

Yours sincerely,
James Lancaster.

And so it ended.

313

In due course, Ann defied her doctors and joined me in Feira. There she and I defied predictions and expectations by thoroughly enjoying our time at the station.

I never settled on a satisfactory explanation of the ghostly drummer. Western people tend to regard the African explanation as highly suspicious: that the drum was beaten by the spirit familiar of a witchdoctor. Of course, the local people of Feira were equally firmly convinced it was indeed the jilombo of Matafwali, just as they were also convinced that Matafwali had been responsible for the death of Elizabeth Drayton.

Looking back on it, I suppose that in one way, he was: it was a strange coincidence that his threat, or prophesy, or whatever you like to call it, was fulfilled. I don't know. It was odd. It was an odd business altogether.

ABOUT THE AUTHOR

Eileen Marguerite Newman was born in 1918, within the sound of East London's Bow Bells (the church bells of Mary-le-Bow in Cheapside), which made her an honourary Cockney. She had seven brothers and sisters, a passion for languages and an interest in adventure, which led to her hitchhike through France and Germany immediately before the outbreak of World War II.

Following the war, she uprooted herself, travelling first to Cape Town by ship and then up to Lusaka by rail. There she took a job, met and married Roylance Arthur Henwick, a District Commissioner in the Colonial Service. Their honeymoon was by barge down the Zambezi to the remote station of Feira.

Several postings for the Henwicks throughout Northen Rhodesia followed, culminating in Broken Hill in 1964, when Zambia gained indepedence, by which time they had a daughter, Gail, and a son, Mark.

In 1970 the family moved to the UK. School for the children and failing health meant that Eileen remained in the UK, while Roy had to travel where his UN employers wished him to.

After a long struggle, Eileen died in hospital in 1975.

Made in the USA
Lexington, KY
16 May 2018